CW01159841

Fun & Games

A Novel

CYNTHIA HARRIS

Copyright © 2022 Cynthia Harris

All rights reserved.

This is a work of fiction.
Names, characters, places, and events are either the product of the author's imagination or are used fictitiously. Any resemblance to actual persons, living or dead, events or locales is entirely coincidental.

The author in no way represents the companies, corporations, or brands mentioned in this book. All opinions expressed in this book are the author's, or fictional.

No part of this book may be reproduced, or stored in a retrieval system, or transmitted in any form or by any means, electronic, mechanical, photocopying, recording, or otherwise, without express written permission from the author and publisher.

ISBN: 9798843328979

Cover art designed by Jared Frank

Printed in the United States of America

In loving memory of **my grandmothers,** both of whom loved a good romance novel

CONTENTS

ONE Introductions

TWO A Kilted Man And The Game

THREE An Unexpected Diversion

FOUR The First Glimpse Of Hope

FIVE Confessions

SIX This Is Fifty

SEVEN My Scot, The Spy

EIGHT A New Beginning

NINE The Bonnie Banks Of Loch Leven

TEN The Other Woman

ELEVEN A Gift Of Inspiration

TWELVE Mythos

THIRTEEN The Hidden Heart

FOURTEEN Old Friends Are The Best

FIFTEEN The Path Forward

SIXTEEN The Last Gift

SEVENTEEN My Home

EIGHTEEN An Unwelcome Offer

NINETEEN We All Win, In The End

GRATITUDE

ABOUT THE AUTHOR

FROM THE AUTHOR

ONE
Introductions

London, England
September 2022

I smiled as I stepped off the lift into the new headquarters of Woodhouse Publishing Group, now in a modern glass-covered building on Victoria Street. I could not help my smile because the original cover art of my first novel, *The Ruins of Dunmara*, was holding pride of place behind the reception desk.

"Good afternoon! Welcome to Woodhouse Publishing," the young receptionist said as I walked in.

"Good afternoon! I have a three o'clock appointment with Kate Woodhouse… Corrine Hunter."

"Oh, of course, Miss Hunter," said the young woman excitedly before she quickly rang Kate's assistant.

"Kate is on her way to meet you herself. I have to say that I am such a huge fan. I am reading your last novel now!"

"Thank you. What is your name?"

"Olivia."

"Well Olivia, my last two novels were not my best work. I hope you have read some of my others," I said, smiling at her.

"Oh, yes! Of course! I have read all of them! They are *brilliant*!"

At that moment, Kate walked in to greet me, and we hugged each other. I turned back and said, "It was nice to meet you. I hope the last novel doesn't change your mind about my work."

She laughed nervously in front of Kate but said nothing back to me.

As Kate and I walked back to her office, she said, "I suppose Olivia told you she is reading your last novel."

"She did."

"I tried to talk her out of it."

"Some supportive publisher you are!"

"You know it was not your best work, my darling!"

"I know. I know. That is why I said I hoped it did not change her mind about me as an author." When we arrived at her expansive corner office, I said, looking around, "I like the new office, Kate. It is very modern, and it suits you!"

"The pandemic freed up a lot of office space in town and it was time to escape grandmother's attic!"

We laughed together as she was not far off with the description of her old office space in Kensington. She always celebrated her authors with images of book covers on the walls. But despite this, the space itself still felt more like a cozy place for an afternoon tea instead of a successful publishing house. The décor here reflects all the sleek lines and furnishings befitting this building and its location.

"Tea?"

"Please! Thank you!"

Kate Woodhouse has been my publisher for the last ten years. Just after I signed with her directly, she became an incredible blessing to me. I have never had a literary agent in between us and while I have my attorney protecting me, our arrangement has worked perfectly for us. After publishing twenty novels together, we have cemented a successful partnership and a lasting friendship. I trust her with my writing, and I trust her advice in my life. She has never steered me wrong, and she is not afraid to correct me when I need it—literally and figuratively.

With a surname like Woodhouse, and all that it evokes of Jane Austen's *Emma*, Kate was destined to be in this industry, surrounded by books and authors. She is a tall, blond-haired, blue-eyed beauty. She had a short stint as a fashion model during college, but quickly decided she wanted more. She started her business just six months after graduating from Oxford and quickly became a force in publishing and online media based on her intellect and keen business sense. I love her as my friend, and I admire her even more as a successful business leader.

"When do you leave?" Kate asked, handing me a clear glass mug with her company logo etched on it.

"Tomorrow. I will be in Edinburgh for half of the time and driving around Skye and the Highlands the other half before returning to Edinburgh for a few more days. I have found on my trips before that this plan works just in case anything I uncover on my travels across the country needs additional research at the library before I leave."

"That makes sense. I am convinced you just like staying at The Balmoral."

"Well, that is partly true," I said, smiling at her honest assessment. "It *is* a lovely hotel."

"I invited you here before your trip to see the new office, but I also want to introduce you to someone that may help you with your current novel," she said while blowing on her tea.

I know where she is going with this line of thinking, and I am not open to someone else weighing in and trying to help me finish the novel that I cannot seem to resolve myself.

I said before sipping my cup of tea, "I will pass, thank you very much!"

Ignoring my statement, she said to me across her desk, "Liam Crichton is one of the most successful business leaders in Scotland. Actually, the entire UK! He made a name for himself—and a *fucking* fortune—investing early in varied tech startups, but for the last decade has focused much of his business efforts on sustainable energy. He has been an important voice and financial backer for many research ventures and government policy decisions related to the impact of climate change and the need to invest more in renewable energy sources."

"Why are you telling me all of this?" I asked, sounding irritated as I sat my cup of tea on the edge of her desk.

"Because the most important thing about him is that he is well-connected at the University of Edinburgh and the University of Glasgow. I believe he can make connections you haven't even thought about for your research. Maybe it is time to seek some outside help."

"Ugh, I don't know," I said, almost rolling my eyes and uncertain if I want to request help from a stranger. "If he is that important of a business executive, helping an author he does not know has to be a pretty low on his list of priorities."

"That very well may be, but he asked me to serve on the board of one of his charitable foundations focused on entrepreneurial mentorship, and I believed every word he said to me about his passion for helping others succeed. He *will* help, I know it! Let me make the introduction. If he says nothing, then no worries. If he reaches out, it might help you finish this damn book!"

"Alright, Kate," I said, giving in to her. "Of course, I trust you. A little *quid pro quo* never hurts, right?"

"Are you accusing me of trading my service on a charitable board to have Liam help your wayward novel?"

"Perhaps," I said with a smile and a wink. I know my friend and she is, in fact, reaching for any help she can find for a friend that is clearly struggling.

"Well, you have a month before the next manuscript is due and if it is like the first, I may ask you to step away from this for a while and work on one of your others. Perhaps, another contemporary one that doesn't need extensive research."

"I understand and I appreciate you giving me one more chance to correct this draft. I believe I am in the right place and time. I just need to fix some things."

"We need to get another successful Corrine Hunter novel out there and quickly to help people forget all about the last two."

I hated to be reminded of them and now I have for the second time this very afternoon. "Fine!" I said, giving in again.

"I will email Liam and copy you. He is based in Edinburgh, and his connections may be just what this book needs."

"Thank you, Kate, for your help… and your tough love."

She laughed and stood up to escort me out. "If Luke and I didn't already have dinner plans with his parents tonight, we would join you at the hotel for a farewell drink."

"I understand, but I have to work a bit and then pack. You know I like to have a low-key night before I get on a plane."

"I do. If nothing else, you are a creature of habit, my darling."

As we walked through the hallways lined with cover art from all the novels Woodhouse Publishing Group had released over the years. I ritually tapped all of mine on our route back to reception. It became a superstition that started with my first published novel. I told myself that if I tapped my own cover in tribute as I passed that the second would not be far behind. Now twenty books in, I look a little silly hitting all the frames from Kate's office to reception... but I need all the luck I can get.

"You *have* to touch them all!" Kate admonished me on the walk, as she always does.

"It is for good luck! But this is not all of them. Perhaps that is why I can't finish the latest!"

"Yes, it is all *my* fault! Decorating the new office has been a deliberate act of sabotage!" Kate said, laughing at me fully now. We kissed each other on the cheek and hugged each other tight when we made it to the lifts. "Be safe during your travels and finish this novel! I will see you when you return. We have a special birthday to celebrate!"

"Oh! Don't remind me! Turning fifty has me rattled. It is no wonder I can't write."

"You can write. Find that missing piece of the puzzle in Scotland and we will publish book twenty-one. You can do this, my darling!"

I walked back to the hotel from Victoria Street instead of taking a car. It was a sunny day in London, and I needed to clear my head. I also wanted to take in the last bits of the city I love. Crossing in front of Westminster Abbey and Parliament Square before heading up Whitehall, I thought about the novel that has perplexed me and why I cannot seem to finish it. If I cannot articulate what I need to fix this struggling story, how can I ask anyone else for help? I can only hope Mr. Crichton is too busy to respond to Kate's email so that I can figure this out for myself.

+++

To: Liam Crichton
From: Kate Woodhouse
CC: Corrine Hunter
Subject: Introductions

13 September 2022, 16:08

Hi Liam! I hope this finds you doing well.

My friend and author, Corrine Hunter, is working on her latest novel and will travel across Scotland this month to complete her manuscript. I am certain you have connections that may help her. I copied Corrine above and will let her tell you more about her novel and her travels. Hopefully, schedules permitting, you two can coordinate a meeting for coffee or a drink.

Best,
Kate

On 14 September 2022, at 16:25, Liam Crichton wrote:

Great to hear from you, Kate! And Corrine, it is nice to meet you. Please let me know your travel plans and if there is anything I can do to help you whilst you are visiting our beautiful country.

Liam

Well, it appears Mr. Crichton wants to be helpful after all! However, I cannot tell if he wants to help me tour his country during my visit or help with my book. I bet it is more the former instead of the latter and I am going to be forced to respond.

> On 14 September 2022, at 18:32, Corrine Hunter wrote:
>
> *Thank you, Kate, for the introduction! And thank you, Liam, for your support! It is nice to meet you! I just arrived in Edinburgh this afternoon. My travel itinerary is below:*
>
> > *September 14-20 Edinburgh*
> > *September 20-27 Isle of Skye*
> > *September 27-30 Edinburgh*
>
> *I set the novel I am currently working on in Scotland during World War One. Seeing the country from a different perspective and spending more time at the National Library will certainly help me make the story richer. If you have any recommendations on places to see or people to meet, that may help me tell a story from that time period, I welcome them.*
>
> *Best,*
> *Corrine*

Just as I expected, Liam sent me a long email about all the places to visit in Scotland, but none of them had anything to do with the Great War. I did not reply to him, so he felt the need to politely nudge me.

I was as cordial as I could be in my response. Perhaps I just wanted to end this email string, or perhaps I felt guilty reminding him I was not in Scotland to be a tourist, but still awkwardly asked about a meeting.

On 16 September 2022, at 19:21, Corrine Hunter wrote:

Thanks so much for your mail, Liam!

Apologies for my delay! I have been to Scotland many times, so I visited some of your great recommendations on other trips. I agree, St. Andrews and coastal Fife is stunning.

On this visit, I have optimized for my research and have booked as much as I can to support my novel from a historical perspective. I welcome any recommendations or introductions that might serve a story set in the early Twentieth Century and the years of the Great War.

I know it is last minute, but if you can make it work, I am more than happy to buy you a drink at The Balmoral Hotel sometime this week before I leave for Skye on the 20th.

Corrine

On 16 September 2022, at 19:46, Liam Crichton wrote:

Well then, if there's anything you want to do but can't seem to get into or access to, please let me know. I have copied my assistant Jenny to see about my diary.

Have a wonderful time on your travels,
Liam

Ah! As expected, he offered no help for my novel and it appears Liam is as reluctant to meet as I am. Hopefully, Jenny will end this episode for us all. Surely there is no way this important man can make a meeting work this week or even in the few days I will be back in town at the end of the month. I bet his schedule is booked out months in advance.

Sadly, I did not have such luck! Jenny confirmed our meeting by sending an official calendar invitation shortly after I sent my email. I am going to have to meet this man and be open to whatever help he can offer. One day, I will make Kate pay for forcing this upon me during what has so far been another incredible trip to Scotland.

On 17 September 2022, at 10:56, Corrine Hunter wrote:

Jenny confirmed a meeting 3PM on Monday the 19th but, I understand you may need to evaluate your schedule as you go through the week. If it all works, the table at Bar Prince is reserved under my name.

See you then!

+++

TWO
A Kilted Man And The Game

Bar Prince, The Balmoral Hotel
Edinburgh, Scotland
September 2022

The hotel reserved the perfect table for me in the back corner of Bar Prince. Even though we are just a party of two, I asked for the last booth to be out of the busy bar top area. It is an ideal spot for a business conversation but still offers a view of the activity in the room.

"Corrine?" The man asked as he came to my table.

I looked up from my computer and asked, "Mr. Crichton?"

"Aye! Liam, please. It is a pleasure," he said with a smile. I stood up so that we could shake hands. "Kate has only good things to say about you, but it is so nice to meet in person after talking on email the few days."

I could not speak. I just smiled and nodded at him in agreement. Liam Crichton is tall and handsome. I expected neither. I am not certain what I expected, honestly. He has thick, dark brown hair and warm hazel eyes to match. But it is his smile and demeanor that you notice the minute you meet him. I can see immediately why he is so successful. I suspect he is not just the brains behind his business ventures, but he is likely responsible for the Scottish charm offensive needed to close them. His mesmerizing Scottish accent is only exaggerated because he is actually standing before my table in a kilt with a tweed sports coat.

I guess he is probably only a few years older than me, but he has more gray hair than I do, which is mostly at his temples and throughout parts of his dark beard. He is not wearing a wedding ring. I took notice of that fact straight away. I was so convinced that we would not meet that I did not even bother to search online about the man or his business ventures. I suddenly fear I have done very little to prepare for this meeting and may end up regretting my total lack of effort.

Before I could say anything, he sat down and said in all of his charming Scottishness, "I was nearly late for our meeting. The general manager met me right inside the door. He was concerned that they did not have any bookings for me today and wanted to help me straight away." He took a moment to sip from the glass of water the server left for him and looked down at the menu, before continuing, "But I told him I was here to meet Miss Hunter and he was immediately relieved. You seem to be known in the hotel as he directed me straight here to your table. I suspect you will get a lot of attention from the hotel staff from here on out and will be well taken care of."

This quickly became one of the most pretentious entrances of all time! First the kilt and now this! I have published twenty novels and have been paying to stay at this fine hotel for weeks at a time on my many trips to Scotland, but apparently the wholehearted endorsement of Liam Crichton is all that I need to be taken care of in this establishment.

"It is a long story, but yes, they know me. Of course, I have been here for nearly a week, and it is not my first time staying in the hotel, so that helps. But just the other day, my room was next to another that needed an emergency plumbing fix in the middle of the night. The team had a great deal of work to stem anymore damage to the room itself and those below it. When I called down to reception to find out what was happening, they offered to move me to a new room. I was quite entrenched and declined. The night manager called me back and would not hear of it. He insisted I pack an overnight bag so that I could sleep soundly in a new room on the other side of the hotel, and I could return to my original room in the morning. He thanked me for being so gracious and understanding. I technically had two fabulous rooms in this hotel at once. That is five-star service all the way!"

"That is for certain! But not unexpected here at this hotel."

"Not unexpected at all! I have to confess though," I said leaning in across the table to share. "Perhaps it is my suspicious nature, but I am convinced they have people monitoring cameras everywhere and informing people in their ear when guests are approaching so that they can call them by name."

"Otherwise, they all have incredible memories."

"Exactly! I can't even imagine how they could keep a constantly changing clientele straight without some sort of clandestine system. But, I have to say, if they have a system or not, I love it! It makes me feel special!" He just nodded as he stared at me, making me suddenly nervous.

"Thank you so much for your time," I said abruptly, breaking the spell he had on me and moving us to the business at hand. His assistant only booked one-hour for our meeting today, and I have a feeling he will honor that time and no more. "I know how valuable your time is and appreciate that Kate connected us."

"Think nothing of it! I had some meetings close by, so stopping here at a hotel bar I love is a simple task. In fact, it was most welcome tonight as I will drive to my house on Loch Leven. It is my honor to help a friend of Kate's, so please tell me how I can best help you, Corrine."

I do not know what to make of his words or the sincerity of his offer to help. I thought about my conversation with Kate—I am a mere quid pro quo between two successful people. But something about how he said my name made me smile. Who doesn't love hearing a Scot roll an 'r'? And my name has plenty of them.

Before I could answer, the server came to us immediately and took our order. I had my regular white wine spritzer and Liam ordered a vodka martini.

"Do you want olives or a twist?" I asked immediately, playing unintentional bartender at the table.

"Good question! Olives, please, and slightly dirty."

The server smiled at me before walking away.

"Sorry, I spend a lot of time in bars." Liam just looked at me, and I started laughing. "I understand how that statement sounds, having just said the words out loud."

He laughed with me and smiled at me again, unnerving me once more. So naturally, I kept talking. "I like the energy of a bar or a pub. It helps me write." He just nodded. I am not sure that he bought my explanation. But his continued stare rattled my nerves. Finally, I changed the subject.

"Like I mentioned to you in email, I returned to Scotland once again to reframe my novel and make it better."

"World War One, right?" he asked as the server delivered our drinks. The bartender must have made our drinks the minute Liam arrived for us to get them this quickly. It is almost unheard of. Not that they are slow here, but they are meticulous behind the bar and in no real hurry. It is part of the experience. I realized at that moment the server did not need my help with Liam's martini. They already know what we both drink.

Looking over his glass, Liam said, "Sorry, I missed the book part and sent you all manner of places to visit. I realize now that you are not a tourist."

"That is correct," I said, trying to hide my initial annoyance at the insinuation. "I set my story in Scotland during World War One. Despite my extensive research over the last eighteen months, I cannot seem to finish it. This will be the twenty-first novel that Kate and I will publish together, and for the first time, I am *absolutely stuck*. I came to Scotland again, hoping to find the missing piece to correct the second draft of my manuscript."

"If you had to guess what is missing, what would you say?" Liam asked me directly before sipping from his glass.

The intent in his eyes made me pause. I thought about my answer for a moment and the core of my struggles with this novel. Finally, it came to me, and I said, "It is missing *heart*."

"Heart?"

"Yes, heart. I cannot find a connection to my main character, my female protagonist. If I cannot connect to her as the author, then how can I expect a reader to connect to her? There are some structural gaps in the plot and pacing, of course, which can be typical at this stage, but I believe that if I can find the heart of the main character and her story, the rest will resolve itself."

He just looked at me, trying his best to understand me and the world of writing novels, as I continued explaining, "I have written and rewritten, but it will not come together. I am close to shelving the whole thing and working on another novel I have started. I would rather make the call myself than have Kate make it for me after receiving another poor draft. That would not instill much confidence in either of us, I'm afraid."

I did not tell Liam how my last two novels were abject failures and how I desperately need the next one to be successful. Otherwise, I risk ruining my reputation as an author and losing a base of readers that I have spent a decade building.

"Don't give up just yet. Let me think."

He sipped his martini and looked deep in thought at the bottom of his glass before asking, "Do you know Dr. Andrew Marshall?"

"I do not know the man, but I have heard of him, of course. I read his books on Scotland's contributions to both World Wars as part of my research for this manuscript and his many books on the history of the island clans for my first series of historical novels years ago."

"He is a good friend and knows more about Scottish history than anyone I have ever met! In fact, the man is a walking history book. It does not matter where or when in Scotland, he can tell you all about it! Do you know how you feel bored in a university lecture hall when academics talk history? Not with Andrew! He is such a wonderful storyteller; he just draws you in! I can make an introduction if you would like. If he is not out on a book tour himself, I am certain that he would be happy to help you."

"Thank you so much! Book or no book, I would like to thank him personally for his work and influence on my writing."

What was supposed to be a one-hour meeting soon became three, as we talked about traveling across Scotland and his passion for how technology can positively address global climate change. As arrogant as his entrance was at the start, I do not doubt the genuine pride he has for his colleagues and his sincere intention to help me—even if it is just a favor for Kate. I wanted to resent him for his wealth and confidence, but I could not. The more we talked, the more I could see that he was a genuinely kind and generous man.

I walked him through my novels and how I split my time between historical fiction that requires lengthy research and contemporary fiction that is easier to write. I explained why having both helped me put out this many books in just ten years.

He understood immediately by saying, "I can see that! I can see that! Changing genres gives your brain a rest."

"That is exactly right! It gives me a chance to just write without second guessing if every single detail is historically accurate for the time or spending hours researching instead of writing. I can just tell the story I want to tell. The research side of historical fiction can easily become all-consuming. That is why I do not want to let this manuscript go just yet. I have invested so much time and effort into it!"

"I understand. How would you say that these books represent you as an author? What do they have in common, if anything?"

I felt for half a second like I was on a job interview, but I appreciated he asked because it told me he was listening and that he was interested in my work. He may know nothing about writing and publishing novels, but he knows the right questions to ask from a business perspective. Essentially, he was asking what my motivation was in writing these books and what made them Corrine Hunter novels, aside from my name being on the front covers.

"It is a good question," I said, thinking about my answer as I sipped my glass of wine. An older woman seated at a table behind Liam caught my eye. She smiled at me, throwing me off for a moment. After publishing so many books, I should be able to answer this question in any press interview. I still had to think for a moment while ignoring the unexpected distraction seated behind Liam.

I finally said, "I set all of my books in England or Scotland. All of them. I have always had a love and appreciation for the history and people of these countries, and I cannot imagine writing about anyplace else. I planned to move to London from Vancouver, but my original relocation was derailed… um, by the pandemic."

He just looked at me, making me uneasy again. That was sadly not the only reason, but it was all I will share of my personal life this evening.

"But, at their core, all of my female protagonists—historical or contemporary—learn something on their journey. Not every novel has a happy ending, but if my main character can learn something about herself and her place in the world, then that is a story worth telling."

I sat back and looked at him with narrowed eyes, trying to gauge if my answer was satisfactory. He nodded his head in understanding as he said, "Then your heroine has a *purpose*."

"She does!" I exclaimed, sitting up tall again and clearly energized by this conversation. "And having a strong female character who can learn and grow through the story is inspiring to my readers because many of them are trying to do the same in their own lives. All of our circumstances are different, but male or female, we are all trying to find our place in the world and make a difference—for ourselves, for our careers, or for our relationships. Some find it easier than others in life, but I try to create and support women in my books who have stories that are relatable and inspiring to the reader."

"Is that what is missing from your current novel then?" he asked. I just looked at him, slightly confused as he continued his thought, "I mean, you said *heart* earlier, but could it be *purpose*? Are you missing the purpose and the lesson for growth?"

"It is a fair question, especially having not read the draft. But no. It is less the story or sense of purpose and more the main character herself. *She* is eluding me."

He looked at me with a furrowed brow, trying his best to follow my thinking as an author and wanting to solve a business problem, and not one of creativity and heart. I am not sure he encounters either of those concepts much in his own work.

"This is going to sound foreign to you, but bear with me. When I start a novel like this one that does not contain established characters from books I have written before, I have a process to find a name for each character. I may have to try many names as I draft the story before settling on one that fits best as the character develops and comes to life of the page. Once that name clicks, there is a point in drafting the story further where they start to talk to me."

We both started laughing at the same time. "I know! *I know!* You think I am raving mad now that I have just talked of hearing voices in my head!"

"Hearing voices is not something I have ever heard positioned as a *positive* trait before!"

"I know it sounds odd. But you must feel who your characters are. Or at least *I must*. I need to hear them and think about them constantly—how they look, how they sound, what motivates them, what they want, what happens if they don't get what they want. All of it! Despite my best attempts, I still cannot *hear* her. So if she doesn't exist to me, she cannot exist to another. Nothing I put on the page will resonate for the reader. In fact, what I have on the page now definitely *does not* resonate! In her current form, I am afraid she would not be a very likable character."

Liam nodded in understanding again and we both sat silently for a moment, thinking about what I just said about the connections between authors and the characters they create. I wondered if I lost him in this moment with glimpses of my maddening process and creative struggles. We sat together silently for a while. Just then, the woman behind Liam raised her glass to me with a smile and startled me out of thinking about the book I cannot finish and the character I cannot connect to.

Liam was staring at me again with narrowed eyes. He noticed I was looking past him again. I leaned in across the table and said softly, "I am *so sorry*, Liam. I am not trying to be rude. I keep glancing over your shoulder because I am distracted by the older woman at the table behind you. She keeps eagerly encouraging me with head nods and smiles. She just raised her glass to me. I believe she thinks we are on a first date."

"Is she encouraging you *or* could she be flirting with you herself?" he asked with a wink before eating an olive from his martini.

Immediately embarrassed, I could feel my cheeks turn red. "*No...* I am certain she is just being supportive."

"Well then," he said, sipping from his glass, "we should give her a show. Put your hand up to my face and stroke my cheek."

"Do *not* make me laugh!" I said, turning bright red in the face once again and sitting back.

"If you laugh, then you lose," he said seriously.

"Lose what?"

"You lose the game."

"The game?"

"Aye, we are going to give the lady a wee show," he said with a sly smile. "Let her staring be worth it. But if you laugh, you will buy the bottle of Champagne I am about to order."

He stopped our young server on his way by and shouted for all around to hear, "Lad, I would like to order a bottle of the 2010 Dom Perignon for the table, if you wouldna mind!"

"Aye, sir! I will get that right away for you!"

The lad left us immediately to retrieve a silver ice bucket stand and the bottle of Champagne. A bottle priced at nearly £300 on the menu, I might add.

"We are *not* on a date," I said in a low voice, leaning into the table. Before he could respond, the server arrived with the bottle and two glasses—once again delivering to our table at lightning speed. He popped the bottle and poured each glass slowly, letting the bubbles settle until each glass was filled evenly. We sat in silence, staring at each other and the server, until he put the bottle back into the silver bucket and walked away.

Liam leaned back to me across the table with his glass in hand and said, "I know that, and you know that, but our nosy neighbor *does not*. Is she still watching us?"

I glanced over his shoulder and the woman was smiling at me, seemingly in approval of the newly ordered bottle for the table. I smiled at her and then nodded subtly at him.

He put his glass up over the middle of the table and said loudly, "To our future!" We clinked our glasses and took a sip, smiling at each other. "Now, put your hand up and stroke my cheek like I said a minute ago."

"That seems a tad forward for a first date, don't you think?"

Liam smiled at me, knowing I was intentionally trying to challenge him. He tilted his head, silently willing me to do as instructed. I do not know where this game is going, but I dislike the idea of paying for this expensive bottle. I sat my glass down and put my hand up to his face. I stroked his cheek and passed my fingers to the hairline above his ear as I brought my fingers back around under his beard.

He smiled and grabbed my hand before turning to kiss the inside of my wrist. I was shocked and immediately pulled my hand away to grab my glass. I know my face was burning much brighter now and I could only hope the chilled bubbly will settle it down and hide my embarrassment at his touch. He just smiled at me, seemingly pleased to cause such a reaction.

"Well? What is Miss Nosy doing now with such an audacious display of affection?"

I could not speak as I thought only of the tickle of his beard and his soft lips on my wrist until I finally said, "Um, she's just ordered a glass for herself now and she is still watching us. She just smiled at me again."

"Of course she did! That is because the show is getting *good* now," he said as he poured more Champagne for both of us and then stood up. I just looked up at him and he walked over to my side of the booth and motioned for me to move over so he could sit next to me.

"What are you doing?" I asked through my teeth and a forced smile with my glass before my face.

"I thought it would be lovely to sit next to you so that I can see the woman for myself," he said, clinking my glass once more and then putting his arm around me. I sat up tall and took a huge gulp of my glass that I nearly choked on. The fine bubbles went straight up my nose, making me cough violently, and my eyes water.

"Och my darlin'!" he said as he rubbed my back, tracing the outline of my bra across my back as he did so. I tried to stop coughing but had a difficult time with all of this attention. His touch was unexpected, and I could barely breathe.

"When is this game over?" I whispered through a forced smile again, trying not to have my face betray me to the woman at the next table.

"It is over when I say it is," he said, filling my glass once again. "Here, calm yourself and sit back."

I leaned back and nestled in the bend of his shoulder. He stroked my arm and whispered in my ear, *"I think she is buying it."*

What started out as a game to entertain a nosy neighbor has now confused me. I just smiled, thinking about how I liked his arm around me and the light tickle of his fingers on my right shoulder. I looked down at his knees peeking from underneath his kilt and felt my cheeks flush again. My hand holding my glass trembled. I took a quick sip and sat it down on the table, hoping he did not notice that he was making me so flustered.

Then Liam boldly lifted his glass to the woman across from us and nodded his head to her in acknowledgement. Suddenly realizing that her staring had not been as subtle as she hoped, the woman did not miss a beat as she smiled and respectfully raised her newly acquired glass back to him.

Once she finished her Champagne, our nosy neighbor gathered her things and stopped by the end of our table on her exit to say in a posh English accent, "You make a lovely couple. Enjoy your evening!"

"Ye are too kind, madam!" Liam said with all the Scottish charm he could. "I think it has been a fine first date, don't ye?"

She smiled and nodded to both of us her approval that it has been a good first date. I started laughing at the spectacle as soon as she walked away through the bar. This must be the most ridiculous night of my life!

Liam said proudly, "You laughed so you lose!"

"No! I *did not*!" I tried to argue. "The game was over when the nosy lady walked away."

"I told you *I said* when the game was over," he said with all seriousness as he filled my glass again. "Here! You can have the last of the Champagne since you paid for it."

"That's *not* fair!"

Laughing at me now, he said, "Are you now a child whinging about how life is not fair? I told you how the game worked, and you clearly laughed before the game was called."

"*Called?* You are making up this game up as you go along, *Liam*."

"That is how the game works, *Corrine*. Och, Fine! I will buy the bottle this time since you have never played before. But you still *lost*."

"No, sir! If you are going to brand me a loser, I am not a sore one. I will pay for the Champagne."

Shaking his head at my insistence on buying the expensive bottle myself, he moved back to his original seat and looked at me with a triumphant smile. He knew I was seething on the inside and his gloating from across the table did not help my increasingly poor attitude.

"I will say that you were an excellent player… until the end, that is."

"You are a *horrible* man!" I said with a slight pout, while enjoying the last of the wonderful bubbly. He has good taste. I will give him that. If I had been smart, I would have set my pride aside, let him brand me a loser, and pay for this damn bottle himself.

"Och, dinnae be like that! It was all good fun," he said, leaning back across the table. "Ye had fun, didn't ye?"

I couldn't help but smile at him as his drink has made his Scottish accent more pronounced. The game was a little fun, but I will not give him the satisfaction of agreeing with him. I said only, "The lady believed we were on a first date."

"Then our *game* worked! But if I ever play with ye again, I will remember how competitive ye are."

"If we ever play again, and I suspect we will *not*, I will remember how you make up your own rules as you go!"

"Ye should thank me for my restraint. I could have ordered the Cristal."

At nearly £500 a bottle, I do, in fact, appreciate his restraint, but I am not about to thank him for it! He seems too eager for that bit of praise.

When he stood up to leave, Liam said, "I will think more about connections to help your novel. I will reach out again on email tomorrow about Andrew and anyone else I think of."

I stood up with him and put my hand out to shake his, saying, "Thank you again for your help! Take your time. I am driving to Skye tomorrow."

As he rejected my outstretched hand and hugged me tight, he said, "Kate knew we would get on, and I thank her for connecting us. I wish you nothing but success and will help as much as I can."

I could not say another word and just nodded politely. Liam walked out, shaking hands with everyone who works in the bar on his way. I smiled, thinking about how much I looked forward to his help and connections, but mostly admired most how he respected every member of the bar staff. I too have my own personal affection for those that work in a bar and restaurant, and I saw a similar kindness in him. I cannot imagine someone this wealthy and successful taking the time to thank not just his server, but the entire team. No wonder they see him approaching and want to take care of him when he arrives.

Once I got back to my room, I kept trying to shake the evening's unusual events from my mind. As the night wore on, my overactive brain kept me from falling asleep. I could not think about anything but touching Liam and him touching me or how a simple business meeting became an unexpected adventure with *the game*.

For the first time in years, a man charmed me. The kilt may have won me over at the very start, and I do not know what to make of my feelings. Three hours with him was more than I expected but was still not enough. My mind continued to race.

I finally got up and traded my restlessness for the warmth of a mint tea and sat on the couch in my room. When I looked at my phone, I saw Liam emailed that he arrived home safe. I smiled that he felt the need to tell me this, but did not dare respond at this late hour.

+++

THREE
An Unexpected Diversion

Isle of Skye, Scotland
September 2022

The drive to Skye was as just as frightening as it was beautiful. The Highlands and Islands of Scotland look like another planet.

No, that is wrong! The Highlands and Islands of Scotland look like the Earth should—pristine, unspoiled, and magical. The moody weather changes in an instant, and I have never seen so many rainbows in my life. At one point on the drive, magnificent rainbows surrounded me on almost all sides! It is a stunning and life-changing view of Scotland and our planet.

However, parts of the drive were on very narrow one-lane roads. Some roads were more paved than others through the most remote areas. I thought for certain that sheep would be my primary worry, but it was actually my fellow drivers that raised my blood pressure more than once. I gripped the steering wheel every time another car or, God forbid, a lorry came toward me, and I hit many potholes on the side of the road. How I did not get a flat tire in the middle of nowhere, I will never know! I am not a novice at driving on the other side of the road, but by the time I got to my hotel in Portree, I was worn out from the stress of my travels despite the majestic beauty I drove through.

I checked in and got settled in my lovely room before walking down the hill to town and the cozy Merchant Bar. When I opened my computer, I saw Liam sent me another email.

> On 20 September 2022, at 16:31, Liam Crichton wrote:
>
> *Corrine,*
>
> *It was lovely to meet you last night. I hope you enjoyed the last of your Champagne.*
>
> *I wanted to let you know that Dr. Marshall is visiting his daughter in France and cannot meet with you while you are here in Scotland for this trip, but he said that he would be happy to meet with you on your next visit, schedules permitting. I have copied him above to introduce you both so you can coordinate. He has also kindly offered to answer questions you might have via email in the meantime.*
>
> *All the best on your travels across our beautiful country and let me know when you are back in Edinburgh.*
>
> *Liam*

I think the mention of the most expensive bottle of Champagne I have ever purchased was a bit of an unnecessary dig. But for some ridiculous reason, I cannot stop thinking about him. Aside from my tricky travels today, I know I am distracted in another way. I held out as long as I could but finally emailed him back—out of complete respect for Dr. Marshall, of course!

> On 20 September 2022, at 20:00, Corrine Hunter wrote:
>
> *Thank you, Liam,*
>
> *I absolutely enjoyed the last of the Champagne and thank you for connecting me to Dr. Marshall. It is lovely to meet you via email, sir. I am a great admirer of your work!*
>
> *Your books have been a tremendous help to me in my research and writing over the last several years. I appreciate the offer to email you directly if I have questions, but I do not want to interrupt your holiday. Please enjoy your time with family! After all we have been through with the pandemic, I can only imagine what a joy it is to be together again. Treasure every moment!*
>
> *I will stay in touch about my next visit to Scotland and perhaps we can meet then.*
>
> *All my best,*
> *Corrine*

Within minutes, Liam replied to just me, and his message sent my heart racing.

> On 20 September 2022, at 22:11, Liam Crichton wrote:
>
> *I am interested to hear how much progress you made with your novel after your trip to Skye. If you would like to grab a drink before you leave the*

> country, I will be happy to meet you. Name the time and place in Edinburgh. I will make it work.
>
> Liam

I do not know what to make of this response. Liam Crichton has become an unexpected diversion, and I do not know that I want to add to the distraction he has caused by seeing him again. I am already in enough trouble with this novel as it is. Thinking of him constantly since we met has made it difficult to make the progress I need to. If this day is any sign, my next draft will undoubtedly be sub-par. I keep adding to my notes or editing but not correcting what I know I need to.

It took me until the next afternoon, but I could not help but reply. I could only make myself ignore him for so long.

> On 21 September 2022, at 15:15, Corrine Hunter wrote:
>
> *If you would like to grab a drink and hear about my progress, let's keep it casual. I have grown fond of the Rose & Crown pub on Rose Street in New Town. How about after 4PM on Wednesday the 28th? I will be there working.*
>
> *Kate will expect more from me than I have. I can tell you more about where I am with the novel and what I have left to do. Perhaps you can help me prepare my ask for another extension.*
>
> Corrine

I worried that I over-shared with him by admitting my failed progress, but if we are going to meet, I should rely on his expertise and help set up another extension with Kate. He will know what to do and I can tell he is the type of man that enjoys being asked for advice.

+++

"It is good to see you again," I said as Liam sat before me with his pint. I saved my work, shut my laptop down, and closed the lid to focus on my guest.

"It is good to see you again, Corrine," he said over his pint with his charming and disconcerting smile. I smiled back at him. Liam causes a physical reaction I cannot completely understand. I have not felt this way in a very long time. I just know that he makes me smile, and I tried my best to ensure I was not smiling maniacally at him across the table.

"I chose a pub so you could not leave me in a bar paying the bill for a £300 bottle of Champagne."

I was intentionally being cheeky with him, and he took the bait, "I should have guessed as much since you are so competitive."

"Or perhaps I am now forced to manage my expenses on this trip with such extravagance at the very start."

He said nothing back but smiled at me over his glass as we both thought about the game we played together in Bar Prince. I am certain he was not worried about my ability to the pay for the bottle but seemed quite proud, that doing so still infuriated me.

We sat quietly for a moment under the watchful eyes of a portrait of Flora MacDonald before Liam asked, "If I may ask, why do you prefer working in a pub or a bar?"

I thought about his question for a moment. It was fair. My thinking has evolved even more so since the pandemic. I answered by saying,

"Like I said the other night, there is a dynamic energy in a bar. People are always moving. Even if I do not watch all the comings and goings, I can absorb all the surrounding energy, and it fuels my work. I can support the staff who work so hard with a smile or a positive word when they are near, and they support me in return. If I wrote in a coffee shop, the library, or even my hotel room, I would most likely be asleep in an hour. If I wrote at home, my household chores would distract me constantly. In fact, I know I could only work in fits and starts and would likely get absolutely nothing done. When I am in a bar, I put my headphones in, listen to my music, and just write."

"What kind of music do you listen to?"

"Instrumental movie soundtracks. I always say that I cannot listen to words while I am writing words. Most bars have music or sports playing on the speakers. Sometimes I also have to drown out the surrounding conversations. So, I put my headphones in and listen to my music. Film soundtracks can evoke emotions without tripping me up on what I am writing or editing on the page."

"I find this all fascinating. Your process, I mean," he said, seemingly genuinely interested. "I appreciated what you said about naming and hearing your characters… now this."

"I do not think it is a perfect plan for delivering a novel, but it works for me, for now." He just nodded his head at me, as I confessed further, "At some point, I need to find another place to write or change my choices here. Otherwise, I am headed straight into the downward spiral that one too many authors have found themselves."

He just looked at me, confused as I continued, "I mean that I have found it very hard to sit in a bar and *not* drink."

"Do you think it is a problem for you?"

The directness of his question stunned me for a moment. "Not yet, but it could be in the future. Deep down, I know I can sit here and take in all the energy and support that I need and sip on a Diet Coke or a soda water with lime, but over the last few years, I have not made such decisions. I stick to my pints or my wine."

"Does that impact your work?"

"I often refer to *The Law of Diminishing Returns* as I am certain that my productivity, clarity of writing and editing wanes as time passes. In contrast, however, I will argue that a drink at the start absolutely helps for a moment of relaxed creativity. I do not know how to describe it otherwise. I can arrive and everything I have thought about since I last wrote just pours out. It is a satisfying feeling, to be sure!"

I smiled at him as I finished my confession and asked, "Have I over-shared?"

"No. You have been honest with me, and with yourself, and I respect you for it. I do."

I just smiled weakly at him and nodded in my understanding of his words, "The last several years have been difficult for me—*personally*. That has nothing to do with the challenges I have faced with this novel. Being alone in isolation during the pandemic, with all the fear and restrictions we had to endure, was difficult. Being here with kind people who support my work helped my spirit, and I hope I have supported them in return. The hospitality and restaurant industries were especially hard hit, as you know."

"Absolutely! Lockdowns, travel bans, distribution challenges, and staffing shortages crippled many industries, but definitely had a devastating effect on the many small, local businesses—including pubs.

Many could never recover, even after government restrictions started lifting. Add the expected cost of energy this winter and it only makes my work even more important. Some businesses and pubs are looking at bills nearly three times what they were last year!"

"I cannot imagine! But the last few years have been difficult for so many, haven't they? We have all had to make choices to cope with a new reality of the world and recalibrate our lives—how we live, how we work, and how to find balance and peace for ourselves. We have all had to look at what makes us truly happy."

"I agree! The last few years have been difficult personally and professionally on many levels for me as well. I have had to learn more as a business leader about how best to support the many employees in my company, but I too have made choices to *recalibrate,* as you said, my own life during this time."

Liam looked at me as he could see and feel my demeanor change before him. I could not ask what he had done to change his life. He would tell me if he wanted to. I just smiled slightly and said, "Life is *too short* to be unhappy."

"Life is *indeed* too short for that," he said, taking a huge gulp of the last of his pint. He immediately picked up both of our glasses and took them to the bar to secure new ones. As he did, I tried to catch my breath.

I can feel the emotional tension between us and that we both have personal stories that we are not willing to share with each other. Even though I shared a lot with him just now, I can tell we are both holding back. For every thought I have of Liam, there is one about my fiancé David, and it weighs heavily on my heart and only adds to my confusion.

When Liam returned, he pushed my new pint across the table. "Now, tell me how you have fared on this trip."

"Oh, I must admit that I have done poorly."

I could not confess how he had been a central part of my lack of focus and just said, "I was hoping you could help me here. I have my fiftieth birthday celebration planned in London on Sunday, October 2nd with my dearest friends. Kate being one, obviously. I need to ask for another deadline extension. I don't know that she will give it to me."

"First, where are you staying?"

"I will be at my favorite hotel—The Corinthia."

"You certainly have fine taste in hotels!"

"I fell in love with it and the people there many years ago. They have always been good to me, and I could not stay anywhere else in London."

"Well, then I know they will take care of you."

"They will."

"I wish you a very happy birthday! You will love your fifties!"

"I heard the same about my forties and I believe you," I said, smiling at him across my pint glass. "A year ago, however, I would have told you I was not so sure how I felt about this milestone birthday creeping up on me. But now, I am ready."

"I am well into my fifties, and I cannot speak to what a woman feels, but I can tell you I feel more confident and assured than I ever have. I wish you the same."

I could not say the words, but I do not tell him that as much as I struggled turning fifty, I too am feeling more confident than I have in a long time. His attention has been a large part of those feelings. I looked at his hand around his pint and, once again, he was not wearing a wedding ring. My diamond band was also opposite where it would normally be in a pub. I am not certain why I keep moving it back and forth.

After a few sips, he considered his words and asked, "Can you complete this novel? Or is Kate right and you should shelve it for a moment? Surely, nothing good can come from forcing it unnaturally."

I did not know what to say back to him. My silence was disconcerting as he leaned into the table and said, "I mean no disrespect, Corrine."

"None taken. I was just thinking about how best to answer your very valid question. I *believe* I can complete this novel. It has taken a lot of research over the last eighteen months to get to this point. I believe in it. I want to finish it. That is not just my pride talking, Liam. I truly believe that if I can find the missing piece, and if I can connect to my heroine, it will all fall into place."

"Then ask Kate for the extension. I know nothing about writing novels, or the steps needed to publish, but tell Kate what you plan to do next. I know you are still looking for the missing piece, but I would avoid mentioning that point for now. If she knows you have a solid plan to correct what you have, she will give you the time you need. *I know it!* If she believes you are still lost and struggling with no plan, or no obvious recognition of what is actually missing, she may not be so inclined. I know enough about business to understand that then you become a risk to her own success—friend or not."

"Ah! The classic *'fake it until you make it'* approach!"

"Aye, stop writing in the manuscript for a moment and spend the time to detail your notes for her. Show her you know what must be done and that you have a solid plan to complete it."

"Thank you, truly. She has given me a lot of latitude because of our history and friendship. I will define my plan and next steps before asking for the extension."

We hugged each other as we said our goodbyes outside the pub. All I could think as he went one way, and I walked alone to my hotel in the opposite direction is that one day, I hope I can tell him everything. Something about Liam makes me *want* to tell him everything.

I could not help myself. Whether it was drink or longing, I emailed Liam later than I normally would.

> On 28 September 2022, at 23:32, Corrine Hunter wrote:
>
> *Liam,*
>
> *Thank you so much for the honest conversation at the pub this evening. You gave me a lot to think about. It was good to see you again, and your sound advice was much appreciated!*
>
> *Corrine*

Liam shocked me again with the speed of his response and the subtle invitation to hear from me again. He made me smile.

> On 28 September 2022, at 23:36, Liam Crichton wrote:
>
> *You are most welcome! Please tell me how the discussion with Kate goes and know that I wish you all the best for your extension. You deserve it!*
>
> *LC*

+++

"Hello, Kate," I said, answering my phone.

"Hello, my darling! How are you doing? Any progress on this trip?"

"Some. I am working this very moment on my checklist of next steps. Thank you for the introduction to Liam! But I have to confess, he has done little to help my book but instead has done a lot to distract me."

"What do you mean?"

"I cannot stop thinking about him. We have met twice now, and I know I should think about other things... like finishing this damn book."

"You need to focus on finishing the *damn* book!"

"I know, but I think he is an amazing man and has suddenly invaded my thoughts. *All of my thoughts.*"

"Corrie," she said with a sigh. "I am pretty certain that Liam is married. No! Let me be more declarative. I *know* Liam is married. He has a wife and two sons, in fact. He told me himself!"

Her words took the air out of my lungs and broke my heart in an instant. I must have expected each one and believe this is why I still refused to look him up online. I did not want to know the truth. I could only say back to her, "He did not have a wedding ring on when we met, and our interactions have been very... *flirtatious*."

"You know well enough that not all men wear a wedding ring out of personal choice and, flirtatious or not, there are also married men that like having women on the side. I am not saying that is who he is, but that is *definitely not* who you are! Please tell me you have not slept with him!"

"Of course not, Kate! You just said you know who I am! How could you ask me that?"

"I apologize! I panicked for a moment. You need to let this infatuation go—and that is all it is! Infatuation! Focus on your novel!"

"You are right," I said reluctantly.

I could not tell at first if she was shocked or annoyed that I did not know what she did. As much as I hated her words, I could not argue with her. Liam has been the first glimmer of hope and interest I have had for nearly five years. Perhaps it has nothing to do with the man, but the moment. I can feel my heart opening up for the first time in a long time, but if he is not available, my infatuation and longing are pointless. But I could not let it go and I was more forward than I should have been.

On 29 September 2022, at 08:32, Corrine Hunter wrote:

Tonight is my last night in Edinburgh. Then I am off to London and Vancouver. I cannot promise a bottle of Dom Perignon, but I'm happy to buy you a drink at The Balmoral if you are available.

C

+++

FOUR
The First Glimpse Of Hope

Bar Prince, The Balmoral Hotel
Edinburgh, Scotland
September 2022

"Do you know this is not a coffee shop, lass?" said the man standing next to my corner stool at the bar top. Despite having one of my wireless headphones in my ear, I heard exactly what he said, and I refused to look at him.

I have heard this line many times before in pubs and bars across the world and rolled my eyes immediately. Sitting with a computer in a bar is annoying to some who believe if I want to work, I should just sit in a coffee shop and not take up a valuable seat in a bar—especially an expensive bar.

"You don't say!" I said rudely, still refusing to look at the man and continuing to type out my notes from my afternoon at the National Library of Scotland. I am clearly working and have no time for this judgmental nonsense.

The man said nothing more but did not move. I could see him out of the corner of my eye, still standing next to me at the bar. Finally, I stopped typing, took out my headphones and looked up at him, clearly annoyed by the disruption. It was then that I looked straight into the gold-flecked hazel eyes of Liam Crichton.

"Well, hello! This is a surprise. What are you doing here?"

"I am here with my colleagues," he said briefly, pointing to a group waiting for him at the host stand. "We are going into the back of the restaurant that we reserved for a private dinner. I saw you here writing in the corner, and I wanted to say hello. I am happy to see you again!"

"I am happy to see you as well!"

"I am sorry I did not respond to your last email and kind invitation."

"Please do not feel bad about that. I expected nothing as I know you are busy, and my invitation was so last minute."

I regretted that email the instant I sent it and thought that as sad as I was to miss seeing him again, he at least saved me the embarrassment of rejecting me outright. But as luck would have it, here the man is anyway!

"I have to take care of my team. We just signed a £500 million deal to revamp the operations maintenance software for two wind farms off the coast of Scotland. Will ye still be here when our dinner is done?"

"I make no promises, sir," I said with a flirtatious smile.

"Corrine," he whispered as he put his hand on the back of my chair. *"I willna ask ye to wait for me tonight, but I have more to say to ye. I just have to take care of my team—they worked so hard for this."*

His thick Scottish accent and glassy eyes told me that the celebration of this deal started somewhere else well before their arrival at the hotel.

"I can only assume this will be a hearty celebration for a deal of that magnitude. Try not to get kicked out of the restaurant or the hotel." I could feel the eyes of his colleagues waiting for him to go into the dining room, secured behind the curtain. I nodded to them before putting out my hand to shake his.

"Congratulations to you all!"

"Thank ye!"

I began mindlessly watering my drinks down, trying to hold on and clearly waiting for Liam to walk out of the dining room. I told myself more than once to go to my room, but I could not seem to leave my seat. I would type for a moment and stare at the curtain in the back, hoping it would move. He was going to have to escape to the toilets at some point. Finally, he did.

On his way back, he said, slurring his words as he sat on the barstool next to me, "Dinnae wait fer us."

"You are drunk, sir! Please tell me you are staying here in the hotel."

"Aye, we all have rooms and think that has added to our freedom with drink. Once we hit the whisky, I knew I was in trouble."

He placed his head on my shoulder in a moment of drunken weariness. I put my hand around his head and patted his warm cheek.

"I leave for London tomorrow and then will return to Vancouver to complete my move to the UK. I will send a note to your email when I have confirmation of the dates for my return to Scotland."

"No," he said, perking up for a moment. "Please stay! And why are we not talking on mobile?"

"We have always just communicated via email," I said, intentionally ignoring his request to stay in Scotland.

"Well, we will correct that *here and now!*"

We exchanged mobile numbers and once we both had them secured in our phones, I said, "Your colleagues are waiting for you."

I was sending him back to the dining room that he came from. He should be there and not here. He said nothing more to me and walked away reluctantly with a side glance at before disappearing behind the curtain to the back room.

I looked down at my phone and typed *'My Scot'* as the name for the number I just gained and smiled at the thought of him. Just then, my phone vibrated, startling me.

> I already regret you
> leaving tomorrow. LC

I did not respond to him but just whispered under my breath as I stared again at the curtain, *"I already regret leaving you tomorrow, Liam."*

+++

I have never been so hungover in my entire life! And that is saying something! Watered down or not, my wait for Liam in the hotel bar last night put me in a fragile state.

After a late-night room service order of a club sandwich and glorious chips, the healing power of fried potatoes did not save me, and I struggled with my ritual departure packing routine.

Despite being mostly packed and setting multiple alarms on my phone, I was late getting to the car waiting for me in front of the hotel. My poor driver, Paul, who has driven me on each trip in Scotland, quickly learned that I was not in the mood to talk when I ignored his question about returning to London. He has always been kind to me, and I tried to make it up to him with my gratuity, but I could not speak to him this morning. I lamented seeing Liam, only to have him walk away from me once again in the hotel bar. In this case, I would have preferred not to have seen him at all. But that is my mind talking. My heart was more than happy to see him once again before I left.

Thankfully, I managed a shower this morning, but I had to do my makeup on the car ride to the airport. I tried to hide my sins and poor choices under a hat and large sunglasses. I only revealed my true, hungover self for the quick trip through airport security.

The one-hour flight to London from Edinburgh was the least of my worries. It was the car ride to my hotel in London that proved to be the most painful. I tried so hard not to be sick in my driver's pristine Mercedes sedan while answering his polite questions. I know he was nervous that I kept rolling the window up and down when I thought I would be ill. But the crisp and cool Autumn air brought me from the brink more than once on the drive into the city.

As we neared the hotel, I realized I had never taken my phone off of airplane mode when I landed. With a restored signal, my phone repeatedly buzzed. I had several preemptive birthday messages from friends around the globe and several texts from Kate about our dinner plans at the hotel on Sunday. There was, however, one text message that stood out.

Travel safe.
I will find you. LC

I could not reply to his text. I do not know what his words mean. I spent the day in my glorious suite with a warm bath, an assortment of spa facial and eye masks, a round of room service, and mindless TV. As much as I wanted to go down to the bar to see my old friends, I could not bear the thought of getting dressed. I also had nothing good to add to my manuscript today. I was in no physical or emotional state to edit or write new and I do not go to the bar without my computer in tow. Instead, I told myself that I could afford a day off. *Finally!*

I benefited from being a repeat customer, as the hotel already gave me bottles of wine and sparkling water with a large bucket of ice in my room for my loyalty and to celebrate the reason I was here. I hope to see them all tomorrow so I can thank them for their generosity.

Tonight, all I can think about is the man I left behind and misery I feel. I tried to relive it all in my head. Looking for clues to tell myself that what I am feeling is not real and that I will probably never see him again. If what Kate said is true about him being married, I may not. The more I thought about that prospect, the more miserable I became. After an evening of wine and self-pity, I retreated to the comfort of my bed.

+++

I heard the doorbell and knocking at the door and wondered who would be so bold when I clearly pushed the *'Do Not Disturb'* button. There should be a small red light on the bell outside my door to signal that I did not want to be bothered.

I opened the door to meet the general manager of the hotel, who said apologetically, "I am so very sorry for the interruption this evening, Miss Hunter, but we were instructed to put these flowers in your room upon your arrival. We made a mistake when we upgraded you to the suite that they were not immediately moved from the original room assigned. I apologize again, but the sender was insistent. *'Do Not Disturb'* designation or not. You *must* have them today. I hoped you would not fault the ringing of the bell for such a lovely bouquet."

"Of course, and I thank you. They *are* lovely. If I may, it gives me the opportunity to give you the room service trolly I failed to put outside my door earlier."

"Absolutely! My pleasure! Let me take that for you, miss!" Visibly relieved that I was not angry about him ringing the bell, he handed me the flowers and walked in to retrieve the cart.

I held the door for him and said, laughing, "I am not sure that this is a fair trade, but I thank you!"

And I did thank him. It was not even eight o'clock, and I needed to stay up longer, otherwise I would be wide awake at three o'clock in the morning. Once he left, I looked at the beautiful white flowers and greenery in a round glass vase and sat them on the table in the entryway. I opened the small card and read the handwritten note:

Happy Birthday!
Until I see you again, LC

I smiled immediately. I have said nothing to Liam about loving white flowers. I do not know how he could know this but took the bouquet as another sign that he was a special man. I tried to find the hope for a future in his message. It will be difficult not to see each other, but we will. I just do not know when. In one day, I was falling back into obsessing about things that had nothing to do with my novel. But this man will not leave my thoughts… or my texts.

Are you there?

Yes, sir.

That is just what I
needed.

Thank you for the
beautiful flowers!

+++

FIVE
Confessions

The Corinthia Hotel
London, England
October 2022

I woke remarkably refreshed after two days of indulgence. I guess that should be expected when you set your alarm for one o'clock in the afternoon. I looked at my phone to see it was now Liam's turn not to respond to a text message.

I went downstairs to see my old friends in the Northhall Bar to thank them for the wine. Tommaso greeted me right away by taking my hand and warmly welcomed me back to the hotel. We caught up with each other's lives since I was last here, and he made my white wine spritzer kit straight away.

I love how some bars give me all the ingredients—the glass of wine, the bottle of soda water, and a container of ice so that I can make my spritzer the way I want it. I made myself comfortable in my favorite seat at the bar and opened my computer to work.

At one point, I stopped typing to take a sip and looked up over my wine glass to see a face I did not expect. The man just walked right through the double doors to the bar and looked around the room. It took me a minute to register his face because it was out of place. He should not be here. Our eyes met and we both smiled. He walked over and stood next to me.

"What on earth are you doing here? You did not tell me you would be in London!"

"I could not let you go back to Vancouver without seeing you again. You told me you would be here, and I told you I would find you."

"You did."

"I also know it is the day before a very special birthday. So I flew down."

"You just *flew down*," I said, almost mocking that he could do such a thing on a whim. I imagined his private jet sitting at London City Airport waiting for him to return to Edinburgh. This is a level of wealth I will never see as an author—no matter how many books I sell!

After a few moments of staring and smiling at each other, unable to speak, I asked directly, "Then you felt what I did when we met?"

"Aye, and I tried to tell myself that you did not or that I could just determine your feelings on your return to Scotland, but the unknown of when that would be became too much for me. I had to come here."

He leaned in and whispered in my ear, *"Walk with me."*

I nodded to him in agreement. Tommaso smiled at me as I signed my bar bill, but said nothing. I only smiled back at him, silently telling him I was safe and not to worry. He would have never said a word, but he made me feel protected. They have always looked out for me in this hotel bar.

I led Liam across town to a pub I found on the other side of St. James' Park—The Colonies. It was a pleasant walk, and it seemed like the most out-of-the-way spot for us. The pub is near Kate's new office and should be quiet on a cloudy Saturday afternoon, as it mostly serves businesspeople in the area during the week.

We walked together through St. James's Park and talked of all that had happened since we last met, my birthday celebration plans with Kate and friends the next day, my return to Vancouver, and my plans to return to Scotland in the future. When we turned on Wilfred Street, Liam took my hand in his for a moment before opening the door to the pub and escorting me through the door. Once inside, I sat down at an empty table in the far corner as he ordered our pints at the bar.

When he returned to our table, he sipped his pint for a moment. I could tell he was nervous. I could see beads of sweat on his forehead, and it was not from our casual walk across town. Seated together and sipping beer in silence for what seemed like an eternity, I finally said softly, "You said in Edinburgh that you had more to say to me."

He looked at me and smiled briefly, acknowledging that I knew he had something to say, but was reluctant to speak. Finally, he bowed his head and said, "Aye. I do. I am married."

My heart sank. I took the longest sip of beer so I could keep from saying anything—so I could keep from saying the *wrong* thing. I expected these very words. Kate already told me the truth of it, but I thought if I could ignore the thought long enough, it would not be true. I wanted the fact that he was here with me now to mean it was most definitely *not* true.

"It is important that you know I am separated and in the process of getting divorced. It has been going on for nearly six months now. We are close, but obviously with my companies, assets, and kids, there is a risk being seen with another woman. The timing of the business deal that I told you about raised the stakes again, but I could not hold the deal back any longer."

I just nodded as he continued, "Being seen with you in the hotels or even here now could completely derail the progress we have made so far. But it was a risk I was willing to take because I wanted to be honest with you. I owed you the *truth*, and it was killing me I did not tell you before. I tried to when I saw you in the hotel bar the night I had dinner with my colleagues, but you know I had too much to drink... and... I was a coward. I feared you would never speak to me again."

"I understand."

It was all I could think to say. I did not like it at all, but I understood. I appreciated his honesty... albeit delayed.

"Like I said, I tried to tell myself that you must certainly not feel the same. Each day that passed, I realized I could not determine what you thought, but I could not lie to myself any longer. I could not ignore my *own* feelings. I have done that for far too long. That is why I am here."

I was relieved by his words and his honest confession, but only a little. I looked around the room to see if anyone noticed us. I looked at him with all the empathy that I could muster and said again softly, "I understand."

"For the most part, my wife Sarah and I are managing this amicably for the sake of our boys. She wants to move on. I know this as a fact because she started this process. She filed for divorce first. But I have no doubt that she or her savvy solicitor would be thrilled to have proof of me with another woman to accuse me of adultery and use that false allegation as leverage in the negotiations."

I looked down at his left hand and the gold band that had reappeared there. I touched his left hand and said softly, "You did not have a wedding ring on when we met."

"Aye! Another point of shame for me! I don't know what made me do it, Corrine, but I put my ring in the pocket of my jacket as I walked into Bar Prince that afternoon. I did it mindlessly. I was not trying to lie to you. I did not even know you and our meeting was for business. Throughout the separation, I have been taking it off and on. I did not have it on the day we met at the Rose & Crown, either."

I nodded to him as he continued, "I am trying to navigate my new life ahead… what it means to be single again. Had I been thinking rationally, I would have also never been so bold to play *the game* with you that evening. Ring or not, I was inviting judgment from everyone watching us in that bar—not just Miss Nosy. The people who work in the hotel know me *and* my wife."

I nodded. He didn't seem to be trying to lie to me. I confessed to him myself, "If it makes you feel any better, I did the same thing."

He turned his head and narrowed his eyes, unsure of what I meant. He looked at my left hand and noticed the diamond band that was now there.

"I am not married, but I have this diamond band I keep on my ring finger hoping it will prevent men from talking to me in a bar, but for some strange reason, I moved it to my right hand just before you walked in that afternoon."

"Aye," he said, sipping his beer again and processing my words. Liam does not know about the diamond band or where it came from, but nodded that we did the same thing. As awkward as this all is, we did the *same* thing before we met. We both made an unconscious choice that we were going to be open to the person we were about to meet, even though it was definitely not a date.

"So much of our talk has been of books and business. I do not want to intrude on your personal life, but tell me about your sons," I said, trying to focus this conversation on what was really important.

"Thank you for asking. Twins. They just turned fourteen and are becoming fine young men, and I do credit their mother for that." I smiled at him for his answer and his honest tribute to his wife.

He continued, "They are incredible individuals, each with their own distinct personalities. Eric is creative and artistic. He was interested in pottery for some time, but has focused on watercolor painting for the last year or so. He has become quite the talent!"

The proud father continued, "Ewan is athletic and, after playing football from a young age, has now become more interested in rugby. He is slightly taller than his brother, and honestly, the sport best suits his temperament. They look so alike but could not be more different. It has been a joy watching them grow."

"They sound like fine young men, finding themselves and their place in this world, as you start to do at that age." I bowed my head and nodded, thinking about such young boys watching their family and the only life they have known change before them.

"I do not want to lose you, Corrine, but I have to finish this part of my life first."

"I understand."

I said the words once again, but I am not sure either of us believed them. We sat in silence and sipped our beer, staring at each other, uncertain of what to say next.

Finally, I asked, "Liam, will I be able to see you when I return to Scotland?"

"Of course! When are you coming back?"

"I failed to complete my manuscript in the way I planned. So, using your advice, I mapped out my next steps. I will ask Kate for my second extension and that includes a return to Scotland before the end of the year—either November or December. I hope to convince her at my birthday celebration tomorrow."

"Then, aye! We may have to make sure that we are with others in professional settings—especially in Edinburgh if my divorce is not final. But we will see each other, I promise you that!" He leaned in towards me and said softly, *"I would hate not to see you."*

"Neither of us expected to meet someone that we wanted to know better. I do not want to get in the way of what you have to finish and if we are honest, we are both old enough to know that nothing good can come from rushing whatever *this* is. At the risk of sounding like an author, I believe you should focus on closing one chapter before starting another."

I heard my voice trailing softly with emotion a little at the end of my ridiculously clichéd response. As much as I believed the words I was saying, I regretted each and every one of them. I am certain he could see the pain in my eyes, despite my feeble attempt at a smile.

Liam took my hand and held it tight as he said, "Spoken like a true author, indeed! Do not be discouraged. We just have to be careful."

He took our empty pint glasses back up to the bar to get us another round, and I leaned back on the bench, trying to catch my breath. It felt like I had been holding it since we sat down. I tried to give myself a peptalk as I watched him politely ask for fresh pints. *This man just flew to London to tell me the truth and to see me before I go home. I <u>will not</u> be discouraged!*

From the moment he returned to the table and sat next to me, my demeanor and tone changed. I expect that my time with him here is short, and I want to enjoy every moment. The beer helped me lose some of my tension and focus on our conversation, which was just as animated and fun as our first meeting. We both like to talk, that is for certain.

Soon, our conversations became low and quiet whispers to each other. His hand sometimes found mine under the table when he made a point or laughed. He looked around and saw that were alone in the pub and took a moment to steal a kiss.

With his hand on my cheek, he brought his lips to mine for a moment. We both kept our eyes open during his tender kiss and laughed at each other. Once again, we did the same thing. It shocked me that he kissed me with all his talk about risk and discretion, but all I could think is that I would give anything for him to do it again. The tickle of his beard and his soft lips melted my heart. I cannot place it, but he smells so sweet—as sweet as his kiss.

"We should head back to the hotel," he said to me once our pints were empty again.

"We should."

As we approached the steps of the hotel. He slid a room key into the pocket of my trench coat. "I have booked a suite here tonight. I planned for us to have dinner together instead of going to the restaurant. It is just a little more... *discreet*."

I panicked for a moment about being in his room with him. We have only known each other for a few weeks. While I am strong enough to know where my personal boundaries are on being with a married man, that restraint could go out of the window quickly if I am in his room—especially after spending the afternoon together.

I put my reservations aside for a moment when he leaned in and whispered, *"Dinner will be ready for us at eight. It will be good to talk more and to celebrate your birthday. Do not dress up. Be comfortable."*

Once in the lift, I looked at the folio and saw that his suite was at the end of my hall, just opposite mine. We exited together, and he walked past me at my door, looked back, and smiled. I wondered if he knew where my room was or if this was a coincidence.

No. If I have learned anything over the last several weeks, there is no such thing as coincidence with Liam Crichton.

+++

I played out all the scenarios in my head and none of them had the outcome I hoped for. We just talked of divorce and discretion, and yet he is inviting me to his suite for a private dinner. We are both saying the right words but then doing the opposite because we are drawn to each other. As much as I love it, I *hate* it! This is going to be difficult, but I made my decision. I walked out and rang the bell outside his room promptly at eight o'clock.

Liam came to the door and asked, "The card key didn't work for you?"

I handed him the folio and said, "I did not try it."

He just looked at me, narrowing his eyes, before taking the key from my hand. He slowly opened the door for me to enter the room. I did not move from the hall and finally said, "Liam, this is playing with fire and not as private and discreet as you think it is."

"Corrine, please come in out of the hall."

"No, I cannot. Finish what you need to."

His initial look of pain and rejection immediately turned to resignation as he hung his head before saying, "I know you are right. I cannot explain what I feel for you—what I felt for you in an instant—but I cannot seem to stay away."

"That is why I have to walk away for us both—even if it is just across the hall." My voice cracked for a moment, and he reached out to me. I stepped back from him. First, there are cameras everywhere. And second, I am afraid that if he touches me, I will lose every bit of my already shaky resolve.

"I am *so sorry*. I wish you a happy birthday! Please have a wonderful celebration with your friends tomorrow."

"Thank you for that. And thank you for coming here and telling me the truth. I respect you for it... truly I do. Good night and safe travels home."

"Good night."

I heard his door shut behind me and I walked into my suite brokenhearted but confident that I did the right thing for both of us and any future we hope to have together.

+++

Look outside your door.

I opened my door to find a room service cart outside. This sweet man wheeled my dinner out for me to enjoy. He ordered perfectly cooked steak and sides. There was a small cake with an unlit candle in it and a bottle of white wine and his handwritten note underneath on hotel stationery that read:

I thought you should still have your supper.

Happy Birthday!

LC

I thoroughly enjoyed my dinner and stood on my balcony with a glass of wine, thinking about how the day unfolded in the most unexpected of ways. Soon I became mesmerized by the light from the crystal chandelier visible through the glass dome in the center courtyard below.

Thank you, Liam!

You are most welcome!

I thought about everything that happened and what keeps pulling me and Liam together. I cannot explain it! Whatever it is, I worry now about seeing him on my next trip and fear we are just setting ourselves up to make the same mistakes again—saying one thing and then doing the exact opposite.

I can only hope and pray that this is the fastest divorce in Scottish history because I all want is to see him again.

+++

SIX
This Is Fifty

The Corinthia Hotel
London, England
October 2022

Against their own rules, the hotel reserved a table for me and my dearest friends in the Northhall Bar. Tommaso met me immediately, wishing me all the best for my special day. Soon, I was joined by Kate and her husband, Luke Matthews.

Luke was best friends with my fiancé David from medical school and has always been so kind to me. I absolutely adore him and, much like the man I loved... he is a gentle soul. He is also the best partner for Kate who can have—let's just say—a more *volatile* temperament. She likes to call herself *passionate,* but she can be a bit of a pill sometimes. Luke can calm her better than any other person on the planet and often does so with only a look or a soothing touch.

"Luke," I said, hugging him tight. "It is so good to see you, my love!"

"Happy birthday, Corrie, my girl," he said, kissing my cheek and handing me an enormous bouquet of roses and his wife her martini.

"Thank you so much! These are beautiful!"

Kate kissed my cheek and said, "You don't look a day over forty-nine, my darling."

We all laughed and said, "Well, I am exactly a day over forty-nine, so it is going to be all Botox and expensive night creams from here on out!"

Just then, our mutual friends Mark and Colin arrived. We all hugged and kissed each other. Between my travels and the pandemic, it has been a long time since we were all in one place together. Two years, in fact. My friends were a welcome sight—milestone birthday or not! This reunion was celebration enough.

Mark Ramsey is also a doctor and longtime friends with David and Luke from medical school. His husband, Colin Peterson, is an interior designer and a gifted one at that. They have been a couple for over fifteen years and married each other in the middle of the pandemic. They postponed their wedding four times because of restrictions, but decided not to wait any longer. They are planning a huge celebration for family and friends in June of next year.

"When are we going to have you finally here in London, Corrie?" Mark asked me straight away as he kissed my cheek. "We miss you so!"

"Well, I don't know, love. I am not sure I want to move to London anymore. I want to live in Scotland. Possibly, Edinburgh."

They all looked at each other in shock as Kate asked, "You want to move to Scotland, now? I thought you were looking at flats in London and had already narrowed the options down to your top two choices."

"Aye, ye got me there, lass," I said in the worst attempt of a Scottish accent ever! Kate nearly spit out her drink at my words. We all laughed with her. I sounded ridiculous!

"I am returning to Vancouver to complete my move by handing all of my belongings that have been in storage to the moving company. I just need to make a call on where to send those items. Edinburgh is smaller than London, but still has all the benefits of city life. I also feel more connected to Scotland after my recent books and travels."

Kate sipped her martini but said nothing to me, but her narrowed eyes and furrowed brow still showed her suspicion about why I had suddenly changed my mind about where to live. She knows based on our conversation that I had become infatuated with Liam, and I would bet she thinks moving to Edinburgh is a foolish notion. In fact, I can see what I saw as suspicion at first is actually judgment as she continued to stare at me over her glass.

"I *love* London! You know that! You all know that without David, there is no reason for me to live here. I can visit you and you can visit me. But I have learned that I want a slower pace of life. So, to be honest, I am actually considering the countryside of Scotland, not just the city. I fell in love with a small town called Banchory on my last visit, so it is on my list for consideration. I have more research to do, but there are many quaint villages in Fife, Perthshire, and Aberdeenshire in consideration."

Before she could say a word, I looked at Kate and asked, "Do the books and my long-standing publishing relationship with your firm give me any hope of a work visa or do I already have latitude with a Canadian passport, as a member of the Commonwealth?

"I actually do not know the answer to that. We would have to talk to the lawyers. You also have your own solicitor to ask. But I would guess that you are fine with a Canadian passport to live and work in Scotland. Either way, I suspect your own wealth and any investments you make in the country—like buying property can help. They will know you will not be a tax on them—meaning you will not move there and live on the dole. You can pay your own way."

"Exactly!" I said excitedly at the prospect of such a move.

"If you can't figure it out, you *could* always marry a Scot," Colin said with a smile and a wink. I smiled back at him. The thoughts of marriage never entered my mind until now and I wondered if Kate said something to the men about Liam. No one said a word, but like clockwork, all three of them stood up and vacated the table on the topic.

Luke kissed his wife's cheek and said, "This is a celebration! It is time for the Champagne! We will be right back, ladies!"

Kate and I looked at each other suspiciously. She knows my mind and I know hers, but we said nothing more to each other about the possibility of my moving to Scotland, visas, or my marrying a man from Scotland.

"Well, you are loved in this hotel, Corrie, my girl," Luke said as he triumphantly returned to the table, followed by Mark, Colin, and Tommaso with flutes in one hand and an ice bucket in the other.

"The 2010 Dom Perignon, Miss Corrine," Tommaso said, presenting me the bottle.

"Oh my! The hotel does not have to do this!"

"No," Luke said immediately. "It was not the hotel. There was a man at the bar that when he heard the Champagne order was for your fiftieth birthday celebration, insisted on buying this bottle for you."

"Liam," I said under my breath.

In that instant, I remembered that this was the same bottle we shared at Bar Prince for the game with Miss Nosy. I stood up to scan the faces surrounding the bar top, but he was not there.

"Luke, what did the man look like?" I asked frantically, but he said nothing.

I screamed at him, *"Luke!"*

He just looked at me and then Kate, confused at what was happening and said, "I did not look that close, but he was um…. Scottish."

"Tommaso! Was it Mr. Crichton, my friend? Which way did he go?"

He pointed in the lobby's direction of the hotel. I ran down the hall and through the Crystal Moon Lounge with the gorgeous chandelier I was mesmerized by the night before and down the quick steps to the front door.

"Can I help you with a car, Miss Hunter?" The kind doorman asked as I arrived on the front steps, completely out of breath.

I did not see Liam anywhere, just the taillights of a black Tesla at the end of Whitehall Place. I looked up and down the street for some sign of him and I finally said, "No. No, sir. I am fine. I just needed some… fresh air. Thank you."

As soon as I arrived back at the table with my dearest friends, Kate said, "Gentlemen, if you will give us a moment. Take your glass with you and, love, find us a table in Bassoon Bar. Preferably in the back corner by the fireplace, or at least as far from the piano as possible."

Luke led the rest of the party down the back hall to the other bar. They were all understandably confused by my frantic behavior, but followed Kate's direction without saying another word to either of us.

My Scot once again played the spy at the bar and my heart was lifted and broken in an instant.

"It was him," I whispered, staring into my newly poured glass of magnificent Champagne. *"It was him.* He should have left this morning, but he didn't."

"Corrie, what was Liam doing here?"

"He came to tell me the truth."

"Liam came all the way to London to tell you he is *married?*"

As my friend, she had every right to break the trance I was clearly in, but I still resented her for it.

"You do not understand! He *wanted* to see me."

"No, I guess I do not understand his foolish rationale for being here or that you continue to be shocked by the truth you already know. But what I know better than anyone is what you have had to endure since David," she said, with tears welling up in her eyes. Her words and the emotion behind them make me finally look at her.

"And I will not let you be hurt again!"

"He is not hurting me," I said in weak defiance.

"Is he not? For Christ's sake, you just ran out of the hotel after the man! *The married man!* And you are sitting before me on the verge of tears!"

My tears were at the very brim of my eyes as I said softly, *"He is getting divorced."*

"They are always getting fucking divorced! Come on, my darling! You are not this naïve!" I just looked at her in pain for the man that left and for her harsh words of judgment against us both. She grabbed my hand and tried to calm us both. "I cannot imagine what it must take to let someone else in, after all this time. But I would not be your friend if I

told you I support this. I see it hurting you and I cannot. Please stop this *now,* before you are hurt even more!"

"I can't tell you what this is. I cannot describe it myself. I have tried over and over and all I can admit with certainty is that since David, no one has touched my heart or mind like Liam. It is that simple, and it happened the minute I met him."

Kate just looked at me as I tried to rationalize feelings that I have not articulated until now. "Liam is not just some wealthy man managing his empire and looking for a mistress on the side. He is looking for the same love and connection that I am. A love that I would have sworn to you just months ago that I was content to have only once in my life. For me to even say these words to you feels like a betrayal to David."

"They are not a betrayal," Kate said softly under her breath. I knew she had more to say. And she did.

"I connected you with Liam to help finish your book, *not this*. I do not..." Kate paused herself mid-sentence and just looked at me with her tears again forming in her eyes to match my own.

"Say what you have to say."

"I do not want to be responsible for another heartbreak in your life. I introduced you to David, and I introduced you to Liam and I will be devastated if he hurts you. What I see before me now is pain, not happiness!"

I had not realized that Kate felt this way about introducing me to David and I reached out my hand to her and said, "You cannot carry such guilt! David was the best thing that ever happened to me, and none of us could have expected what happened to him. It is too early to tell about Liam, but I will be fine. I will be *just fine*!"

"Will you?" she asked me over her own tears now falling on her cheeks. Mine quickly followed.

"Yes! You cannot keep me in a glass cage, protected from heartache and pain. Life can hurt sometimes, but if I have love on my journey, that has to be good, right?"

She just nodded to me but said nothing. "I told Liam last night that we could not be together until his divorce was final. It hurt me to walk away from him, but it was the right thing to do. It really *hurts*! He should have left this morning, but his staying in London today and buying the bottle of Champagne which we shared the day we met was a kind gesture. I should not have caused a scene, but all I could think in that moment was that I did not want him to leave me. That is the pain you see. We both want to do the right thing, but keep finding it difficult. I should not be with him now, but I also did not want him to leave. I am my own contradiction."

"I am glad you are going back to Vancouver for a bit. It will be good for you to wrap things up there."

"Are you going to give me the *'absence makes the heart grow fonder'* speech?" I asked, trying to make her smile and lighten the mood between us.

Kate did smile briefly before continuing her advice. "No. But settle your life while he settles his. And please do not move to Scotland for a man! Go because you truly want to live there."

"Understood."

Kate is right. I am avoiding London because of the painful memories I have here but I need to determine myself if the pull to Scotland is truly because I have fallen in love with the country or if I have fallen in love with the thought of a man in the country. A man who is *not* mine."

Kate's demeanor totally changed, and she said excitedly, "Tonight is your birthday! Your *fiftieth* birthday! We are all here to celebrate with you and love you! We should join the men and enjoy the last of the evening. What do you say?"

"I agree with that. Thank you, Kate."

"You are an absolute pain in my ass sometimes, but I love you, my darling!"

"I love you! But I have one more thing. I hoped to say it earlier, before we got distracted by birthday celebrations. I am glad it is just us here now."

"Oh, God! I am not sure I have had enough bubbles for anymore heartfelt confessions tonight," she said, draining the last of her glass and trying to make me laugh this time.

"It is fine," I said, taking her hand in mine. "I need another extension. I know I can finish this book. I can't give you another broken manuscript. I won't give you another broken manuscript. But I am not ready to give up on what I have just yet. Please, Kate! Give me until the end of the year. We both know that everything will slow through the upcoming holidays, anyway. I can email you my plan to finish it. I mapped it all out."

"You have it. But I want to know more next week about what to expect from you because you are now affecting our production and marketing schedule for next year."

"Absolutely!"

We hugged each other tight and walked hand-in-hand down the back hall and joined our party before the perfect table in front of the fireplace in Bassoon Bar. We not only finished the bottle of Champagne Liam left us but had much more to drink before we were the last to leave the bar as it shut down for the night.

+++

"I think this should be the last of our celebration, friends," Kate said, finally protecting me and the rest of our party. We all over-indulged and were over-served, but it was a wonderful birthday. I love each person sitting with me here and I felt their genuine love for me.

Fifty is a milestone. It could be very easy for a woman to get bogged down in doubt and insecurity, especially as she ages, but I felt good tonight. *Really good!*

I decided that whatever happens with Liam, I thank him for boosting my confidence over the last few weeks. It has been like the fog has lifted a bit and while it was painful to say goodbye and watch him leave, I believe we will see each other again.

Finally, I said, raising the last of my glass, "Thank you all for making my birthday so special. I would not want to be with anyone else this night!"

Luke immediately said, "We love you, Corrie, my girl!"

Kate followed with, "We do, my darling!"

Each member of our party hugged and kissed each other at the front door as they got into their black cabs home. I walked back to the elevators and thought to myself that my words and sentiment were true, but there was one more person I would have enjoyed spending my special birthday with. Unfortunately, he left tonight without saying a word to return to Scotland.

+++

SEVEN
My Scot, The Spy

The Balmoral Hotel
Edinburgh, Scotland
November 2022

Bar Prince at The Balmoral Hotel in Edinburgh is bustling this evening. It is so nice to be seated at the bar top once again after many of the pandemic rules have fully relaxed in Scotland since the start of the year.

Sitting on a stool at the bar top and watching the people come and go is fun again. Things are finally feeling more and more *normal*. While I like to keep to myself and usually avoid talking to people over my drink or my computer as much as I can, I welcome the camaraderie at the rail versus being at a table in the corner all alone. It was difficult to be removed from what was happening at the center of the bar. I naturally gravitate to bar staff for support and felt so disconnected from the people who work so hard to take care of me during all the COVID restrictions. I have one more month in Scotland before resubmitting my manuscript, but welcomed the company and the chatter tonight.

The bartender said as he dropped off my spritzer, "You work a lot, Miss Hunter and we have enjoyed having you here the last few weeks. This glass is on *us*."

"Thank you so much, Simon! Please call me Corrine. I work a lot on my computer, but it is *fun* work. I am an author."

"*I knew it!* Are you a travel writer—perhaps writing about the hotel or Edinburgh, then?"

"Oh no! Though I would have nothing but good things to say based on my stay here. My view of the castle is stunning! Every time I look out my window, I am reminded of how blessed I am to be in this hotel and this city. And of course, I have found another home here in the bar. You are all so kind to me as I sit here on the corner seat with my computer."

"You are most welcome. All of us here in the bar say that we are glad when you are here because you are friendly, kind, and make no demands."

I took a sip of my drink and said, "To answer your question, I write novels and I am here in Scotland again conducting research for my latest. It is based during The Great War—World War One."

Just then, the older gentleman next to me said in his thick Scottish accent, "Aye! I could not help but overhear ye, lass. Scotland fought hard in that war and sadly lost an entire generation of lads."

"You did indeed, sir. I have learned a great deal about the sacrifices Scotland made during the war. All this research will not only improve my novel, but I hope to honor their memory."

"Another Negroni, lad, and let's make it better than the last!" He was clearly no longer interested in Scotland's contribution to war or my writing and immediately started talking about what makes for a good Negroni.

"Do ye know what makes for a good Negroni, lass?" The man asked me pointedly and loudly. I doubt he cares if I know what makes a good Negroni, but likely wants his beleaguered bartender to hear his thoughts and correct himself.

With a brief smile between Simon and myself, I understood instantly his comment about not being a demanding customer at the bar. He has his work cut out for him, as he clearly is not meeting this man's expectations. I would say from my perspective that it was not for a lack of trying. Thankfully, before I could answer the gentleman—or hear what makes a perfect Negroni—my phone started vibrating with an incoming call.

Even before I saw who was calling me, I welcomed the well-timed interruption that would surely excuse me from this conversation. "Please excuse me, sir! I apologize. I just need to take this call."

"Of course," the man said with complete understanding. Though he was more focused on the construction of his next drink than me. When I looked down, I saw *My Scot'* on my screen and smiled. This was a most welcome interruption!

"Well, hello there," I said sweetly to the man on the other side. I was happy to hear from him, to be sure, but equally relieved for the break from this mindless chatter at the bar. We texted regularly but could not see each other because of schedules, his own travels, and my general aversion to tempting fate once again.

"Who are ye talkin' to, Corrine?" he asked. It was hard to be offended by his cold and direct question against the warmth of such an accent.

"To you, sir."

"I mean at the bar."

"Where are you?" I asked and looked around, pulling my glasses down from the top of my head for a better look on both sides of the restaurant and bar. I did not see him anywhere. He remained silent. It was in that silence that I could hear he was outside as I heard the wind rushing around him. I knew he was walking on the street.

"Answer my question and I will answer yours," he finally said.

I could tell he was being playful, but I could also tell there was still an air of suspicion underneath. Still, I looked anxiously for any sight of him. I stepped away from my seat at the bar top so that I could get a better view of the room and outside the door to Princes Street. I also wanted to be away from my company at the bar so that I could speak freely without being heard.

"I have just talked to the bartender and some older gentleman who keeps chatting to us both about the best Negronis in the world, when we would rather, he didn't. Especially since he has not positively ranked the Negroni young Simon has put in front of him twice now. There are five versions of the damn thing on the bar menu here, but somehow, he is still unhappy. *Where are you?*"

"Settle everything there and meet me at the Rose & Crown."

"Liam, if you can see who I am talking to, walk with me to the pub. I can hear the traffic around you and the chime of the tram. You are already walking on the street now. Wait for me!"

"I will have a pint waiting for you when you arrive."

I gave in on my argument, as he did not sound willing to walk with me. "Alright. I will meet you there shortly."

I ended the call, shut down my computer, signed the bar bill to my room, and set out for the Rose & Crown. In the dying light of the evening, I looked up, down, and across Princes Street, hoping to see Liam walking ahead of me. I cut across to Rose Street a few blocks early. Surely, a tall and impeccably dressed Scot would be noticeable even on the crowded streets of Edinburgh.

Unfortunately, Liam Crichton was nowhere to be found.

+++

When I walked into the pub off brick-lined Rose Street, I immediately saw Liam seated at the same wobbly table under the watchful eye of the portrait of Flora MacDonald where we sat together weeks ago.

"Well hello there, Corrine," Robin, the bar manager, said. "Welcome back!"

"Thank you, Robin! It is always good to be here with my friends at the pub. Are you well?"

"Very. Tennent's?" She asked, already pulling a glass from underneath the bar for me.

"No, it appears my pint has been secured. But thank you."

True to his word, Liam had two pints of Tennent's on the table. As I slid into the seat opposite him, his eyes immediately softened. There was a candle burning and dripping wax down the sides of an empty Glenammon whisky bottle on the table, making the scene even more romantic.

"This is a surprise!" I said, putting my glasses in my bag, now under the table, and raising my pint to his. "I did not think I would see you on this trip."

"I had to see you, but I could not go into the hotel bar."

"But you were spying on me at the hotel bar… from where?"

His mouth twitched slightly on the word *spying* as he took a sip of his beer. "Aye, I was on the front steps outside the entrance. I started to walk in, but that is when I saw you talking to the man, and I felt a wave of jealousy that I have not felt in a very long time. I wanted to walk here to the pub alone so I could settle myself before seeing you."

I reached out to touch his arm and said with a smile and a wink to reassure him, "He's not my type."

I sipped my beer as he smiled, finally letting go of all the jealously and suspicion about the older gentleman in the hotel bar. I do not know what I think about him being jealous. I felt immediately flattered, then appreciative that he knew his thinking was not fair, and that he confessed the truth of it.

"I have missed you," I said.

"Aye, and I have missed you. I regret that you have been back here in Scotland, and we have not seen each other."

"Well, I finished everything in Vancouver and returned as quickly as I could. You have work to do, Liam. I get that. But the Rose & Crown is not exactly a *professional setting with others*."

"It is not," he said as a matter of fact before taking a quick sip of his own pint. He knew I was throwing his own words back at him. I could not tell which he hated more saying them in the first place, or that I reminded him of them.

After sitting together in silence for a moment, he said, pointing behind me, "If you need to go to the loo, it is just there."

"I introduced you to this pub, Liam. I know where the toilets are."

He just smiled back at me over his own glass. After my quick retreat from the hotel, I did, in fact, need a moment. I kicked my bag further under the table and stood to excuse myself. I climbed the two short steps to the next landing and walked to the back corner of the pub. The doorway on the left went into a short hall that split into men's and women's toilets. I had not crossed the threshold of the hall before he grabbed me from behind. With one hand around my waist and the other moving my hair to the side, he started kissing my neck.

"Liam!"

It startled me at first, but I knew full well that he was sending me back here for a reason. I welcomed it and resented it all the same. He then turned me around to face him. Breathless, our hands and mouths were desperate. We both missed each other and the game of cat and mouse this afternoon only added to the tension of seeing each other again. I swear! He smells so good! I cannot place it, but his scent is sugary sweet and absolutely intoxicating.

"I'm sorry! I wanted to see you and when I did, this is all I thought about," he said in my ear.

"And you can't kiss or touch me in the pub and definitely not at the hotel," I said, finishing his thought and breaking the spell he had on me.

"I cannot."

His tone and demeanor turned despondent as placed his forehead to mine. I felt his pain, as I was equally sad at the reality of our situation. His divorce is still not final, and we remain trapped in limbo.

I touched his cheek and said, softly, *"Please, go back to our table. My passport and computer are inside my bag. I will be screwed if I lose either tonight."*

He reluctantly let go of me and did as I asked. I needed the loo after leaving the hotel so quickly, but I also needed a moment to think. His work and travel schedule had been a blessing. I made much more progress with my novel by not having the constant distraction of seeing him.

As much as I want this man, I am not interested in being anyone's mistress. I am too old for that game. And I do not want to live in the shadows or the back toilets of pubs across Scotland. Apparently, I need to say more, and it is going to hurt us both. We both keep saying we must stay apart, but clearly cannot do so.

I am as guilty as he is! Simply by being here with him now, I have gone back on my insistence that he finish his other life. Leaving him in London was painful, and it is going to take all the strength I have to do the right thing and leave him again tonight.

When I sat back down at the table, I was thankful that we did not lose my bag. We talked freely over our beer of all we accomplished during the weeks we had been apart. I officially left Vancouver for the last time but have still not decided if I want to live in Scotland or England, so I just move between my favorite hotels in Edinburgh and London. Luckily, my belongings will take another twelve weeks or more to make it to the UK, so I have a bit more time to determine where I want to land.

We talked about my research at the National Library of Scotland and how further immersion in the country has improved my book, but it remains unfinished. His sustainable energy ventures have become even more profitable as the country continues to find its way out of pandemic restrictions that plagued many companies during the last few turbulent years. It may be too early to help many this winter. There are, however, encouraging signs for next year. But what I will remember more than anything is how easily we talked and laughed together.

I watched Liam walk to the bar top to secure us one more round of beer as I prepared myself to say the words I dreaded. Once he returned, he gently touched the top of my hand wrapped around my pint in a quiet moment. I pulled my hand from his and sipped my beer. I smiled at him and refused to put my glass back on the table for a bit, before finally setting it aside and putting my hands in my lap.

"We cannot do *this,* Liam. *Not now.*"

He seemed startled by my words, but did not speak.

"You have something that you must finish first. I think about you all the time. You *know* that! In fact, the mere thought of you leaves me as breathless as your hands and mouth on me just moments ago."

He smiled for a moment, thinking the same, but he knows what is coming and his face now shows me he is not happy about it.

"But I will not cause you any trouble with what lies ahead for you with this divorce. I understand the situation you are in; *I do!* I don't like it one bit, and I do not know how long it will take before you can resolve it all, but I *understand.* I hope you will respect me for saying that I do not want to live with you in the shadows. Finish what you need to and then come to me. I will wait for you."

I took the risk and gripped his hand. He leaned back from the table and away from me. Now it was my turn to feel a twinge of rejection as I looked down at my hand resting alone on the table. He sighed, thinking about my words for a moment, and leaned back to me, taking my hand in his again.

"I respect you and your words. You are reminding us to live up to the values we have. I do not want you to feel anything less than you are. As much as it hurts, right now, I have to respect both you and my family… my lads."

"That is the thinking of a man I could love."

"Like you said, I dislike it, but I *understand*. If ye walk away from me again, my heart will break, but I know you deserve better."

"I deserve *you* when it is right, Liam. We just met each other too soon."

"*We met each other too soon*," he said quietly and nodding at the truth of it.

The very act of walking away could risk ending this—whatever *this* is—forever, and that scares me. Even though it started in an instant, I believe what we feel is real. Once we can be together openly, I truly hope we can try this again.

We just met each other too soon.

I gathered my things, and he reached out his hand to mine and asked, holding it tight, "Can we still email and text with each other? I like knowing you are… *there*. It is a comfort to me."

I had to fight the tears welling in my eyes. "Of course! I like knowing you are *there* as well."

"I am so sorry for all of this."

"I am *not* sorry. And at the risk of detection in the middle of the pub, I will leave you with this when you are ready." I leaned down and kissed him with the most passion I could muster while fighting back the tears forming in my eyes and the deep sorrow and regret I felt in my heart.

I could sense that he was also emotional, but he said nothing as I walked out of the double doors of the pub. I walked all the way back to the hotel in tears. I had foolish thoughts of him running after me like some horribly predictable romance movie, but I knew he would not. He could not.

I spent the evening at the bar at the hotel, frantically typing in my books. The sadness and heartbreak I felt was rich fodder for my other stories. I tried to capture my feelings as best I could between my tears and my wine.

Simon, the kind bartender from earlier in the evening, and ever the professional, kept the glasses coming without instruction or intrusion into my work. He only smiled at me sympathetically when I asked him for the bill just before closing.

+++

EIGHT
A New Beginning

Bar Prince, The Balmoral Hotel
Edinburgh, Scotland
December 2022

"**I would very much like to kiss you, Corrine,**" Liam said, **standing next to my chair at the bar.** His presence shocked me as he arrived here unexpected and unannounced. I tried to keep myself composed as it had been nearly a month since we last saw each other.

We had kissed before, but he did not seem certain of where he stood with me. Despite his declaration, he seemed shy. I looked at him and asked, "Are you sure you want to do that in the middle of this very public hotel bar?"

"I suppose I deserve that," he laughed and shook his head. He knew my rebuke—while lighthearted—was anchored in truth. "It is over. It is all over! So, aye! I would like to kiss you in front of every person in this very public hotel bar."

"Well, then…" I said softly to him as I placed my hand on top of his, resting on the back of my chair. He pulled up his other hand and wrapped it under my hair and around my neck. His thumb came to rest on my chin, just before my ear, and pulled me to him slowly. He brought his lips to mine, and we both met each other and breathed in deeply. It was a simple kiss, but tender. It was emotional and long overdue. I am not sure what it is, but he always smells like sugar.

He tilted my head slightly to rest his cheek on mine. I could feel the slight tickle of his beard and the warmth of his face as he whispered in my ear, *"I have wanted to do that for a long time."*

"Perhaps you should do it again."

He did and hugged me tight. I could feel his relief along with my own. I whispered in his ear, *"I leave for London tomorrow."*

He pulled his head back and said, looking at me, *"No. No, you don't.* You will cancel your hotel and change your return flight to open. Or you could cancel your commercial flight all together. I can fly you private when you need. We will leave tomorrow for my house on Loch Leven, just north of here."

"Is this *really* happening?" I asked, smiling up at him.

"It is," he said, kissing me quickly once more and taking my hand in his. "Before I even met you, Corrine, I dreamt of finding a woman who would love me for me and who would support and challenge me to be a better man. A woman that I could love and support in return. I knew the minute I shook your hand and talked with you in this very room that the woman I was looking for was right before me."

I smiled at him, in a haze of emotion and desire as he sat in the bar stool next to me, and said, "When I met you and you left me in this bar to go home, I told myself that I hoped you would never walk away from me again. But, as much as it broke my heart, I have left you more than once."

"Aye, you have!"

"I thought leaving you in the hotel in London was the hardest thing I have ever done, but nothing compared to walking away from you in the pub! I was absolutely gutted! I cried all the way back here to the hotel."

"You had to. What I was asking of you was selfish. Your words hurt me, but I deserved each and every one. I was, as you said, relegating you to hiding in the shadows. I am *so* sorry. Can you forgive me?"

"There is nothing to forgive. I knew you weren't trying to hurt me or disrespect me. You wanted what I wanted—which was to be together! But, we have too much respect for each other to live a half-life and too much self-respect as individuals to live a life that could hurt others. I knew you would come back to me when you could… *and you have!*"

He squeezed my hand in his and brought it up to his lips to kiss. "Finish your drink and then *walk with me.*"

I smiled at the invitation I heard once before. I wanted to go wherever he would lead me. We said very little, but stole silent glances at each other. Even in the middle of the crowded bar, he was the only person I saw or heard. It felt like we were starting over, but we never felt tentative with each other like we do now. Tonight, we both seem nervous and uncertain despite the freedom finally offered to us.

Once he paid the bill and stood up, I said, "My coat is in my room. Will my wrap be enough for where we are going?"

He placed his hand on my back, leading me to the door out to Princes Street and said, "I will keep you warm."

When we stepped outside, he wrapped his wool coat around my shoulders and kept his arm around me. We walked with intention. We were not just on an evening stroll.

"Where are we going?"

"You will see."

Once we crossed in front of the festive Christmas market at Princes Street Gardens to Hanover Street, we turned left onto quiet Rose Street. I knew he was taking me to the pub. The smile grew on my face the closer we got to the Rose & Crown. We stopped outside the door, and he took off his tie and unbuttoned his collar as he said, "There are times for fancy dinners and drinks and then there are times you just want a beer with a friend."

"Thank you for bringing me here! You know I love this pub!"

We walked in and by some miracle, my table was available. Once we entered, Michael said loudly, "Here comes trouble!"

I immediately felt at home. I smiled and said, "It is good to see you again too, Michael!"

With a slight nod of respect to Flora MacDonald's portrait over the table, I placed Liam's coat over the chair next to where I thought he would sit. But when he came back to the table with two pints of Tennent's in hand, he told me to move over so he could sit next to me instead of opposite.

I realized that what he said was indeed true about being at the pub. Sometimes you do just want a beer with a friend. Liam was smart to bring us here. It helped take some of the edge off of our reunion, and I slowly became more relaxed. He kept his left hand around me on the back of my chair and his right hand on his pint.

"Are you happy, Liam? That it is all over? The process, I mean. I am sure nothing about what you and your family have had to go through makes you *happy*," I asked, trying to correct myself mid-sentence.

"I am sad that my boys have to deal with the aftermath of the choice my wife—*my ex-wife*—and I made." His sudden correction reflecting the new reality of his life sounded pained in a way. It was another signal that part of his life was over, and it was new to him. "But it was the right decision. We were unhappy for a long time. I can already tell my sons sense that the tension they felt at home has lifted. That gives me some comfort that perhaps we made the right decision, and they will eventually understand that this was the best decision for all four of us in the end."

"I have never been married myself, but I can imagine all the ways relationships can change as people grow and change on their own. But I cannot imagine what it means to have children involved and what that adds to the emotion of it all."

"I admit that has been the hardest part for me. There is a lot of resentment and pain underneath what Sarah and I feel about each other, but trying to be amicable for the sake of the boys has been a shared goal, but still a difficult one. I confess some days are better than others."

I said nothing back to him and after a brief sip of his beer, I let him continue. "To answer your original question, I am glad the process is over. There is freedom in the finality of it and I can be here with you now without constantly looking over my shoulder and calculating every point of risk in my head. But it will never *truly* be over. We have sons to raise and based on the settlement terms, I will pay spousal support and for the care and education of my lads for many years to come. Sarah and

I are no longer married, but we will always be their parents. Nothing changes that."

"Of course, even if expected, an ending is an ending, and it is sad."

I asked no more questions. It was none of my business. And the mere mention of spousal or child support and money was *definitely* none of my business.

"Are you glad that I am here?" he asked with the initial shyness that I thought we lost when we walked into the pub.

I took his face in both of my hands and I kissed him and hugged him tight. Pulling back, I said, "I am so happy you are here! I have missed you! Tonight, I was miserable thinking that you would let me leave Scotland again without a word. I was ready for another lonely night in the hotel bar, drowning my broken heart in all the Sauvignon Blanc they have."

"I am sorry," he said, placing his hands on top of mine.

"Everything works at it should," I said, taking the last sip of my pint.

"I will be right back," he said, kissing my cheek before taking our empty pint glasses back to the bar for another round. Upon his return, he took off his sport coat and threw it on top of the wool coat already resting on the chair opposite us. He rolled up his shirt sleeves and sat back down next to me.

We raised our glasses and said in unison, *"Sláinte."*

Once we both took another sip of our beer, I said, "Now tell me all about where we are going tomorrow."

"Aye!" he said, turning to me excitedly. "I will drive us up to the house at Loch Leven. I inherited the house and land from my parents, so I got to keep it in the settlement. It is not a long trip but is a beautiful and relaxing spot out of the city. You will love the house! It is large and sits right on the loch. It has plenty of walking trails and I have a boat that we can take out any time. I thought we could stay there for a bit and get to know each other more… but as I say the words, I realize I should have asked you if you *want* to join me at the house."

I smiled but said nothing. I can tell he is nervous, and I admit it is endearing to see him in such a state. Liam took my silence for acceptance and kept selling me on the house on the loch.

"You will have your own space, and I understand that you have a process to write each day. The location might inspire your work. I also thought I could invite some people over one day and you could meet some of my friends."

I did not think about assumptions, but I wondered about being in a family home and now meeting friends. I could see he was excited about it, and I wanted nothing more than to share that feeling with him. So I became excited about it myself. He observed me as I processed my response.

"It sounds wonderful! I would very much like to see this house. You may not remember, but you mentioned it the night we met. I also want to get to know you more and meet your friends, but I think having my space is important for work… and… *this is all so new*."

"Do not worry! I already asked for the guest suite to be made up for you," he said, silently acknowledging my sudden shyness.

"Asked who?"

"I have a house manager and a chef," he said almost apologetically.

"Of course you do!"

Liam ignored my judgmental response and said with a proud smile, "Mrs. Elizabeth Norman—or Miss Betty, as we call her—runs everything at the house. She will see that you have anything you need to be comfortable. And Chef Dan Garrett is incredible. I stole him from a Michelin-starred restaurant here in the city that shall remain nameless. He will want to talk to you right away to understand your preferences and allergies to ensure your suite is stocked and that our meals together are stellar."

I got nervous as he spoke and tried not to show it. I wanted to be in his life, but before now, that life did not include others. I immediately felt my personal insecurities at the very thought of accompanying a man I had only known for a few months to his family home just after his divorce was final.

Putting his arm around me, he said, "I can see—and feel—that you are thinking and worrying. You will love them, and they will love you. We will all be glad to welcome you as our guest."

"Then I should go back to the hotel, cancel my trip to London, and get packed. What time do you want to leave tomorrow?"

"Let's plan on checkout. Noon. I know I just surprised you with this so you will have tonight and then the full morning if you need it, to prepare. I have a room in the hotel for the night. They will have my car waiting for us out front."

"I think that sounds perfect!" I said, smiling at him.

"Let's go," he said. He placed the half-empty pints on the bar and put on his sport coat. I let him place his wool coat over my shoulders once again, and he kissed the top of my head and took my hand. After saying our goodbyes to my friends at the pub, we walked all the way back to the hotel hand-in-hand. We said very little to each other, but enjoyed the newfound freedom to be together.

In the hotel lift, I handed his coat back to him and said, "I will see you at noon tomorrow."

He kissed me on the cheek and smiled.

I got out on my floor and turned back to smile at him. He smiled back as the doors shut between us. I ran all the way down the hall to my room. I had a lot of work to do to be in Scotland longer and I had to pee something fierce! Leaving the Rose & Crown without going to the loo first was a mistake for a nearly mile-long walk. Thank God, I made it!

I laid across my bed wondering how this day just unfolded and how it resulted in me staying longer in Scotland with Liam at his country house. I am excited and just as nervous. I could never have expected such a thing! Just then, my mobile phone rang. I saw the name *'My Scot'* on the screen and I smiled.

"Missing me already, are you?"

"Aye! But I realized I let you walk out of the lift, and I did not say good night. So, *good night* to you and sleep well."

"Good night, and I will see you at noon tomorrow."

"Noon tomorrow."

I hung up the phone and yelled as I laid back on my bed, *"Here we go!"*

I packed strategically, planning country days and potential nights. I wished I had known this was going to be the plan, as I would have had more laundry done at the hotel. I could only hope that Miss Betty would help me on that front. After drinking the water left at turndown, I slipped into bed and canceled my London travel.

I worried again about what was ahead of me, but my last thoughts before falling asleep were of Liam's lips on mine, how he makes me feel wanted, and how much I want to kiss him again.

+++

NINE
The Bonnie Banks Of Loch Leven

Loch Leven, Scotland
December 2022

"Your chariot awaits, Miss Hunter," Liam said, taking my luggage from me before the tartan and Harris-tweed-clad doorman could. He placed my bags in the back of his black Range Rover plug-in hybrid with his own luggage as the doorman helped me into the passenger seat.

On the winding route out of Edinburgh, we talked about nothing but traffic, wayward pedestrians, and discourteous drivers. I have driven enough in Scotland to identify the tourists who cannot cope with the roundabout or driving on the other side of the road. We laughed together at some mistakes our fellow travelers made in their newly acquired rental cars.

Once we made it to the Queensferry Crossing Bridge headed north, we were quiet for a bit as we both took in the calming views of this glorious country from the high perch over the Firth of Forth. I reached across the middle console, took his hand in mine, and smiled at him. He smiled back and held my hand tight.

I said very little, but remained connected to him for most of the drive. Once we exited the motorway, he needed both hands to navigate the narrow roads and country lanes leading to the house. So, when he let go of my hand to take the wheel, I moved to place my hand down on his thigh. He looked at me and said, "Don't make me lose control of this car!"

We smiled at each other, but I kept my hand exactly where it was. Thinking about all the nervousness I had going on this trip, I wanted him to know that I was here and that I welcomed his invitation to join him in his home. I will do everything I can to not let fear get in my way and will combat any notions of my insecurity trying to block me from happiness. I cannot predict where this will go or for how long, but it is worth trying with an open heart and mind.

We turned off the narrow road onto an even narrower tree-lined lane. We passed through a gate that he opened with a button under the rearview mirror, and once we went around a curve, the lane led to the most beautiful house I have ever seen. Part of it has an old stone façade from whatever ruin existed here before, and the rest was modern in all kinds of glass and wood glory. The house would have fit in perfectly with the grand homes of the Pacific Northwest.

We pulled into the circle drive as an older woman came out to meet us. Two young men, possibly brothers, and around sixteen years old, by my guess, took their positions dutifully behind her. I smiled at Liam and laughed silently to myself because of the spectacle of it all. It was like we just arrived at some sort of modern version of *Downton Abbey*.

Liam stepped out of the car and gave Miss Betty a warm hug. I exited on my own and came around to the other side of the car to join them.

He put his hand on my back and said, "Miss Betty, I would like you to meet Corrine Hunter. She will be my guest here at Crichton House."

She immediately lost her smile and said coldly, "Of course you are most welcome, Miss Hunter. We have your rooms ready, sir."

I said graciously, "I cannot wait to see the house, Miss Betty. Upon first impressions, I can only imagine my room is beautiful. This is a stunning home."

She did not respond to me and did not smile again. I just looked at Liam and he moved his hand from my back to my elbow, which he squeezed in support and winked at me. He opened the trunk and told the nameless young lads my bags from his so they could place them in our rooms.

Miss Betty and I stood looking at each other in awkward silence, until Liam came back around and took my hand, saying, "Come with me! I will give you the grand tour!"

We left the nameless lads to deal with the luggage and Miss Betty to direct them. I asked as I touched the stone once we climbed the stairs to the front door. "What was the ruin? Do you know?"

"It was an old fishing cottage, as best we can tell. You can still see some logs from the old docks by the new boathouse we built. We were told at one point there was a mill here, but we have seen no evidence of that."

"I would have thought you would have researched this extensively."

"I did, but it had been a ruin for hundreds of years. Just getting the deed to the property took my father nearly a decade. What you see of the old stone outer walls was all that remained when he bought the land. He specifically asked the builders to reclaim every stone and piece of wood that they could. My father instilled a sense of sustainability before I ever knew what the term meant. I did not realize until now that he was a man ahead of his time."

"Then he taught you well."

"He did. I had the house completely gutted and remodeled about three years ago to bring it up to a more modern standard but preserved as much as we could again."

"It is absolutely beautiful! I love you kept what you could from the ruins. Not just from a sustainability perspective, but an architectural one. The mix of ancient and modern is striking."

"I will show you on a walk, but there are remains of an old stone wall on both sides of the house in the woods, and you will also see inside that we took some of the stone rubble from the grounds for the fireplaces."

Liam squeezed my hand as we walked up the stairs, into a grand foyer. I could tell he was proud to show off his house, and once we walked into the next room, I stopped in my tracks. The back wall was all glass from floor to ceiling, bringing the loch and the surrounding woodlands into the house. It was so peaceful. Any place away from the frantic hustle of life in the city and obligations should be peaceful and restorative. In the short time we have been here, I already feel calm.

"Oh, my! Look at that view! It is gorgeous, Liam!"

A massive fireplace on the right with the stones he mentioned dominated the main living area, and a large and open kitchen was just to the left. Just then, the chef came around the kitchen island to greet us. I was so captivated by the view before me, I had not even noticed that he was standing there when we walked in.

"It is good to see ye, man!" Liam said, first shaking the man's hand and then hugging him.

"LC, it has been too long!" the chef said. He was another tall Scot, but he clearly has a good relationship with Liam calling him by his initials instead of his name.

"Dan, may I introduce you to Corrine Hunter? She will stay here in the guest quarters for a while, and I want to ensure she has everything she needs. Corrine, this is Chef Dan Garrett."

"It is a pleasure to meet you, chef," I said, putting my hand out immediately. "I have heard only great things about you and your cooking."

"The pleasure is all mine, Miss Hunter," he said respectfully and shaking my outstretched hand. "I have read some of your novels and I am quite a fan."

"Are you *really*?" I asked in disbelief, thinking that he wouldn't even know who I was, let alone have read any of my books. Liam smiled and nodded his head.

"Aye! I love historical novels. Especially ones about Scotland."

"Then you will like the next one. It is a story set in Scotland during World War One," I said proudly, supporting the wayward novel I cannot seem to finish.

"Och, I cannae wait to read it, then! Now, Miss Hunter…"

I interrupted him and said, "Corrine, please."

"Miss Corrine, my goal here is to ensure you all have the food and drinks you want during your stay here—formally at mealtime and in your suite."

I nodded to him as Liam said, "Ask Corrine what you need to, and then I will take her on the rest of the house tour."

Liam then stepped away to open some of the broad accordion glass doors to the outside. Despite a slight December chill, the fire was raging, and the cool, fresh air was welcome. He was bringing the beautiful surroundings even more into the room.

Chef said as he opened his notebook. "First, I need to know of any allergies."

"Just shellfish. I have an EpiPen, but I have never had anaphylactic shock or needed to use it. I had a progressively worse reaction to shellfish—mostly scallops and shrimp—about a decade ago and stopped eating them out of an abundance of caution based on the advice of my doctor. Since then, I have the occasional oyster or bite of lobster during the year that has never caused me any reaction. I would say, just give me an option. I will not fall over if you make a dish for others at the table or use in a fish stock. And like I said, I have managed the occasional bite with no consequence."

"All the same, it is good to know. I will keep things clean for you, but if you choose to have a bite here or there, you can make that choice. Just make certain LC knows where your EpiPen is!"

"Understood. It is in my bag, Liam," I said as I smiled and nodded my head to both of them.

Chef Dan is a very engaging man. He is probably in his mid-thirties and handsome, with reddish brown hair and bright blue eyes. Much like Liam, he is naturally talkative and his Scottish accent, while softer, is just as mesmerizing. He takes his job seriously and is most welcoming to me here in this house.

"Now, let's talk about preferences," he said, turning a page in his little black notebook. "Breakfast, or no?"

I looked at Liam as he nodded to me. I answered honestly, "Most days, I prefer just plain toast and butter, maybe some jam. I can certainly manage that myself. But, after a night of drink, sometimes I like a full-on eggs and bacon breakfast. And you cannot dismiss the miraculous healing properties of fried potatoes."

"Add some beans, mushrooms, tomatoes, and even some haggis and most Scots would agree with you," he said as the two men laughed at the thought of the universal hangover cure of a full Scottish Breakfast.

"I can also manage that in a kitchen if needed. I am not the best cook, but I am great at making eggs."

"Good to know," he said, still smiling at me and back at his boss. I blushed for a moment, as I doubt I will ever make anything more than toast in Chef Dan's kitchen.

"I will never want porridge or cereal."

"Understood. How about a European breakfast?"

"If you mean a meat, fish, and cheese board, then yes, sir," I said. "Any time of day, I find a meat and cheese board perfect. In fact, I could nibble all day on them and never have a full meal until dinner."

"I knew I liked you the minute you walked in," he said, laughing as he leaned toward me. "LC also prefers snacks to meals. You can imagine that it makes my job as chef at this house quite *easy*."

"Exactly!" I said, smiling back at Liam, who seemed amused that we were both snackers. "I need little. The exception being the healing traditional breakfasts I mentioned… and maybe the occasional fine dinner. Of course I defer to the master of the house on that."

He wrote this all down in his book as I asked him, "What type of food do you prefer to cook, chef?" He seemed pleased that I asked him about his own preference. He smiled and leaned across the counter to me and said directly, "I can cook anything you want, Miss Corrine, but my specialty is Mediterranean. Mostly Greek and Italian."

I repeated his own words back and leaned toward him, saying, "I knew I liked you the minute I walked in, and we will be fast friends. Greek and Italian are my favorites!"

"Then you will like dinner tonight—it is risotto."

"I will certainly like that!"

Liam nodded to me, and I felt like this was a good start.

"Last question—let's talk drinks. Alcoholic or no, what do you *prefer*?"

"White wine!" Liam said, laughing aloud before I could say the same.

I nodded to him and said, laughing myself, "I do like a white wine, usually crisp and light—a Sauvignon Blanc, Pinot Gris, or Sancerre, *never* a Chardonnay—but with ice and soda water mixed in."

"A spritzer then?"

"That is right! A spritzer! I also like the occasional Diet Coke or just plain water handy. I like hot tea but rarely drink coffee."

"No whisky then?" Liam asked before the chef could, as he was still busy recording my preferences.

"I am not knowledgeable enough about whisky to direct there, so will abide by house rules. But…" I said, looking at Liam with a smile of remembrance. "I do sometimes just like a beer with a friend."

Liam smiled back at me, as Chef Dan said, "That is all I need for now, though I suspect we will both learn more about each other. When you get to your suite downstairs, I think you will be most pleased that you have a small bar area in the sitting room. We have provided cheese, crisps, nuts, water, and Diet Coke for you. You have your own tea kettle and a coffee machine there as well. You will not have to come up to the kitchen if you do not want to. The most incredible thing about this bar, however, is that you have your own ice machine. You will never want for ice!"

"Thank you so much!" I said with genuine appreciation that Liam and Chef Dan have provided me a room with my own mini bar. "I do like my ice."

Liam said, laughing at me, "That you do!"

"I will go shopping shortly and come back to prepare for dinner, now that I know what I want to make for you both."

"Aye Dan, we appreciate it. I will take Corrine into town to add to our white wine selection in the cellar because of her preference. Let us take care of that today. We will have dinner in the dining room, aye?" Liam motioned to the room on the other side of the kitchen, though he did not show it to me.

"Aye," Dan said. "I already set it for dinner."

Liam said with his hand taking mine, "Come with me! Let's continue our tour."

"Thank you," I said with a smile back at Chef Dan, who just smiled and nodded to me.

We walked through the rest of the house. On the main floor, only a guest powder room and the enormous master suite remained. Liam's luggage was already in his room and Miss Betty was there unpacking for him. I smiled briefly at her, though she did not smile back. We walked quickly back out and up the stairs.

I worried that she may have unpacked my unruly mess of a bag. We passed several rooms with closed doors he said belonged to his sons. I respected that he kept their personal bedrooms private. We then arrived at a cinema room that had its own well-stocked bar, drinks fridge, and popcorn station. A small game room was next to it filled with multiple TVs, gaming consoles, and a billiards table. We walked back downstairs together and then to another set of stairs that looked like they were leading to the basement but revealed an entire suite on the ground floor.

The graduated slope of the house on the hill meant that this area had the same beautiful views of the loch as the floor above. We arrived in a large living room that had the mini bar chef mentioned, a seating area, and a desk. I had a gas fireplace that separated this room from the bedroom—warming both. The guest room and bathroom—with my own massive steam shower and tub—rivaled all the grand hotels I have stayed in. My luggage was placed on a rack in the walk-in closet between the room and the bathroom. Thankfully, it was not open or unpacked.

I took Liam's hand and said, "It is absolutely beautiful! I cannot wait to explore more with you. When is dinner?"

Looking at his watch, he said, "We won't eat until after seven, but I can direct Dan as needed. Like I said earlier, I thought we would take a quick drive to town for wine before."

"I will need only an hour to get settled. Will that work?"

"It does! And no need to be formal. Remember, we are relaxing in the country."

"That's right! I just need some time to get cleaned up and situated at the desk. I can text and meet you upstairs when I am ready."

"Of course, and I know you may want to do some work. The Wi-Fi information is in the top drawer of the desk. Do you have a mobile signal?"

Taking my phone out of my bag, I said, "I have not even looked! I do!"

"Oh good, it can be hit or miss here. Take your time and no need to text unless you want to. I want you to feel welcome in this house, so come upstairs whenever you are ready."

He kissed me on the cheek and walked back up the stairs. I looked again at my phone to see who had reached out today. Kate sent me a text wishing me safe travels. I think I will leave her thinking that I am headed to London for now. Even I do not know how to describe what is happening as I sit on the edge of my bed staring out at the sun peeking through the clouds and dancing on the glassy waters of the loch.

+++

I broke my spell with the gorgeous view outside my room and set up my computer and power cords at the desk and then unpacked and organized my clothes. Luckily, I found a steamer iron already filled and ready to use in the closet. I removed the wrinkles from the freshly laundered clothes that had to be put back into my luggage this morning and tried to revive the other items that might be one more wear from needing laundering.

There was a quick knock at the door. I opened it to find Miss Betty standing before me... reluctantly, as best I could tell.

"Do you need anything, Miss Hunter?" she asked out of her own obligation because of her position and not that she actually cared if I needed anything.

"No, but I would like to thank you for the steamer iron. I have steamed all of my clothes and think I am set."

Miss Betty looked both annoyed and crestfallen that perhaps Liam might find out that I tended my own clothes. She still said nothing to me.

"I do have one question for you. I could not see on the panel if there were any other controls for the temperature in my room, other than the floor tiles in the bath. Can you help me?"

"Aye. Are ye cold then?" she asked with a somewhat dismissive tone that seemed to indicate she did not think that I would be in my room tonight.

"Yes, ma'am. I do like a cooler room to sleep, for sure, but it feels a little cold in here unless I am standing just before the fireplace."

"You have controls just here," she said, pointing to the digital control panel and screen next to the bedroom door. "You can set the room temperature and raise and lower the gas flames of the fire."

"Oh!" I said, as she punched effortlessly at the display several times to set the room temperature a few more degrees warmer. I could see the flames in the fireplace raise slightly. "I thank you! I only saw the floor tiles setting for the bathroom on the panel and completely missed the settings for the room and the fireplace itself."

"Anything else, Miss Hunter?"

"No, ma'am. This helps me considerably and I thank you." I knew I had to earn her trust and respect, but she was clearly wary of me. I need laundry done but did not have the nerve to ask her for help for that on my first day here.

She closed my door as she walked out and up the stairs. I cleaned up and got ready for our trip to town. I can only hope that Liam and I will be on our own tonight because I dread seeing Miss Betty again.

+++

TEN
The Other Woman

Loch Leven, Scotland
December 2022

We parked just down the street from a charming wine and whisky shop in Kinross. On my travels, I had not been here before, but I loved everything about the town. I hoped that at some point I could find a day to explore it more.

Once inside the shop, the owner eagerly met Liam the moment he walked in. In fact, I have never seen someone move that fast around a till to greet a customer in my life! I can only assume that he is a valuable customer to this tiny shop.

"Mr. Crichton," the lady said excitedly, with a huge smile as she took his hand. "This is a surprise! We just recently shipped wine to your house. Surely you are not out already!"

"No, we have a good bit still in the wine cellar, but we need to rebalance the white wine selection for my guest. Mrs. Giles, may I introduce you to Corrine Hunter?"

The woman lost her smile almost immediately and said, "The author?"

I put my hand out immediately and said, "The same. It is a pleasure to meet you, Mrs. Giles."

She reluctantly took my hand. I could not tell if she was most disappointed that Liam has a female house guest so soon after his divorce—or that his house guest is me. I wondered for half-a-second if she had actually read any of my books. But I am not sure that I care. In a split second, she made it clear that I was not welcome.

I backed away from her immediately and started wandering the aisles of wine in the shop on my own. I am certain Liam felt the icy chill in the air, but he walked slowly behind me without saying a word. The whisky section soon distracted him and left me to determine which white wine I preferred.

I took a bottle of the Sancerre to the front and said, "Mrs. Giles, I would like to know if you have a case of this Sancerre on hand."

"What is out in the shop is what we have," she said curtly.

"Well then, I can make a case out of this along with the New Zealand Sauvignon Blanc. You have six bottles of each. That will do just fine! Let's package that up and deliver to Mr. Crichton's house. I would also like to have a case of Pellegrino, please."

"I will only deliver orders for *Mr. or Mrs. Crichton*," she said coldly.

I breathed in as I was stunned by her words and her tone. I could not think of a response quick enough, so just stood there with my mouth half-open on the breath. Rather than being defensive and causing a scene in front of Liam, I deferred to my gentler nature.

"I understand. I wanted to pay for this order myself if I could... including any delivery fees, of course."

She ignored me and asked across the shop, "Mr. Crichton, will *you* be asking us to ship this order to *your* house?"

I am not sure if he heard our exchange, but he walked over and said, "Of course! That is what we always do."

"I wanted to pay for my wine, Liam," I whispered.

"No, I cannot have you do that. Mrs. Giles, just put it all on my account and deliver Corrine's order to the house this afternoon. We will need it in time for supper tonight."

I could tell that his tone was more direct than when we walked in. Perhaps he heard what was happening here and set the woman on her task, albeit begrudgingly. She said nothing else to me, and I said nothing to her as she set about following his orders.

"Thank you," I said in a whisper to Liam and touched his arm before walking out of the shop and onto the street. I stood patiently in front of the car alone until he came out. I could not stay in the shop any longer and needed a moment to recover myself. Mrs. Giles is now the second woman to make me feel like a homewrecker and a whore in a few brief hours.

We drove back to the house in silence. Just as we turned onto the lane and stopped at the gate as it opened, I put my hand on his thigh again and smiled weakly at him. I did not want him to think that I was going to let his house manager and a local wine merchant ruin our first evening together.

But they did hurt my feelings. I knew the transition would be difficult and perhaps seen to others as happening too soon, but despite the truth, I could not escape the pain of judgment. Before dinner, I took some time to write in my room. By retreating to my suite, I thought I could compose myself and set my attitude in a more positive direction. Unfortunately, the more I thought about the frosty reception from Miss Betty and what happened in town with Mrs. Giles, the more upset I became.

+++

"Chef, if I am not interrupting your prep for dinner, I would like to get a glass of wine. Do you know if my order was delivered from town?"

"Aye, Miss Corrine," Chef Dan said. "I have a bottle of the Sancerre and a Pellegrino for you in the chiller here. How do you prefer your spritzer?"

I looked at the freestanding bottle chiller built into the countertop and smiled at him before saying. "It is easy! It is a lesson in thirds. A third wine, a third ice, and a third sparkling or soda water."

He handed me my wineglass, and I said after my first sip, "You have mastered the white wine spritzer in one go! Thank you!"

"Come right back here anytime you want another!"

"Absolutely!"

I am more than happy to pour my own glass, but I will not challenge Chef Dan in running his kitchen. I walked with my glass to the water's edge and the start of the dock leading to the boathouse. I shut my eyes as I breathed in the fresh Scottish air and settled on the soothing and rhythmic sounds of the lapping water below and the wind and birds in the rustling trees above. I tried my best to settle myself. This is my first night here with Liam and I do not want to be miserable, but I could not stop the tears I swallowed all afternoon. They had to come.

With his own glass in hand, Liam joined me. He stood silently next to me, but I could not look at him. My best attempts at righting myself this afternoon failed miserably. I prayed he would not look at me, but he did.

"No, Corrine! *No*," he said, turning me to take my wine glass once he realized I was standing next to him, silently crying. He sat our glasses down on the dock and came back to wrap both of his arms around me. I cried into his chest and held on to him. "*What is this?* Please, do not cry!"

I said nothing because I could not speak. I just shook my head in his chest and cried more. He held me tight and ran his hands up and down my back, trying to calm me.

I am convinced that you cannot stop crying enough to speak until you are supposed to. Whatever the emotion—happy or sad. In my fifty years, I have never cracked the code. But, upon his question, I could not yet speak. My time was not up for this crying spell, and I needed a moment before I could say anything to him.

"Was it what happened in town this afternoon?" he asked softly, with his chin on the top of my head. I just nodded into his chest. He held me even tighter. "Och, Corrine."

I could finally speak and said, "We did everything we could to stay apart and be respectful, but I am just the other woman… *the whore*."

"No. Stop that. You know that is not true."

"I understand the thinking and the timing of my being here so soon after your divorce, but it hurt my feelings. Like you said about correcting yourself after seeing me talking to the older gentleman at Bar Prince, I just needed a moment to correct myself. I am sorry to cry."

"Never apologize for showing your heart. And do not let that nonsense hurt you. Some people, like Mrs. Giles and even Miss Betty, need to learn who you are and how you had nothing to do with my divorce. I met you when I was already going through the process. You were not the cause of it. We do not owe anyone an explanation or an apology for trying for a new start so quickly. You and I both know the truth of it and that is all that matters. We just met each other too soon." I smiled up at him at the mention of the words we shared in Edinburgh.

"We met each other too soon," I whispered.

He hugged me tight and continued, "You will build your own relationships here and in town. Be true to who you are, and I know they will all come to love you as much as I do."

I appreciated he spoke of Miss Betty and that he noticed she made this transition difficult at the very start with her coldness. I never complained about her, but it was both her frosty reception and the time in town today that rattled my confidence. The afternoon made me emotional and embarrassed. It was a quick mention, but this was the first time he had ever spoken of love. His words and his gentle reassurance were welcome.

I hugged him tight and pulled back to put my hand on his face. Stroking his beard, I said, "I know you are right. My emotions got the best of me. That is why I came out here. I kept trying to right myself and I did not want to burden you with it, but you have made me feel much better. Thank you."

Liam leaned in to kiss me and said, "They will come to love you. I promise." He then brought up his hands to wipe the last of my tears from my face and retrieved our glasses. He put out his left elbow for me to take as he escorted me back up to the house for dinner like a proper gentleman.

+++

Chef Dan did not disappoint. The mushroom risotto was divine. Liam had the largest seared scallops I have ever seen on top of his plate and the chef made my cod medallions almost look like seared scallops.

I usually choose a cheese plate over dessert, but I made the exception tonight when Dan said he made tiramisu. He left a small cheese plate on the kitchen island for us, but the tiramisu was more than enough. The wine selected for dinner was the Sancerre that I decided not to water down with ice and soda. It was so lovely and cold on its own, having sat in the chiller.

We skipped the dining room on the initial house tour, but I could now see that the back side of the room had a glass wall and door to a lighted and temperature-controlled wine cellar stocked with some of the best wine I have ever seen. At first, I doubted we needed to add to the white wine selection until I saw on our tour before dinner that Liam's wife must have preferred a Chardonnay. I may defer any future orders to Chef Dan or Liam with Mrs. Giles, but I will *not* be drinking Chardonnay.

Like the rest of this incredible house, the construction of the wine cellar honored the past but was exceptionally modern. It had an intricate computer system mounted to the stone wall that tracks the bottle inventory by vineyard and date. Liam or Chef Dan can order more wine directly from the preferred vineyards on the panel when the local wine merchant or stores cannot meet a specific need. The panel also controls the temperature and even the lighting in the room, which offers a beautiful view into the cellar while you are dining at the table.

+++

"Come with me," he said.

We both took our glasses into the kitchen and filled them again, before moving to sit together in front of the grand fireplace.

"Do you feel better?"

"Yes, thank you," I said, leaning into his shoulder. "I thought taking a moment to work when we returned would help me, but it did not. I just wallowed even more in my feelings. You helped me let it all go."

"Never hide your emotions. Honestly, I don't think you could anyway…"

I laughed and said, leaning away from him now, "What does that mean?"

"Aye, you give off an energy. Whether you are just thinking or are uncomfortable, happy, or sad. In the short time I have known you, I can feel what you feel just being near you. It is a powerful thing!"

I could not argue with him on this observation because what he said was true. But I was most intrigued that this man of business and titan of industry talking about feeling energy from another. Perhaps it was another sign of the intense personal connection between us that was established from the very moment we met.

"I heard how Mrs. Giles spoke to you in the shop today and I could feel how you felt with her words. I should have said something to support you right then. I honestly did not know what to do. I did not want to make it worse. I suppose I am learning how to navigate all of this myself."

"I tried to ignore the woman's rudeness in the moment. I have never shied away from defending myself, but I thought the same thing. I did not know what to do. I did not want to make the situation worse or embarrass you on my first day here."

"Once you left, I signed the delivery order, and I told her I was disappointed, and I expected more kindness from her."

"You *did not*!"

"I did! And would say the same thing again."

"What did she say back to you?"

"Nothing. She stared at me, mortified that I called her out on her rude behavior, and I did not give her much of a chance to respond as I walked out of the shop immediately."

"Thank you," I said, touching his hand. I appreciated him defending me. I did.

"Dan said she had a full case of the Sancerre delivered. She sent it along with the Sauvignon Blanc and Pellegrino you ordered."

"Well then. Perhaps six extra bottles of wine *may* serve as an adequate apology."

"It is a start, anyway! I cannot believe she lied about not having it!"

"She was protecting what she knows, and if that includes you and Sarah…," I barely completed my thought before he agreed.

"Aye," he said, acknowledging another area where he was going to need to rethink his new life.

We sat silently for a bit, enjoying the fire and being together. I cannot believe how my life has changed in just one day. I should be at my hotel in London, but here I am with Liam in his gorgeous house on Loch Leven.

Liam put his glass down and then put his arm around my shoulders. He kissed me on top of my head. It was still a very comforting embrace with his warm body next to mine. I know he felt terrible that I got so upset earlier and, even worse, that people would be so bold to treat me poorly.

"Thank you for bringing me here, Liam. It is a lovely house, and you have made me feel *more* than welcome."

"I am so happy to hear that. I knew you would like it here and hope that it is a good place for you to write."

"Oh, of course! I have everything all set at the desk and staring out at the water is perfect. Water has always inspired me."

"Your books are by the sea, are they not?" he asked. I smiled that he remembered what I told him about my novels during one of our talks.

"My very first historical novel was about the ruins of a castle by the sea on the Isle of Skye, but water is prominent in almost all of my books. I am most comforted by the sight, sounds, and smells of being near water. It always finds its way into my stories somehow—even if it is just a character who thinks and feels the same."

"Are you close to finishing this novel? The one about World War One?"

"I am currently trying to clean up some areas on my own so that my second manuscript is not as bad as the first. Kate gave me an extension until the New Year. Thank you again for your advice there! Being here in Scotland and doing research at the National Library has made everything so much richer. It is a good problem to have, but I desperately need to move some of my fresh notes into the story. I have to admit to you, this book remains a challenge for me."

"Your heroine, still?"

"Yes."

He said, holding me tight again, "You must keep up your work! I want to make certain you tell me when you need to write. Otherwise, I will selfishly try to fill up your days."

"I need to write, but I want you to show me everything. What is the plan for tomorrow?"

"Well, I thought we would have a slow morning. We can both work and then I would like to take you on the boat to town. I told Dan that we would have lunch there so he would not come here until he was ready to prep for dinner. I hope you do not mind, but I invited Dr. Marshall, who has a house about ten miles from Kinross, to join us."

"Oh my goodness! That is wonderful!" I said, sitting up and turning around to him, now excited at the prospect. "I will have to prepare for that meeting in the morning. I have so many questions for him!"

"I thought he could be of help to you, and he could not meet in Edinburgh when you were there last. Plus, he is just a lovely man. His wife, Clara, died about eighteen months ago."

"Oh, bless him! I did not know."

"She was already battling breast cancer for the second time, but she caught COVID and was taken too soon. With the restrictions, Andrew could not even have a suitable funeral for her. I believe that and his isolation added to his grief. Clara was also a historian and was just a lovely woman. She was a perfect match for him in every way."

I had a twinge of remembrance of grief I carried in my own life, and I remained silent as Liam continued, "It will be good for him to get out of the house for a bit. I must warn you that the man is a massive flirt. I am going to have to work hard to ensure he does not steal you away from me with his knowledge of history and natural Scottish charm."

"I don't think you will have to work that hard," I said as he kissed me quickly in appreciation. I love Liam's tender kisses. They are loving and kind and he always smells *so good*!

"Then, after that, I believe Dan wants to prepare you a Greek feast."

"You did well on that one! I will think about tonight's meal for quite some time."

"The very first time I ate in the restaurant where he was working, I determined immediately that I had to steal him away. I knew I could pay him more than he was making there, and he would have much more freedom to run his kitchen and make his own food instead of being under the thumb of another ambitious chef who was only there part of the time."

"What does he do when you are not here?" I asked, thinking about how often Liam and his family may have been here in this house during the year versus in the city. Surely that could not be enough for a man who had been leading a busy restaurant kitchen.

"He used to work for us in the city as well, but he is preparing to open his own restaurant in town. I will show you tomorrow. So, while I am sad that he will leave at some point, I know he is not going far. And occasionally, I can still pull him for events or important dinners here or in Edinburgh."

"That should help keep him going as he starts out, I suppose."

"Aye! I will help him as much as I can. He is an excellent chef and has become a good friend. Do you know, I just realized I *won* Chef Dan in the divorce?" We both laughed together for a moment at the prospect of such a thing. From our brief interactions, Chef Dan seems quite loyal to Liam. I am not sure he would be anywhere else—Sarah or the new restaurant aside.

Liam got up to adjust the flames down on the panel near the stone fireplace. I watched him and I thought... I am in awe of this man. With his money, position, and power, he could certainly have a *new start* with someone younger and prettier than me. I shook my head at my own thoughts, still teetering on the edge of negative after my arrival here. I do not know why my insecurities keep invading my thoughts. Instead of telling myself all that I am not, I returned to my original thoughts of how blessed I am to have him in my life and to be here with him now.

Once he sat back down, we sat quietly together for a bit. He put his hands through my hair and on the back of my neck. I already lost a lot of my stress when we arrived at this beautiful house on the water and now his hands and the wine eliminated any I had left. I bowed my head slightly under his hands and said softly, "That feels *so* good!"

He wrapped his hands in my hair and turned me to face him. "*Liam.*" I whispered as he kissed me passionately on the mouth. *"I am so happy to be here with you."*

"I have asked a lot of you to be here and to say longer in Scotland at my house. I know today was challenging for you, but I hope you will be happy here. I *want* you to be happy here!"

We said nothing of how long we would stay in this house and what our next steps were. I dared not ask. I did not want to think of dates and deadlines for the bliss I feel now. I cannot look too far into the future, and tonight I do not want to think about a future away from this man or this country. I also want to be happy here.

"I know I will be."

"Let me walk you downstairs. I want to ensure the fire is warming the room for you and that you have what you need."

I respected he was so kind to me and made no assumptions that I would stay with him. We know that there is a passion between us, but neither of us felt the need to prove it on our first night in this house. I think our restraint and shyness have actually helped temper some of our nerves.

He held my hand all the way down the stairs, and I said, "I can already tell it is warmer down here. I had Miss Betty help me with the temperature control panel this afternoon."

"Did she help you unpack?" he asked. I can tell he is still disappointed that Miss Betty was not as welcoming as she should have been, and I did not want to get her in trouble—or any *more* trouble.

"I beat her to it! I found the steamer iron in the closet so I could refresh my clothes."

"You unpacked and steamed your own clothes?" he asked, now sounding more agitated than ever.

"Please do not be cross about that. We arrived, and I had plenty of time to get settled on my own. I honestly did not have any expectation that someone would do that task for me, so I just did it myself. I am not upset about it, so you should not be either."

"Please ask her to do what you need. You are my guest here."

I could tell he was not happy and immediately regretted telling him that Miss Betty did not help me with my clothes. He had every right to protect me from her coldness at my arrival, but the unpacking was my doing. I could only hope that if he says anything to her, he remembers that I did not give her the chance to help me.

"Now that I am not going back to London, I need to do some laundry for sure! I will ask her tomorrow for the help I need."

He said nothing as he advanced the fire on the panel, immediately warming the guest room even more for me. He came to me with his hands around my waist and he kissed my cheek and then my neck as he held me tight.

I hugged him and said, "Thank you for today. I cannot wait to see more tomorrow."

He kissed me and with our cheeks together, he whispered in my ear, *"I will see you tomorrow. Good night."*

"Good night."

Once he went up the stairs to the main floor and shut the door, I could hear him walk to his own room, over mine. I went straight for the water chef had in my mini-fridge and sat for a moment at my computer to record what I could of the day.

I took a quick shower and brushed my teeth before I slid into my comfortable bed with pillows and soft linens to rival all the glorious hotels I have been in the last few months. Before I fell asleep, I thought about all that had happened in the last twenty-four hours and became overwhelmed.

My mind kept moving between thoughts of hope and bliss to my own nagging personal insecurities. Wherever this is going, I need to settle myself so that I can enjoy all Liam is offering me right now because the most important thing I realized tonight is how much I have missed having a man in my life.

+++

ELEVEN
A Gift Of Inspiration

Loch Leven, Scotland
December 2022

I woke up in the early morning and heard no one moving about on the floor above. I tied my unruly curls into a bun on top of my head, put on my glasses, and climbed the stairs to the kitchen. I was relieved not to see anyone else and made my toast with butter and what appears to be homemade raspberry preserves. I heard Liam talking in his room and went back downstairs to enjoy my light breakfast with my tea before showering and getting ready for the day. I worked at the desk, looking out across the loch, until about noon. I finally heard footsteps above me and watched Liam walk out toward the dock.

I opened my glass door and walked to him. I kissed the back of his shoulder, as I put my arms around him from behind.

"Well hello there," he said, bringing his arm around to hold me next to him. "Did you sleep well?"

"Yes, once I finally fell asleep, that is. Between being the first night in a new place and that you were in the room above me, I had a hard time *falling* asleep."

"Och, I also had a hard time. It took everything I had to leave you in your room last night. I almost walked back downstairs—more than once."

I smiled at him and appreciated that he felt the same.

"Chef Dan left me what I needed for toast this morning. I could hear you talking on the phone in your room, so just took everything downstairs so I would not disturb you."

"You would not disturb a thing! I did not work as much this morning as I thought I might. You likely heard me on the phone with Pete at the restaurant we are going to for lunch. Have you been writing this morning?"

"Yes, lots of writing. Something about the ruins of this house made me think about another historical novel. If there is anything there, it will come together. It is important to record thoughts and lessons when you can. Sometimes notes and ideas become full novels and sometimes they become stories in other books. I worked on my other manuscript a bit, but I also took some time to make my list of questions for Dr. Marshall. I cannot wait to meet him and talk with him!"

"Your process is fascinating! When we walk the trails, you will see other ruins along the old stone wall. We can see if that adds any inspiration to what you have written. Today, we will go back to a restaurant near Kinross just across the loch, but we will take the boat. I have asked for my table which has a perfect view of the loch back to the house."

"I can't wait!"

He kissed the top of my head again and said, "Meet me at the boathouse in about thirty minutes. I don't know what it is, but once we get to the middle, the temperature drops. You will want to wear more than just that jumper. Bring your coat and a scarf."

"Interesting," I said, looking at the calm water before me on a sunny and relatively warmer December day.

"Aye, the ancient legends of the depths of Loch Leven and the kelpies bringing the cold water to the top to rattle the fishers persist," he said, clearly enjoying telling me about this house and location. "It will be much colder on the water."

"I will meet you at the boathouse," I said, walking away from him with a smile.

+++

I joined Liam at the boathouse where he had everything ready, including a thermos filled with hot tea and warm wool blankets. He helped me down into a beautifully restored wooden boat and I immediately sat in the chair opposite the captain. I kept my scarf handy for both the expected chill and wind in my hair if needed.

He confidently drove us across the loch toward the village. Between the sound of the boat's engine and the wind, it was difficult to talk to each other on our journey. Also, the views were so beautiful that I was constantly looking around, trying to take it all in, and taking pictures with my phone even at the risk of forgetting about my handsome driver. When we got to the middle of the loch, it did indeed feel significantly colder! I wrapped up my head and neck with my scarf.

"I told you," he said, laughing at me.

He pointed out Loch Leven Castle, as we passed the island in the middle of the loch and told me all about how Mary Queen of Scots was imprisoned there in 1567. I only heard half of what he said and told myself that I could look it all up online when we returned to the house.

Once we got to the other side of the loch, we parked the boat at his private, reserved dock below town. Apparently, he has special permission from the city to have a private landing in this spot. He did not elaborate, and I did not ask, but I am certain he has probably invested a great deal of money in this town. We walked up the hill and just at the top was a beautiful restaurant and inn, looking out upon the water.

Pete, the restaurant manager, welcomed us immediately at the front and escorted us to the large table at the window. I suspect his regular table could accommodate his family and any guests but seemed large for a party of three. Despite this, the staff made it look intimate with place settings closest to the window. Two on one side and one on the other. I do not know why I chose the single seat. Perhaps it was out of habit, as I am so used to being a party of one.

"This is lovely," I said, as Liam pulled out my seat for me. Pete quickly followed with the linen napkin across my lap.

We sat silently for a bit while I looked at the menu. I looked up to see Liam staring at me.

"I assume you know the menu."

"Aye!"

"Do you already know what you want?"

"I *do*," he said, leaning into the table with a mischievous smile. Based on his look and phrasing, I am not sure if he is talking about food or me. Perhaps a bit of both.

"Do you want to help me choose?"

"I want to kiss you first. *Regrettably,* you are on the other side of the table."

"Come sit next to me then," I said, leaning back and placing my arm around the empty chair next to me.

"Select the drink you want first and I will move."

"I would like a glass of Sancerre and I need ice and soda water," I said, reminding him of my preference while pulling out the empty chair next to me slightly.

"Pete, we will have a *bottle* of the Sancerre and Miss Hunter will need ice and soda water on the side. I will have a Laphroaig neat. Our guest will take the same. I will move to the seat next to Miss Hunter so we can both sit across from him."

"Of course, sir! I will get the order to the bar and move the settings for you myself. Just give me a moment."

"Wait, no! Sorry! It will be easier for me to just move next to Mr. Crichton. You do not need to move a thing, Pete."

As the bar worked to complete the order, I moved to sit next to Liam. Once I was seated, I said, "I believe you owe me a kiss."

"I do," he said and kissed me with such passion I could have fallen out of my newfound chair. I was almost embarrassed for the other guests having lunch in the restaurant to see such a display.

I caught my breath and asked in a whisper as I stroked his beard, *"What should I order?"*

"I think you should get the fish and chips."

"Liam, you just ordered a bottle of Sancerre, and you want me to get the fish and chips?"

"It is the best for lunch."

"Then that is it. Fish and Chips with a side of Sancerre."

"You are *ridiculous*, madam," he said, laughing at me and my mismatched choice. I am sure my face showed my disappointment at his light-hearted admonishment.

"What are you having?"

"I always have the burger here for lunch."

"Why should I not order the burger, then?" I asked, putting my hand to his face, wishing he would kiss me again.

He kissed me again, but on my wrist, as he said, "You can get that the *next* time we are here."

I smiled at him, thinking about a next time. Despite the fine service and atmosphere, we were having pub food that should be just perfect for lunch on a bright and beautiful Scottish day on the water.

"I should have waited to order lunch before thinking about my drink."

"Do you want a pint instead?"

"That may be best. The wine would be suitable for fish, of course, but I think I would prefer a beer with fish and chips," I said, looking over his shoulder at the taps on the bar. "Tennent's please."

"Consider it done."

+++

Suddenly, standing at the end of our table, was the brilliant Dr. Andrew Marshall. Liam and I stood up to welcome our guest. I could feel myself become nervous suddenly being in his presence. I am such an admirer of his work.

"Liam! It is so good to see you again, lad!"

"It has been too long, hasn't it?" Liam said, first shaking the man's hand and then hugging him. "How have you fared since Clara's passing, my friend?"

"It has been hard to live without her, but it was harder still to be so isolated in lockdown. I missed my friends and my work routine. I felt like I would wallow in grief alone forever. But, you know I got to spend time with my daughter and her family in France, which helped me considerably. And being here with you today is an absolute joy! An *absolute* joy!"

Liam and I nodded in understanding at what too many families had to go through losing loved ones during the last two years of restrictions and rules for gatherings, including funerals.

"Thank you for the beautiful flowers and donation to the university in her name. Your kindness and generosity touched me." Dr. Marshall nodded to him in reverence and appreciation.

"You are most welcome! Like I said, it was the least I could do to honor Clara and her contribution to the university."

Liam put his hand on my back and said, "Dr. Andrew Marshall, may I introduce you to Corrine Hunter?"

"It is such an honor to meet you, sir! I have enjoyed your books and they have been a great help with my own writing."

"Miss Hunter, I am so glad to meet you as well. I am familiar with your work, and I am happy to be of any help you need!"

Dr. Marshall is a slight man, well into his seventies but with the brightest blue eyes I have ever seen. He took off his tweed cap and sat across from us, smiling. Everything about him was warm and inviting. He has not said a single word about history yet, but you can feel it the minute that you meet him that he is a brilliant scholar and historian.

Dressed in all manner of Harris Tweed, he is only missing the corduroy or suede elbow patches on his blazer to make his look of a university professor complete. His Scottish accent is subtle, like Chef Dan, but you can hear it behind his soft, slow, and deliberate phrasing. Liam was right! He is a charmer, and I was under his spell the minute he arrived at our table.

We ordered our lunch and then I said, "I have so many questions for you, sir. I hope you do not mind."

Liam sipped his whisky and said, putting his arm around the back of my chair, "You did not realize that you were walking into a lunch quiz, mate! I hope you are adequately prepared!"

"I am ready for all of your questions, Miss Hunter!"

"Corrine, please," I said, opening my Moleskine notebook as he nodded at me. "First, Dr. Marshall, I should tell you about the novel I am currently working on and where I am struggling with my manuscript. That way, you will understand the rationale behind some of my questions."

"Aye," he said, sipping his whisky. "But I will say the same back to you, Corrine. Please... call me Andrew."

"Of course! Andrew, my next novel, is based in Scotland during the years of the Great War, 1914-1918. My female protagonist is a young woman who's fiancé is sent off to war. She has to keep his business, the local newspaper, running in town while he is gone and does so brilliantly. When she eventually loses him, she moves to Edinburgh and becomes a force in journalism... a calling she never expected. It is a love story. It is a war story. And it is a story of female empowerment at a time of significant societal change."

"Interesting," he said. I could not tell if he was truly interested or just being kind. Liam nodded to me. I think this is the first he has heard about the premise of my novel, other than that I cannot seem to finish the thing.

"Where is this novel set in Scotland?"

"Inverness. I wanted to be far enough away from the big cities of Glasgow and Edinburgh, but large enough for its own newspaper. My research landed me in Inverness. But I am open. I just need to ensure there is enough of a population for such an enterprise to exist there. I know that Dundee could be strong possibility as well."

He just nodded to me, thinking about whether this was a good place for this novel before saying, "We often read stories through both world wars about how women advanced in the fields of medicine or took on typical male industrial and factory roles of the time as a supplemental workforce, but we hear little about women's impact on the field of *journalism*."

"That is correct, but where I am struggling is that there is no heart to my story. I hope I can fix that myself. But I wonder if this is the story I should tell. Do you know if there are any models for a story like this? Any women I could research more as true inspiration in journalism during this time in Scotland? I have struggled to find any in my own research, but I know they *must* be out there waiting to be discovered."

"I cannot help you with heart, Corrine. As you know, I write non-fiction, but I can go back and look for any points of inspiration for your heroine. I do not have any names that come to mind right away, especially in Scotland. The minute you mentioned journalism during wartime, I thought of Martha Gellhorn."

"Ernest Hemingway's wife?" I asked.

"Aye, but that would be World War Two, wouldn't it?"

"It would."

"Let me go back through my notes. Martha may still help you on some level. I would not ignore her. In the Twenties, you may find an inspirational woman in journalism in Scotland that helps you develop your character. Her backstory can be fictional, as you described, but having a real-life reference during these pivotal years can make her real to you. I understand that."

"Thank you so much! That would be wonderful! That is exactly what I need, just a little real-life inspiration! I have researched the war, its impact to Scotland, and even the mechanics of the printing process of the time, but I am struggling to make her an inspiration to the reader. Dr. Marshall, I mean Andrew... I try in all of my novels to have the female protagonist learn and grow, so that by the end of the book, the reader is inspired."

"Not all stories are told and sadly, throughout time, often stories of women were forgotten as it was usually the men who recorded history. But, moving into the twentieth century and more modern times, perhaps we can find something to help you."

I immediately thought about the cheeky saying, *'well-behaved women rarely make history'* but his words were true. For centuries, unless a woman was of royal or of noble birth, or did something outlandish, there could be little documentation of her existence in the world, let alone her contributions. Even as we moved into modern times, sadly, not all of the incredible stories of women are documented.

Liam and I listened to him intently, almost mesmerized, as he continued slowly, "There are always tales hidden in the human experience, especially during wartime or times of great societal change, that can inspire."

"Are there other stories during this time period that have inspired you, sir? They do not have to be stories involving women."

Liam looked at me and nodded, realizing that I was asking this brilliant historian to tell us a good story. And I was. I was captivated and wanted to hear all he had to say to us this day.

"Aye, there are many. Through your own research, Corrine, you know Scotland lost a generation of young men in the Great War, only to be followed by the Spanish Flu pandemic. It was believed that the illness came into the country with the returning servicemen. You can imagine the immense impact such a loss of so many men and women could have on a country as small as Scotland and what that profound loss meant in the many years that followed."

I forgot about how the Spanish Flu pandemic also affected the post-war period globally and how communities already reeling from the loss of many men in wartime struggled. Liam and I shook our heads at the profound loss. We could not relate fully, but having just lived through the COVID global pandemic, the loss could indeed be staggering and heartbreaking. Andrew and Clara's own story told us that much!

"One story that touched me as I studied the time was about the lads of Aberlour Orphanage. Have you ever heard of it?"

I shook my head and said, "No, sir."

"I have heard of the town and whisky, of course, but not the orphanage or how it relates to the Great War," Liam said.

I smiled at him and thought of his words to me that Dr. Andrew Marshall will draw you in with his storytelling. He was right! And I love that the man sitting next to me is as interested as I am in what this historian has to say.

"You can find much of this in the National Library of Scotland or from the Aberlour Child Care Trust should you wish to research more yourself," he said, taking another sip of his whisky. I put his words in my notebook.

"Aberlour, a small town in Moray, was the site of the Aberlour Orphanage. It closed in 1967 and is no longer there. At the time of the Great War, many *'old boys'* from the orphanage were deployed across the armed forces and the varied theatres of battle. What was truly fascinating is that some of those lads wrote letters back to the headmaster, staff, and even the other children still living in the orphanage."

"That is so lovely," I said, looking at both Andrew and Liam, intrigued by this story and abandoning all of my other questions in my notebook that no longer seemed relevant in this moment.

"Think about not having a mother or father to write to or to write to you, to pray for you, to support you while you are away serving your country. So the sending of letters and the *receiving* of letters from the only home and family they had growing up was a blessing to the lads."

Liam and I just nodded to him about this thought. It was a blessing!

"There is a book you can reference at the National Library called *The Only Home They Knew* by Anne Black and it details the letters and the stories behind them. What is truly remarkable is that they printed many of the letters in the Aberlour Orphanage newsletter, and this prompted an outpouring of letters and acts of incredible generosity from supporters and staff. They sent the lads everything from homemade treats to handmade socks or scarves. Whenever a letter was shared, it helped shine a light on the struggles and realities of war. And aye, even some points of humor in stories relayed by our fighting lads."

"That is so uplifting," I said, thinking about his words.

"Unfortunately, many young men died in the Great War, but what was truly remarkable was how the community surrounding Aberlour shared in the genuine celebration of the lads that lived and returned home and the grief when a lad was lost. There is a granite marker that stands outside St. Margaret's Church in Aberlour where the dead are memorialized. Sixty-two of them, if my memory serves. What I cannot seem to remember is if this is all the *'old boys'* that died or if it was just those that wrote letters. The book can clarify that for you, and I will send you the notes that I have."

Between the actual story and Andrew's soft and respectful delivery, the story moved me. I could not help but tear up. Liam could feel my emotion and took my hand in his. I smiled at him, but my tears still fell upon my cheeks. I have only been with him for two days and here I am crying again! Thankfully, I could tell that the story Andrew told also moved him as he squeezed my hand again and smiled back at me.

I said to both men at the table, "That is a remarkable story! We often hear the horror stories of children in care homes, but these boys felt like Aberlour *was* their home *and* their family. And they were not forgotten orphans in the broader community."

"Aye," Andrew said. "I suspect that no place like that is perfect, but the lads who wrote back to the orphanage seemed to have had a deep connection to the place and the people there."

We enjoyed the rest of our lunch and Liam and Andrew caught up with each other. I listened intently as they discussed all that had happened in the last several months, including Liam's divorce. All the while, my mind raced! I thought about all I could do to reframe my novel. Perhaps the story Andrew shared should be told from the Great War, not that of my fictional journalist. I began thinking about how to rethink the plot, or possibly merge the two stories, and how much more research I would need to complete incorporating this newly discovered piece of history.

Finally, Andrew stood and, with his tweed cap in hand, said, "I wish you all the best, Corrine! I hope I was a help to you today."

I reached out my hand to touch his arm and said, "Thank you, sir! I wish you the same and you were *absolutely* a help to me! Your story touched my heart! I am thrilled to have met you in person and you are an extraordinary ambassador for Scotland and its rich history."

"You are too kind!"

Liam said softly, hugging Andrew, "Thank you, my friend!"

"Andrew, if I may," I said, putting my hand on his arm again. "I want to say that I hope that the memories you have of your late wife are a blessing and comfort to you. I am very sorry for your loss."

"Thank you very much. Clara is gone from this world, but she will never truly leave me."

I knew all too well what he meant and smiled at him in sympathy. Those we love and lose remain in our hearts and in our minds forever. He put his tweed cap back on and we watched him walk out of the restaurant.

I immediately turned and hugged Liam. I said with tears in my eyes once again, "Thank you so much for this! I absolutely adored him, and he gave me an incredible and most unexpected gift today!"

"He did?"

"Yes, he gave me the gift of inspiration."

+++

TWELVE
Mythos

Kinross, Scotland
December 2022

"Pete, I thank you and your staff. My fish and chips were the best I have had during my travels across Scotland!"

"It was our honor, Miss Hunter! I hope you will come back again," he said, shaking Liam's hand while looking at me.

"I intend to, sir. Next time, I want to try the burger. It looked delicious!"

"You will be most welcome," he said, nodding to me. "Mr. Crichton, we corked the bottle of Sancerre and delivered it directly to your boat."

"We thank you again," I said as Liam took my hand in his own. My errant order resulted in this action, and I was so happy that they both corrected it for me. We now have one more bottle for our white wine collection. Perhaps this will delay another trip to the judgmental wine merchant.

"Let me show you where Dan is building his restaurant. If we are lucky, he may be there now, since we did not need his help for lunch. I have not seen the space he has been building in months."

After a short but welcome walk to work off our lunch, we found ourselves at the other end of High Street. Walking hand-in-hand, we passed people on the street who clearly knew who he was and clearly knew that I was not his wife. Perhaps news of the divorce had not reached all of Scotland just yet. They unsettled me, but I hid my anxiety behind my sunglasses. When we arrived at the restaurant, Dan was overseeing the decisions on variations of table settings. The best I could tell, the difference was setting for lunch versus dinner.

"Chef, it is so good to see you again," I said, shaking Dan's hand. "Thank you for a wonderful supper last night. When Liam told me what you were building here, I wanted to see it for myself!"

"Aye, Miss Hunter! Sorry, I mean, Miss Corrine! I am so glad to see you again and appreciate the support," he said, before dismissing the others in the dining room.

The men shook hands and Dan said, "I think you will be pleased with the progress we have made, LC."

"Aye!"

"We are close. I am so proud, and we have already secured stellar staff in front and back of the house. My new sous chef is coming to us this week after a successful stint at Gleneagles. Everyone is training now, but I have to say that I am very impressed with the team so far. They all seem to be invested in our success by helping each other, and that makes me proud."

"Then that shows have made good hiring decisions," Liam said.

"What is your vision, chef?" I asked. He already told me his preference was to cook Greek or Italian, but I did not want to assume anything about his own restaurant. The dining room had a very Scottish country look with lots of blue and brown plaid which complement the view out to a beautiful garden on the back but definitely does not look overtly Mediterranean in its décor.

The tables were well spaced, and the chairs and banquets had tall backs, creating an intimate feeling at each one. You could imagine shielding yourself from the sounds of the table next to you to just focus on your own while still enjoying the view of the sizeable garden out of the large windows to the back.

"Mythos is going to be the only Mediterranean fine-dining restaurant in Kinross. You will have to go to Edinburgh or Glasgow for anything that comes close. But, even then, we hope to stand out."

"Mythos? As a storyteller myself, I can get behind that name."

"Aye! We experimented with a few names, but I finally settled on this one. If there is anything the Greeks and Scots have in common, it is a long history of myths, deeply rooted in the folklore of our people and lands, and kept alive through generations of storytelling."

I nodded to him as he continued, "I remain true to my Scottish heritage, but the menu blends the excellent Scottish larder with my Greek influences, flavors, and cooking methods. You will see this on the lunch menu, which is very much inspired by the mezze plates we love, then a more refined dinner menu."

"I think the view out to the back is beautiful," I said, admiring the large and well-manicured garden and patio before us.

"Aye, we are so fortunate to have such a large space, and you can imagine alfresco dining and drinks in the back during the summer months.

Liam weighed in and said, "I can see how much progress you have made since I was here last, and you should be proud."

"I thank you, sir," Dan said before turning back to me. "I believe LC told you I am making a Greek feast for you both this evening."

"He did, and I am looking forward to it!"

"I admit I am also serving my own interests here. Some items I will make are actually on the menu and I would like your feedback after dinner, if you would not mind."

I appreciated that in such a short amount of time he would value my opinion. "I am happy to give you the feedback you need. Your salad, risotto, and tiramisu last night were all divine. I especially loved that you made my fish almost look like seared scallops."

"Aye! I wanted you to feel you both were having the same meal."

"It was a stroke of genius! I am certain there is something to be said of fileting the fish in such a way, but I appreciated it. I have tried to negotiate this allergy for many years and some fine restaurants make me feel like I just ordered off of the children's menu or that the chef begrudgingly has to change everything about their precious dish. You did not! You accommodated my allergy but made my plate look exactly like Liam's and I thank you for it."

"I appreciate you noticed that. I believe it is a principle in this restaurant and for the very reason you mentioned. I never want us to treat someone with an allergy like they are less than because of something they cannot control. Your experience should not be any different from someone with no allergies."

I nodded to him as he kept talking, "I want this restaurant to be inclusive and other ways we show that is how accessible the floor is. You can see that we replaced the original stairs down to the lower dining room with a ramp. We have also hired a local young man who is on the autism spectrum to help us on the line. The lad's passion for food and attention to detail is astounding! I wish we could bottle his enthusiasm and his laser-sharp focus on timing and delivery and give it to every member of staff. I hope every customer has an enjoyable experience here—not just good food."

Liam said, "I admire your conviction, Dan. Are you on track for your opening?"

"Aye! We are still on track for mid-January. I wanted to get through the holidays, but coming out of the pandemic, we will have to work to ensure we get the shipments we need each week for the larder and the pantry. I am still waiting for much of my glassware that is overdue, and you likely saw on your way in that we do not yet have our sign outside. We can adjust as we need to and revise menus accordingly. Aside from that, we have already decided that we will continue on our plan for some preview days to work out the process for the kitchen and for service. I welcome you both to join on one of those nights if you would like."

"Aye!" Liam said as we both nodded in agreement. "We are happy to support you."

"Thank you! I know I will get *all* of your feedback—good and bad!" Dan smiled as he continued with a wink to me, "If you do not already know this Miss Corrine, LC loves to give feedback."

"Well, to be honest, so do I. So, prepare yourself, chef!"

As Dan walked us out, he said, "I am going to make most of the dishes here at the restaurant to guide the team through the prep and serving elements as part of our training, but I will finish everything else at the house. I will give you more than you would order on your own, so consider it a tasting menu. Do not feel you have to finish everything on your plates."

Liam reached out his hand to Chef Dan and said, "We will see you tonight."

+++

We returned to the house, and each retreated to our rooms to work a bit and get ready for dinner. I had so many notes in my head and notebook from our meeting with Andrew that I had to get in my computer. I also wanted to look again at my draft and think about a how to make some sort of combination of stories work. I met Liam before the great fireplace and looked a little more dressed than country-chic in my leather skirt, boots, and cashmere turtleneck sweater. He immediately took my hand and kissed my wrist.

"You look beautiful, love!"

I just smiled up at him and thought how nice it was to hear such kind words. I wanted to say he also looked beautiful, but the fire dancing in the gold of his eyes captivated me. I could not speak. He kissed me gently and led me to the kitchen island where Chef Dan had wine and a small selection of olives and almonds waiting for us. We watched him prep for a bit before walking into the dining room. For the first time, Dan provided us a small, printed menu card at our place settings to help guide us through his dishes tonight.

Starters & Salads
Cured Fish Platter for Two

Smoked Salmon, Eel with Beetroot, Cured Halibut

Fried Courgette Flowers

Stuffed with cheese—lightly battered and fried, topped with sea salt

Greek Spread Trio

Tzatziki, Taramosalata, and Ktipiti served with assorted raw vegetables and grilled pita

Greek Salad

Tomatoes, cucumbers, olives, onions, peppers, Greek feta, with an olive oil and white wine vinaigrette

Chef's Grill

Fresh Mediterranean Cuttlefish—or Langoustines

Smoky grilled, served over Parmigiano-Reggiano risotto

Lamb Chops

Grilled, served with fried potatoes and seasonal steamed vegetables

Dessert

Baklava

Selection of Greek cheeses

It was all masterfully done, and Liam and I both ate too much—especially after our hearty pub lunch. After dinner, and with a copy of the menu in hand and a pen, Chef Dan sat with us at the kitchen island. Liam poured all of us a fresh glass of wine as we complimented the chef and prepared to give our feedback on his menu.

"Alright, I would like to walk through each item and record your thoughts. Aside from staff, you are the first people outside of the restaurant to taste some of these dishes and the current preparations. Ahead of our tasting days, I want your opinion to help refine the menu even more."

Liam and I nodded in understanding. Chef Dan and I sat on the barstools next to each other and Liam just came to stand next to me with his arm around the back of my chair, occasionally lovingly stroking my back.

"Let us start with the easiest... the salad."

I spoke up first and stated the obvious, "No challenge here on my side. It is simple, fresh, and perfect. If anything, I wanted a little ground pepper, but that is just preference."

"Agreed," Liam said. "If I had anything else to say, it is that I would have preferred more feta. But like Corrine said, that is just personal preference."

"We will certainly offer fresh ground pepper on delivery with the servers and can ensure a tad more feta in prep."

"Chef, you know I am *all in* on the starters!"

"I knew you would love those, Miss Corrine! I told you I know you would not order this much food to start, but I added extra just so that you could try a variety. And you and LC do like to snack."

"The cured fish—unreal! I am not sure if this is the plating you would have in the restaurant, or because you were giving us so many options."

"It is the planned plating."

"Then that is my only feedback. It is too small of a portion for two! It is so good! I wanted more! Especially the halibut! I had to fight Liam for the last bite."

Liam laughed and said, stroking my back, "She *stole* the last of the halibut and I will never forgive her for it!" We smiled at each other before he said, "My favorites were the fried courgette flowers. You gave us both versions with cheese and without, but the fry batter and sea salt on both were light and perfect!"

"The ones without the cheese would be for someone who cannot have the dairy. We would not normally serve them together that way. If you do not have an allergy, you would only get the ones with cheese. What did you think about the spreads?"

"Incredible!" Liam said immediately.

"I agree." Looking at the menu myself now, I asked, "Which one was the cod roe spread, chef?"

"The Taramosalata."

"I have never had it before. I thought it was a tad salty, but perhaps that is natural considering what it is. It was still delicious. The last note for me is that as good as they all were, I would suspect that most people will still expect a hummus."

"That has been my biggest concern," Dan said. "We have considered adding hummus as a fourth spread flavored by what is in season and balanced with the seasonal menu. We can rotate that one in with the assortment." Liam and I nodded to him in agreement. Even with all we had, we both wanted a little hummus.

"Finally, let's talk about the fish, lamb, and dessert so I can leave you both for tonight," Dan said as he finished the last of his wine.

"I will tell you the langoustines were beautifully cooked. They were huge and the smoky grill and light seasoning enhanced the taste of the sea. They were perfect, man!"

"For me, I would say the same. The smoky grill on the fish over the risotto was beautiful. And the portion size was right, but I also had a ton of starters, so maybe think about the person who just has a salad or one starter. I could see it as a small main portion. But if the goal is to get the customer to dessert and coffee, then it may be just right. You are the expert here."

"I agree," Liam said. "I would say the same for the langoustines. Not everyone orders most of the starter menu. I could have had one or two more. They were *so* delicious."

"And what do we think of the lamb?"

I spoke first and said, "I am going to defer, because lamb is not my first choice for a main, but it was a beautiful plate and tasted fine to me."

Liam helped me here by saying, "The cook was over for me, but it was just fine. Clearly, Corrine and I are not the best to judge this dish. I, too, don't gravitate to lamb as my first choice either."

I changed the subject from the lamb Liam and I did not fully enjoy by saying, "The cheese selection was fine, and I loved the addition of the fig spread and honeycomb. Honestly, the fresh honeycomb was absolutely *incredible!* It was so pure. I could have had a bit of that and the oat crackers and been fine. Forget the cheese!"

Liam continued his thought, "I think for some people, knowing what the cheeses are called and what they are made of on the menu would be helpful."

"Of course, LC! We should note that on the menu."

"That is a good point. Not everyone is well-versed in the varieties of Greek cheeses, so knowing if it is soft or hard, made from goat, cow, or sheep's milk, can be helpful in deciding for the plate against allergies or preference. I also like knowing the name of something new if I want to remember it when I am in the cheese shop or market to create a board at home. A fine restaurant is a great place to learn new things."

"And the baklava?"

"Heavenly! I would typically go for the cheese board straight away at the end of a meal, but after indulging in such rich flavors tonight, the sweet treat was welcome. That is why I wanted even more of that honeycomb!"

Liam nodded to me and said, "I told myself that I wish I had saved some for my tea tomorrow, but I ate everything on my plate."

"I think I can hook you up!" Dan said as he stood from his stool. "I left you both a little tray of both the baklava and the rest of the cheese in the fridge. You both can snack all day tomorrow. Thank you again! I am most encouraged by your feedback."

"Chef, if I may add one point before you go."

Liam and Dan just looked at me. I laughed and said almost apologetically, "I told you I like to give feedback!"

Dan nodded and said, laughing, "You did warn me, Miss Corrine!"

"You talked this afternoon of celebrating the Scottish larder, and I would call that out on the menu as well so that the diners can appreciate that with you. You mention all the Mediterranean or Greek items but not the Scottish items. If I am in your restaurant, I want to know that our Scottish fishermen and farmers are contributing to this bounty. Just tell me where."

"Great point! The full menu will have a description of the vision for Mythos, which I shared with you, but I can easily call out Scotland's contribution to the menu items. For the cured fish, both the salmon and halibut were Scottish, as were the langoustines. Some things like the honeycomb and sea salt are not only Scottish but locally made, as well."

"Well then, let's celebrate it all!"

"Aye, Miss Corrine!"

Liam kissed my cheek and then walked Dan out. He came back to fill our wine glasses once more. We moved to the couch and sat together before the fire.

"I thought Chef Dan did really well. I love the name Mythos, and the thought of storytelling being an inspiration and a connection between the Greeks and the Scots—not just the food."

"He did well. And you were right about giving feedback."

"Are you trying to tell me I gave *too much* feedback?"

"Not at all! I was interested that we were so aligned throughout the menu." And we were, but it was clear he had more to say.

"But…"

"I have a feeling I am going to have to go into the restaurant business."

"Why?"

"Because I am going to want to eat there every night. I might as well own it."

We laughed together and I thought the same. I could eat like this every night myself. We sat together quietly, holding hands, and sipping our wine.

"Is that how you make all of your business decisions? You just buy what you like?"

"It has worked for me so far!"

I nodded. It has indeed been a good plan and worked for him so far.

"Corrine, I…," Liam said nervously and shaking his head. "I do not know what to say."

"What is it?"

"Please do not go downstairs. Stay with me tonight."

+++

THIRTEEN
The Hidden Heart

Loch Leven, Scotland
December 2022

"I brought my water up," I said nervously in front of Liam's **open bedroom door.** I went downstairs to get ready for bed before coming back upstairs to meet him. Normally, I would just sleep in a tank top and shorts. I did not even think about this scenario when planning my original trip, so I had nothing but a black satin pajama nightshirt as an alternative. Even then, I am definitely not winning any awards for sexiness tonight. Thankfully, this man is standing in his own formal pajamas. I almost laughed at the sight of us. We are unintentionally showing our age and he looks as ridiculously formal and stuffy as I do!

He came to kiss me, and he did so hard and with such passion, but stopped himself mid-way. He just put his forehead to mine and sighed. I could tell that he was nervous. This was a marked contrast for a man who traced the outlines of my bra over my sweater in a hotel bar the night we met and put me up against a wall in a pub in Edinburgh just a month ago.

Nothing about Liam Crichton is shy, but everyone has their own insecurities. Some are just better at hiding them than others. I could not imagine how a man who had been married so long and had only been with one woman his entire life must feel. I also had my own nerves. I have not been with another man since David.

"Come with me," I said, taking his hand in mine and leading him out of his room and down the stairs to mine. Luckily, I left my room without turning off the fire, so the room was still quite warm.

"Does this help?" I asked.

"It does, but…" he said, clearly still uncertain and unnerved.

"There are no rules here, Liam. We do not have to rush things. Which side of the bed do you sleep on?"

He silently pointed to the left side, closest to the door and the bathroom. I bit my bottom lip for a moment, as that would be my side, too. Actually, as someone who mostly lives in hotels, it truly depends on the room configuration and the proximity to the bathroom in the middle of the night. Sometimes, I have to sleep on the right. But to be honest, when you sleep alone, it all becomes the middle, eventually.

"Come," I said to him, leading to that side and pulling the covers back, inviting him in. I tucked him in, kissed him quickly, and turned out the lamp on his bedside table.

"Where are you going?" he asked as I walked away.

"*All* the way to the other side of the bed," I said, almost laughing at him and his genuine concern about being left alone for a moment. I turned out my light and slipped under the covers and put myself right next to him. He put his arms around me, and I nestled myself effortlessly in the bend of his shoulder. We fit together perfectly. Just like that first night in The Balmoral. He kissed me on top of my head, and I smiled back up at him.

"*Sleep well.*"

"*Aye, sleep well, lass.*"

+++

I woke in the early hours of the morning with Liam wrapped around me, breathing softly on the back of my neck. He had to be awake. I turned over and looked at him face-to-face across our pillows.

As he kissed me, I smiled at him. I knew he was willing to try again, not being in the bed or in the room he used to share with his wife. I rolled him over and sat astride him.

"*Corrine,*" he whispered, as I took my nightshirt off. I kept on the black lace bra and panties I had on earlier in anticipation of this moment. I had to spice up this boring night shirt somehow!

"Och, Christ," he said as he sat up and came to my chest immediately and began slowly tracing the scalloped edges of the lace before kissing the tops of my breasts.

"*I thought you would like that,*" I said in a whisper as I ran my hands through his thick hair and down his back.

"*And you thought right!*"

He flipped me over and pulled off his pajama top over his head. As he did, I pulled at his pajama bottoms and my panties at the same time. We could not hold back any longer and he eagerly helped me with both.

"You are so beautiful," he said with a smile. He was sincere, but I laughed nervously.

"Everyone is beautiful in firelight or candlelight," I said, thinking about my historical research but also vocalizing my own insecurities.

"No. Look at me! You are absolutely beautiful!"

"Liam… I want you, now. Please!" I whispered as I raised my hips to his and pulled my right leg up around him. He took me with such passion that we both could barely breathe. I have only had only one true love in my life, but Liam made me cry out in a way I have never done before. We needed each other and this release. It had been too long… for both of us.

When he moved over to lie next to me, I turned to him and ran my fingers through the hair on his chest as we both caught our breath. He took my hand in his and gently kissed my wrist. I appreciated the tickle of his beard and his sweet kisses. We did not speak, but we both knew that this was just the beginning, and we would never be the same.

+++

We stared at each other across our pillows. The firelight made our faces barely visible but just enough to still light up the gold in his eyes. His face was so sweet and kind. He was clearly happy and so was I, yet still neither of us could speak. We had no words. We could only stare at each other and lightly touch each other.

"If I may ask, why did you never marry?" he finally asked as he pushed my hair over my shoulder before taking my hand in his atop the pillow. "I cannot imagine that you did not have plenty of men knocking down your door."

It was a fair question, and his compliment was genuine. I am fifty years old and never married, but I had to think for a moment about how best to answer. It was not a story that anyone outside of my close circle of friends or my friends at the hotel in London knew, and I worried about my ability to tell it without resurrecting all the hurt and pain that goes with it.

"I was engaged once."

Liam said nothing but gave me the room to tell him what I wanted to, what I needed to. I wanted to tell him the truth of it, but I worried about talking about David with him here on our first night together. But he asked and deserves the answer. He deserves the truth.

"Kate had a dinner party one night. Her husband, Luke Matthews, who I absolutely adore, is a doctor. Do you know him?"

"No, I know *of* him, but have never met Luke."

I continued with a smile, "He is a lovely man! He invited a dear friend of his from medical school, David, to sit next to me. I was being set up without knowing I was being set up. I am certain Kate and Luke were proud of themselves. They had to know that I would never agree to attend the dinner if I thought that a blind date was their objective!"

"Aye, I do not see that being something you would enjoy."

"I would not! I was in my mid-forties and had already convinced myself that I was better off being more invested in my work than in any relationship. At that point in my life, I had built a successful career as an author, and love and marriage were just not something I ever saw for myself. I certainly did *nothing* to look for it on my own! So I did not care who was seated next to me. I was going to enjoy being with my friends that evening."

It took me a minute to speak again. "David Bryant was a pediatric surgeon at Great Ormond Street Hospital in London. He was smart, enormously talented in his field, and he was kind. He was everything you would hope for if you entrusted your child to his care. He was also ridiculously funny! I mean, *goofball funny!* The man lightened up my serious nature in an instant and made me happy."

I smiled at the thought of my own words and the memory of David. Those times, just laughing together, in the silliest of ways, are cherished in my heart and my mind forever.

"We hit it off immediately and fell hard for each other. Perhaps it was our close emotional connection at the very start or our ages, but we wasted no time. Within weeks, I moved out of my hotel and was living with him in his flat in Mayfair. Not even a year later, we were engaged."

I could see that Liam did not expect this story, and it is not one that I have told before. Our new intimacy tonight only added to the honesty of such a conversation. If we are going to be together, he needs to know the truth of my past. Liam stroked my hand, and we laced our fingers together while staring at each other.

"He was everything to me. We were madly in love and fell into a rhythm of life together. While it was quick, I already had plans to move to London from Vancouver, and our engagement made such a move even easier. We would marry and build our new life together, loving, respecting, and supporting each other. We started looking for a larger flat together in the area of the city we both loved."

Liam said nothing, but he was listening intently, keeping my hand in his. I breathed in and said, "One night, David came home late from a long night of emergency surgery and quietly got into bed. His words to me were, *'I am home, Corrie. I love you.'* I remember his voice and his words, but I barely said anything more than a half-awake whimper back to him, acknowledging that he was there before I fell back asleep."

I sat for a moment thinking about the rest of the story and willing the tears back behind my eyes. In my silence, Liam whispered, *"You do not have to tell me the rest if you do not want to."*

"I *do want to tell it* because it is the truth. It is the truth of my past and of me. If we are going to be together, you should know it!"

"Aye," he said, as he kissed me on my forehead, releasing me to tell the story.

"In the middle of the night, I woke up and went to the loo. When I came back to bed, I slid in right next to him, so thankful that he was there, and put my hand across his chest. Still in the fog of sleep, it took me a minute to realize that he was not responsive. Even in a deep sleep, David would make a soft sound on my touch and eventually his hand would find its way on top of mine. Then I realized that my hand was not moving. I called out his name and there was still no response. I stood up immediately turned on the lights to find his lips blue and his eyes open."

"Och, Christ above," Liam said, holding my hand tighter, and kissing it over and over.

"He had a massive heart attack in his sleep, and that was the end of it. He was only fifty-four years old."

I cried at the loss and the story I could have never imagined myself.

"I am *so sorry,* love! I did not know that you had suffered such a loss," he said as he tried to wipe the unending tears from my cheeks. "I have selfishly talked of my own life changes. I never expected a story like this with my question! Never!"

"I found David late in my life, and I lost him in an instant."

I cried again for a moment before finding my voice again. "After they took him away that morning, I just sat on the couch numb to everything that happened and despite my own powerful sense of independence, felt suddenly so afraid to be *alone*. Once I could escape the shock I felt, I packed up everything I owned and moved back to the Corinthia."

Liam wiped my tears again, but said nothing as I continued, "That is why they take such good care of me there. Not that they wouldn't anyway, but most of my friends at the hotel know why I returned suddenly, and why I choose to stay there whenever I am in London. And now, you know why I understand why you cannot be with me in your own bed."

"That is *not* the same."

"I know what you are thinking—that the finality of death differs from divorce. But in some ways, it *is* the same. It is a *loss*. It is a *transition*. Memories and moments surround us from our past. I could not stay in that flat knowing David died there... in that bed. And you could not be with me in a bed you shared with your wife."

"I understand, but my darlin'... it is *not* the same."

"Are you not mourning a life and a love you once had?"

"Aye."

Even if he did not make the same connection himself, Liam would not continue to argue with me on this point. It was not something that needed to be measured. We were both grieving a part of our life that was no more. We don't need to debate who's loss was bigger.

"I had not thought about it that way. I appreciate you showing more of your heart and telling me the story of David and his role in your life."

"You would have liked him," I said, smiling, but with tears still streaming down my cheeks.

"If he was the type of man who loved you and made you happy, I know I would have," Liam said, kissing me and wiping the remnant tears from my cheeks, "but I would have been *jealous as hell* of him!"

I laughed through my tears as he held me tight. I honored the thought of the love I lost and the new love before me.

+++

I had more to say. I wanted to tell Liam everything. *I have to tell him everything!* I have held back so much since we met. For this new relationship to work, I want him to know all of me, and that includes the rest of the story.

"Grief is a powerful thing. I had a hard time. A *really* hard time. David's parents had him cremated at his request in his will, but they could not bear a service. I think his friends from medical school and the hospital had something, but I did not attend. I could not bear a memorial service either. I had to deal with the finality of his life alone in that flat with him. I meant no disrespect to his memory, but I was not in a place to share my grief with anyone else and despite the loving comfort offered me, I could not engage. Once I got to the hotel, I locked myself in my room, talked to no one, and let my sorrow consume me. One day, the hotel manager and head of hotel security escorted Kate up to do a welfare check, as I had not left the room, ordered room service, answered the phone, or had housekeeping for nearly a week."

"*Och, love,*" Liam said, squeezing my hand again and kissing it over and over.

"I was not in a good place. I existed on all the minibar offered... when I was awake, that is. Honestly, I spent most of that week in bed asleep. Kate walked in and gently woke me up. She never said the words to me, but I know she was relieved that she did not find me dead in that room."

Liam kissed my hand again as I continued, "I could not even speak to her. I could only cry. I was grieving my loss and was perhaps even a tad embarrassed that she found me in such a pitiful state. I was broken!"

"I am so sorry!"

"She ordered me a proper lunch, made me eat it, and helped me shower. I could barely stand on my own between my emotions and my physical weakness from a week in bed. Kate dressed me, brushed my teeth and my hair, and forced me to leave the room by taking a walk around Trafalgar Square. I cried the entire way. My body hurt. My heart hurt. We had to stop and sit on the steps of St. Martin in the Fields Church for a while so I could collect myself and find the physical and mental strength to walk back down to the hotel. It mortified me to walk through the hotel lobby distraught and weak with grief."

Liam held my hand tighter but said nothing.

"Thankfully, housekeeping quickly cleaned my room while we were on our walk, so that I would be comfortable when we got back. They had fresh flowers and a full tea service waiting for us. Kate and I had tea together in silence, and then she helped me get back into my comfortable bed. Before she left, she told me she would meet me at the same time the next day to walk again and that I had better be dressed and ready to go on my own. Each day, we walked a little further around London and each day it became easier for me to get up, get dressed, and go on those walks. With each walk, it became easier to feel like I was alive again."

"Kate is a true and loyal friend."

"She is. I love her more than anything. I swear, she saved me! Kate Woodhouse saved my life! I want you to know that I did not have thoughts of harming myself, but I would have happily died in that bed, and sometimes wished for it. I could not do it myself but willed my grief to end me."

"Corrine, my love, I do not know what to say."

Liam let me recover myself a bit before I continued. "I returned to Vancouver to prepare to sell my flat and move to London as originally planned. It took a lot longer than I expected and perhaps I made it so. I did not want to return to London. I had no reason to return to London. Then COVID happened, and travel restrictions delayed me even more. I wrote two contemporary novels while I was there. They were both dark and depressing. Kate published them anyway. I am certain she hoped I had enough fans to buy them in order to break even, but I doubt she did. I refused to do any press to support the books, and the reviews were understandably horrible. In fact, after the second book release, one headline was *What Happened To Corrine Hunter?*"

Still holding my hand in support, Liam remained quiet.

"The diamond band that I told you I moved from my ring finger before you arrived at Bar Prince, is my engagement ring," I said as I spun my precious ring now consistently on my right hand around. "David protects me when I need him to."

"I simply do not have the words. What you have endured is beyond anything I could have imagined, and again, I am so sorry for your loss. I am also sorry to bring it all back to you with my question."

I nodded in receipt of his genuine sympathy and continued, "I had to wait for travel restrictions to lift before I could return to the UK, and in the meantime, I started researching the current novel."

"How did you settle on World War One?"

"I honestly don't remember! It was just different from what I had done before in the historical fiction genre, and I started reading and researching. I think there was a book on the history of pipers in the Scottish regiments that got me thinking about the military and war. The more I read, the more intrigued I became. I also realized how much I did not know about the time period. Suddenly, I was reading more about World War One and the impact of the Great War on Scotland."

"You buried yourself in research, then?"

"I did, and it kept me going," I said, thinking more about his words and all that had happened since David's death.

"Liam, I never thought about it until now, but perhaps what happened is why I cannot find the *heart* of my protagonist."

"What do you mean?"

"I cannot find her heart, or the heart of the story… because I *lost my own!*"

"Och, my darlin'!"

Liam held me tighter and let me sob into his chest at the memory of my beloved and this moment of stark realization.

No amount of research could summon the emotions that I could not feel myself. No amount of writing or time in Scotland could ever uncover the missing piece of the puzzle for this wayward novel, because *I was* the missing piece! I have been the missing piece all along and I see that now.

When David died, I lost my heart, and it left me broken and empty. I had nothing to give this novel or my heroine other than historical facts, research, and a lot of words. Liam is opening my heart, and I am overwhelmed with all the emotion he is bringing back to me. It is no wonder I have cried so much since we arrived at the house on Loch Leven!

I got up to find tissues and put cold water on my red and puffy eyes after my late-night confessional. Liam gave me the time I needed and waited for me in bed. Once I returned, he placed his arms tight around me again.

"Thank you for listening to me," I said softly and stroking his loving arms, holding me tight. "As difficult as it was, I wanted to tell you my story. I felt like I owed you my truth as well."

"You told me that the last few years had been hard for you. Thank you for telling me the story of David," he said before kissing the top of my head. "I know nothing about writing novels, but I hope your realization tonight gives you what you need to finish this one."

I cannot speak the words just yet, but I nodded in agreement. Liam could have easily resented another man being mentioned and mourned on our first night together, but he did not. He was compassionate and respected David's memory and the loss I felt. The loss I still feel. I feel loved and supported. That is who this man is, and he is filling me with all the feelings and emotions I have suppressed for many years.

I hope that finding my heart again with Liam will not just lead me to a safe and loving comfort like I had with David in my own life, but that he is right—it will lead me to the heart of my novel and the story that deserves to be told.

+++

FOURTEEN
Old Friends Are The Best

Crichton House
Loch Leven, Scotland
December 2022

The air is lighter. I feel lighter with my confession of David's story and my past. I feel relieved that Liam respected my sharing it and has been so tender and supportive since. We are falling in love and becoming more comfortable together each day. I am also falling in love with this beautiful house and location. I would have thought that I would miss the busy energy of a bar, but I don't. My office area, with its incredible view across the water, has not only become a calm place of inspiration but has focused my work.

"I will write this afternoon," I said to Liam over my cup of breakfast tea in the kitchen. "I have notes from the visit to the library, and Andrew sent me some of the additional notes he mentioned at our lunch. I haven't had a chance to read them all, but the story of Aberlour Orphanage is fascinating!"

"Andrew loved speaking with you!"

I looked at him and he continued, "I did not tell you, but he sent me a text after our lunch. He said you were an absolute delight to talk with and had clearly done your research. I think you earned yourself a new fan, love."

"I could not think of anything but how to change everything in my manuscript based on his story about the old boys of Aberlour. It touched me so."

"That is wonderful! I could see how it made you emotional, but admit, I was also touched. Andrew is a powerful storyteller!"

"I knew something was missing from my last draft. And it was! I told you that my manuscript had no *heart*. You are helping me find mine again, but I feel compelled to honor these young men. The story could also better show the human toll of sacrifice during this time. It will change everything I have written so far, but I will try my best to salvage as much of my previous work as I can."

"You will be just fine, I know it! I can see the determination in your eyes, and I can feel your passion for your work."

He kissed me again on my forehead and held me tight. After a moment, he said, still holding me, "Andrew also said I should hold on to you and never let you go."

"That is sweet of him! Perhaps it is only natural for a man who recently lost his wife to be so sentimental about the hope and promise of new relationships."

As soon as I said the words, I worried it sounded like I was diminishing our new relationship. Luckily, I do not think he heard my words in that way.

"True, but there is also something to be said sitting across from a smart, beautiful woman who truly wants to hear you talk to lift your spirits. He has been so sad, and I could tell the lunch meeting made him happy. For the first time in a long while, he looked and sounded like the old friend—the incredible man—that I know."

"I found him fascinating! Though I expected nothing less."

"I enjoyed seeing you both happy and in your element. I know nothing about writing books and researching history, but you both impressed me with your conversation. Though, I too expected nothing less!"

"Thank you." I did not say the words, but I completely agreed with Dr. Andrew Marshall. I should hold on to this man and never let him go.

+++

Suddenly, I heard a large commotion on the floor above me. I left my desk and walked up the stairs to see the two unnamed lads being directed by Liam on the removal of his bed.

I smiled at him and asked, "What is all of this?"

"Sorry to disturb your work, Corrine. I know we are making a mighty loud racket up here. But it is time for a new start."

I smiled at him, and he kissed me in full view of Miss Betty, which understandably gave me as much pleasure as the removal of his old bed and the new one being brought in the front door. I went to the kitchen to refill my hot tea from the kettle and watched the lads—all of them, Liam included—negotiate corners with mattresses and assemble a new headboard and bed frame.

I could not hide the smile on my face. It *is* time for a new start. I finally returned to my room and left them all to the arranging of new furniture.

+++

Liam came downstairs and said as he handed me another cup of hot tea, "I thought you could use a break."

"Your timing is perfect! I made progress today and think I am at a good stopping point."

"Then let's finish our tea and go for a walk. It is a beautiful day."

"I stared at the sun reflecting on the water moments ago and thought to myself that it is *indeed* a fine day for a walk."

We looked at each other over our cups. I kept thinking about how everything has changed and how happy I am to be here with him. I hoped he was thinking the same. We finished our tea and walked around a portion of the loch for what seemed like forever.

"Is all of this land yours?"

"It is. It is about six and a half acres in total. But nature reserves surround us on both sides, so not having any close neighbors makes it feel much more expansive."

"That is wonderful! Why don't you live here instead of Edinburgh? It is not that far of a drive to the city."

"Well, *technically*, I do live here. I had to move out of the house in Edinburgh early last summer, and this has been my home ever since. The exception has been when I need to be in the city, then I try to stay at The Balmoral."

"I'm sorry. I didn't think about that."

"I have been trying to decide what I want to buy in the city. I haven't found anything that I like yet. I was hoping…" he said suddenly stopping himself. I just held his hand and smiled. He didn't know what to say.

"I was hoping being here with you would help me decide. I don't want to rush anything, but I would be crushed if you went back to London. Have you ever considered living in Scotland?"

"I have. In fact, I told Kate at my birthday celebration that there was no reason for me to be in London, as I have fallen more in love with Scotland on each of my trips here." If I am honest, I have fallen in love with more than this country. I suspect he knew what I meant with my words as he smiled at me.

"I was trying to decide what would be best for me—Edinburgh or a smaller town. There are so many great towns and villages I have grown to love on my travels. My things are sailing across the ocean as we speak, and the moving company is just waiting for me to tell them where to deliver them. Otherwise, what is left of my home in Vancouver will go straight into storage."

We stopped by the old stone wall and looked out at the peaceful water before us with our arms wrapped around each other. After an incredible day exploring his property, coupled with our physical connection, I feel even closer to him. I looked up at him and could only think that wanted him more than anything. I turned toward him with dreamy eyes and brought his face to mine with both hands. I kissed him long and hard.

"Well, that is a pleasant surprise," he whispered to me at the end of our kiss.

I thought to myself that if it was a surprise he wants, I might as well give it to him. It is a beautiful day, and we are far enough from the house that no one would see us—or hear us. With the next kiss, I moved my hand slowly down his chest to the front of his trousers.

"What are you doing?" he asked through his kiss with a huge smile on his face.

"What does it *feel* like I am doing?"

I kissed him deeply again as my hands unbuttoned and unzipped his trousers before moving my hand inside.

"*Corrine,*" he said with a low groan as he kissed my neck.

"I want you to take me over the old stone wall," I said breathlessly before I removed my hand and backed away from him with my own huge smile.

"Do ye now?" he asked, smiling, and following me to the wall, managing his now loose trousers.

I had on a long tweed skirt and tall boots but had not put on any tights or underwear. There would be no barrier to slow him down. I leaned over the stone wall and with my back to him, slowly lifted my skirt so that he could see that I was more than prepared for this moment.

"*Och, Christ,*" he said, came to me and pulled up the rest of my skirt. Once he took me, I knew he was happy. Our rhythm was slow, but there was no denying the intensity of the passion between us. This is all so new and welcome as we keep learning how to please each other. We both called out at almost the same time. Against the cool wall of stone, he laid across my back, still holding my hips to his. I tried to catch my breath and steady myself as my legs were weak and trembling.

"You are a remarkable woman!" he said, buttoning his trousers. I let my skirt fall down as I turned around to face him. Before I could repay the compliment, he took me in his arms and kissed me. With his cheek to mine, he continued in my ear, *"One that I will try to make as happy as you have made me."*

I smiled and kissed him back, and said, "If you ever want to meet at the old stone wall again, Mr. Crichton…"

"Same, my darlin'! There is *no* question about that!"

Taking my hand in his, we walked back to the house with huge smiles of satisfaction on our faces.

+++

After another fantastic and filling dinner from Chef Dan of comforting Scottish fish pie for a chilly December evening, we sat together before the fire. This time he had music playing throughout the house speaker system. As best I could tell, it was instrumental movie soundtracks, but they were soft and low. I loved that he listened to me about this type of music being essential to my writing process. His arm was around me and we sipped our drinks in silence, just enjoying the comfort of being with each other.

"You surprised me this afternoon," he said, finally running his hand through my curls. "Before today, I would have told you I do *not* like surprises. But that was the most incredible thing I have ever done, and I can't stop thinking about it."

"I probably should not ask this, but I assume you and your ex-wife did not do such things?"

"Well, that is an understatement," he said as he stood up to refill our glasses in the kitchen once more. I looked over the back of the sofa at him. He took a moment to think about his words and said, "When Sarah and I first met, we were much younger, and the passion was there, but there was very little in the way of spontaneity or variety."

I said nothing, but nodded my head at his words as came back around and handed me my newly filled glass. While my question may have been intrusive, he seems to want to talk. He sipped from his own glass and said, "By the time we married, it was all fairly basic, and I freely admit that I did not know any better. I felt fortunate to have a woman who wanted to be with me. I told you she is the only woman I had been with until you. So my thoughts on that part of our life are as much of an indictment of myself as her."

Since being together, I have found Liam to be a tender and considerate lover. Being intimate with someone new can sometimes be tentative and awkward as you get to know each other emotionally and physically. As we have grown to learn more about each other and what made each other happy, the thing I loved most was how present and attentive he was. There was a level of intimacy that made me feel safe and loved as much as wanted.

"After kids, it became even harder to connect and then I would say that we both were not looking for it as much. Something changed between us personally, not just physically, and we stopped trying. We *both* stopped trying. We no longer found comfort in each other. I can see now that was because we no longer loved each other. We had a past. We had two beautiful children. But we were done."

Before I could respond, he said, "I know what you are thinking. You think that a successful man with money meets his needs elsewhere—and perhaps anywhere."

I kept my mouth shut and bit my bottom lip. But he read my mind exactly, and his thinking was my very own. I only assumed he had mistresses scattered across the United Kingdom. Those thoughts often fueled my own personal insecurities and doubts about why he would want to be with me, and magnified the risk I was taking each time I walked away from him. I was deeply afraid he would stop trying to see me and just move on to another.

I nodded my head as he continued, "My wife eventually found what she needed with her tennis coach and maybe even her yoga instructor. I withdrew into work; somewhat thankful I suppose I did not have to be responsible for it. That is the other thing that was remarkable about today! You initiated sex, and it was so new for me. I *always* started it with Sarah, and I can tell you she rejected me more often than not. If she engaged, it felt like an obligation or a chore. We got what we both needed in the moment, but there was no… connection. Any physical relationship became just that—*the occasional need met*. It became easier and easier to ignore that part of our marriage and, not surprisingly, the marriage was no more. With all of my work, it also became easy to ignore that part of my life all together."

I looked at him with empathy, but still said nothing. I wanted to let him tell me what he felt he needed to.

"I had desires, of course, as a man. But I was consumed with *conquests* in other places—with work or the causes that I support. Each success made me happy and satisfied in a way. It wasn't just money or the next big deal to top the last. I enjoyed helping other businesses that I believed in succeed. My own financial success is a by-product, to be sure. But it was more than that. I also wanted to know that I was honorable enough of a man not to hurt my sons or my wife with scandal or betrayal. I am not ignorant or naïve. I know I am visible. The first transgression not only ruins my family, but it also ruins my reputation, and possibly everything I have built. That was not a risk I was willing to take."

I smiled at this. Liam is an honorable man. Even with his struggles to live his words of discretion with me, I know he was working through his own changing and conflicting emotions when he knew his marriage was already over.

"I have never been married but can imagine that it is easy to fall into the routine of life—especially over that many years—and with children, you have another set of commitments, routines, and schedules. The passion we feel now with a new relationship and how we were brought together and stayed apart has fueled our emotions now that we can finally be together. But you have to attempt to connect at some point and that doesn't always have to be physical. It can be as simple as stopping for a moment to check on each other or sitting before the fire like this to talk about the events of the day. I love spending this time with you."

"*That is right!* One thing I have loved most about having you here with me in this house is talking before bed. I feel connected to you here in our talks in a way I have never felt before. I feel you supporting me, and I hope I am a support to you."

"You support me in so many ways," I said in agreement. From the very moment we met, Liam has been nothing but a support to me... and my work.

"You have also slowed me down a little. I would normally be on my computer or phone late in the evening. I want to tell you *everything*, though I fear I am blethering too much."

"You are not. I appreciate that you share your thoughts and emotions, even if you are unsure of them. You are open and honest in that respect. I *want* a man who cares enough to share his thoughts with me, even if he is working through those thoughts himself. And I *want* a man who wants to listen to my own thoughts and feelings. This time is valuable and needed—no matter the stage of a relationship—for honest, human connection."

He just smiled at the compliment and said nothing for a moment. He thought more about my words and finally said, "I appreciate that, but I would say that I have not been honest about my own feelings for a long time. You have brought that honesty out in me because I feel safe talking to you. I do not feel *judged*."

I smiled as I thought to myself that I would hate for us not to want to be together and tell each other what we are thinking and feeling. We have become both friends and lovers. The mere thought of not talking to him made me sad for a moment. He sensed the shift in my demeanor and squeezed me tighter for a moment and kissed the top of my head, silently reassuring me.

"Will you work tomorrow?" I asked, clearly changing the subject.

"I need to attend a call with my business partner Tom Preston at nine o'clock as we have another deal in the works. He just has to give me a status, so unless things have suddenly gone off the rails since our last call, it should be a quick conversation. I will keep my mobile handy if I am needed. I have the luxury here that the signal is not consistent, so I can choose when I engage. Things are also slower with the approaching holidays."

I nodded in understanding as he continued, "I should tell you I invited Tom and his wife, Elaine, for dinner tomorrow. Chef Dan knows that we will have two more join us and we will keep it casual.

Tom has probably had nothing but a burger, chips, and beer every night of his life, so nothing fancy!"

I laughed at the thought for a moment, and said back to him, "Sometimes you just want a beer with a friend."

"Aye, that is right."

"Tom sounds like that kind of friend, and I think I already love him. But how are we on beer?"

"You are a quick study, love! We have plenty of beer. We will have to once *he* arrives. Did you not see the kegs in the wine cellar?" I shook my head that I did not.

"Look back at the kitchen. Do you see the taps in the back right corner?"

I immediately turned around on the sofa to look back in the kitchen to see the beer taps for Tennant's and Innis & Gunn in the corner.

"I never noticed that, but think it is the most amazing thing I have ever seen! Liam, you have your own pub!"

We both laughed at the notion, and I asked, "What can you tell me about his wife? I mean no disrespect with the question. I am just a little nervous about meeting your friends for the first time."

"We all went to university together and have been friends for over thirty years! Do not feel left out once they arrive. We have just known each other so long that we have our own stories, history, and way of speaking with each other. You will also hear us gravitate to our nicknames—Tommy, Laney, and they both sometimes call me just Lee instead of Liam."

I silently nodded in understanding.

"Elaine is an absolute force, and she is so good for Tom. They have been married for nearly thirty years! Prepare yourself! She will march right into this house like she owns the place because that is just who she is!"

"I am sorry. I did not mean to laugh! She sounds like a big personality!"

"You have that right! You should also know that she never liked Sarah! I would bet you £50 right now that she arrives here with her own bottle of Champagne! Perhaps two!"

"I trust your word, so I will *not* take that bet."

"Aye! Trust me, she is celebrating this divorce being final more than anyone else on the planet!"

+++

After another great day of writing and editing, I joined Liam and Chef Dan upstairs to prepare for our guests. When the bell rang, I sat up tall on the barstool with nervous expectation. Liam kissed me quickly and said as I breathed in, "You will be just fine. These are my oldest and dearest friends. Be yourself. I thought we would start here and then decide if we want to know anyone else."

I nodded to him and thought about my own friends we might add to this group as he walked to the front door to receive his guests. Before they entered the room, I could hear the usual pleasantries in the foyer.

I almost choked on my spritzer as Elaine did indeed bring her own Champagne. In fact, she had a bottle in each hand! Liam called it perfectly and I could not help but smile and wink at him, thankful I did not take his bet.

"Tom and Elaine Preston, may I introduce you to Corrine Hunter? Corrine, these are my oldest and dearest friends."

"I am so happy to meet you, Tom and Elaine," I said, shaking each of their hands eagerly. "It is an absolute pleasure."

For certain, Elaine was a big personality and a tall woman. I thought I was tall, but she was taller than me. Her height was magnified because she was a good two or three inches taller than her husband. Her bright red hair and green eyes only added to her striking presence. The first thing I noticed about Tom was his smile. It was so genuine and lit up his face. His hair was completely gray and despite being shorter than all three of us, he stood tall in our company. Something about them walking in together told me instantly that they have a loving partnership.

"When Tommy said who we were meeting tonight, I nearly fell over! I brought my copy of *The Ruins of Dunmara* hoping you would sign it for me, if you wouldna mind, Corrine," she said eagerly, in her thick Scottish accent and handing me her own worn copy of my first novel.

"Of course! Let me find a suitable pen. Liam, do you have one? If not, I can get one out of my computer bag downstairs." I saw a flash of a look between Elaine and Tom at the notion that I might be staying downstairs, and I bit my lip to keep from smiling. The new bed upstairs meant my suite downstairs was only for work.

Liam pulled a black marker out of a drawer in the kitchen and handed it to me with a smile. I wrote on the inside of the title page and handed the book back to her.

To Elaine and new friendships
Best, Corrine Hunter

"Thank you! I am thrilled to bits with this!" she said, showing Tom, before putting the book in her bag. "Now, we are here to celebrate, Lee!

Pop the cork on this bottle and put the other one in the chiller for you both to have later with our compliments. Tommy will look for his beer soon, but let us have a toast first!"

"We are so happy to meet you, Corrine," Tom said, raising his glass to me first. "I want you to know that we welcome you as a friend."

Elaine nodded cheerfully in agreement, and Liam put his arm around my waist and held me tight as he handed me my own flute. He had been smiling all day and I could tell he was pleased to have his friends here. It made me happy to see him so happy. If I have noticed anything since arriving here at Crichton House, is that he shed some of the pain and worry about his divorce and has become a lighter version of himself. Now, in the short time Tom and Elaine have been here, he seems even more relaxed. These new glimpses of who he is as a man make him even more attractive to me.

"Thank you so much, Tom! Like I said, I am so happy to meet you both and welcome the opportunity to get to know more about Liam by knowing his dearest friends."

"Lee has not been himself for many months, but I did not realize that it was you that changed him," Tom said before nearly choking on his Champagne. Elaine hit him hard on the back as he corrected himself. "All for the positive, of course!"

We all laughed at his quick recovery and Liam mocked like he was hitting the man in the arm, only to have the two men hug each other tight.

Elaine said, raising her flute to us all, "We are so happy for you, Liam. Truly. You know we love you and the lads with all of our heart, but this divorce is for the best. Sláinte!"

"*Sláinte,*" we all said in unison and clinked our glasses together.

"Let's get out of Dan's way here in the kitchen," Liam said, moving us all out to the patio and nodding to the chef, who just returned from lighting the outdoor grill for our burgers.

Liam set the outdoor heaters and fireplace on full blast for our comfort, and the chairs had beautiful wool tartan throws over them now. I suppose Miss Betty helped prepare for our dinner party, as I clearly did nothing.

The warm heaters coupled with the view across the loch as the sun set made for a great night of pleasantries about the weather, the house, and the drive here. Eventually the men moved down by the loch talking business, leaving me and Elaine talking about my next novel alone on the patio.

After a moment of silence, she said, "I do not know you, Corrine. But my friend is happier than I have seen in a long time, and I thank you for that."

"I appreciate your kind words and your love for your friend," I said, reaching out and clinking my glass with hers once more. I looked at Liam talking with Tom and said, "You should know that he has made me happy as well."

"That says a lot to me, because you both deserve such happiness."

I just looked at her and wondered how, in meeting me for the first time, she could make such a declaration. She answered my silent question, with, "Again, I just met you, but if I have any talent at all, it is that I am an excellent judge of character. I can tell you have a loving heart. In our short amount of time together, I can see your love for Lee, and he *deserves* that love. I can only *assume* that you deserve the same."

I smiled at her and then looked at Liam standing with his friend by the boathouse and thought that he does deserve my love and I deserve his. He looked right at me like he could read my thoughts at that very moment and smiled sweetly at me.

"My husband told me to keep my mouth shut about it, but I want you to know that this divorce is the best thing that ever happened to him. Well, perhaps the second-best thing!"

I just nodded to her in appreciation that she meant me, but said nothing back to her. I do not want to comment on Liam's wife or his divorce, though I could not ignore the fact that it has been perhaps the best thing to happen for both of us.

"The lads know I am outspoken, as I am sure you have already heard."

"Well, I heard some musing on the fact. It turns out Liam knew you would show up with two bottles of Champagne tonight if that gives you any indication."

She threw her head back and laughed loudly before saying, "That lad knows I love him, and he knows that despite that love, I *seriously* disliked his wife!"

I nearly choked on my drink with her words.

"It is the truth! I can count on one hand how many times I have even been to this house over the last twenty years. It hurt Tommy to no end to feel excluded, but Sarah knew not to invite us to many events—here or in the city—because we did not get along. Seeing the two men that I have known for most of my adult life talking together at the boathouse there makes me want to cry with happiness. I *love* them both so!"

I could see the emotion on her face and the tears form in her eyes. She meant every word she said. Her love for the men standing before us was apparent and genuine.

"Why would they not socialize together? Why would *you* not socialize together? I mean, I understand you did not like her, but…"

"Sarah would not allow it."

I just looked at her, still confused about how that could be so.

"You are thinking rationally, Corrine. You are thinking that a man has his own friendships say nothing of the fact that these old friends work together. But if you are *not* rational, those close friendships are a threat to you. Especially if those friends are not friends of yours."

I just nodded in understanding of the concept but asked, "But what does she gain by keeping you apart?"

"It is all about power and control. She chose where she could lead, and their personal life was one area where she could tell him what to do or not do. And Lee let her. I will not give him a pass on that other than in any relationship you learn to pick your battles, I suppose."

I just nodded and looked at Liam, still talking with his best friend at the dock as she continued, "They dated off and on for years but married later, well into their thirties. The lads almost came to blows when Lee said he asked Sarah to marry him. Tommy had always followed Lee, but he never felt second to his best friend. They balance each other. He knew Lee was making a mistake and spoke his mind and said so. I supported him being honest with Lee and he said as much in their conversation. The three of us did not speak for a time because of it. We were still invited to the wedding, which we attended. We kept our mouths shut from that point on, but Sarah never forgave either of us."

"I can't imagine," I said, shaking my head.

"She loved Lee's money and influence sure enough, but I am not sure that she ever really loved the man. Tommy struggled to support his friend's choice. In the end, he had to let it go. He loves Lee. We both do. So they remained business partners, but we did not see each other much. Business was business and old friendships became mere history. They silently found a balance that kept them connected—and that was at work."

"I can tell you, Elaine, that Liam has been so excited about you both being here tonight, if that helps in any way."

"Aye," she said as we both sipped our glasses. "That mends my heart. It does."

She continued, "Last year, they had a Christmas party here at this very house and Sarah invited all the senior leaders from their company except Tommy."

"Oh, my!"

"We only found out about the party because Lee texted Tommy and asked when we were arriving so that they could do the Champagne toast to the team together. It was then Lee found out we were never invited. He genuinely did not know, and I think it broke his heart. He sent us the largest Christmas hamper I have ever seen and wrote a personal note of apology to us both."

"That had to hurt," I said, thinking about the Prestons feeling excluded and for Liam to see that his business partner and oldest friends were deliberately the only leaders in the company excluded by his own wife.

"I'm all for keeping a man grounded. Tommy knows that no matter the number of pounds in our bank account, I will not let him stray far from where we were raised *or how* we were raised. I love him with everything I have, and I will always support him, but I will check him in an instant if he becomes arrogant or boastful. Sarah did not keep Liam grounded—she was horrible to him."

Elaine saw her choice of words confused me and continued as she sipped her glass again. "Aye, she was never a kind woman, but she was exceptionally harsh to Lee."

"Thank you for telling me this, Elaine. You are helping me understand Liam more, but this is all so new for me. I do not want to get in the middle of his relationship with his ex-wife."

"That is fair, and those are the words of an honorable woman. I do not intend to put you in the middle. I just want you to understand what this man has gone through."

"Gone through?"

"Aye!"

"Tell me," I said, topping up her glass once again.

"We have all watched her destroy the man when she could for many years. His own professional success was matched by personal misery in equal measure."

"What on earth did she do?" I could not help but ask. I truly did not want to get in the middle, but I am now intrigued by the story she seems more than willing to share.

"Under the pretense of not letting success go to the man's head, Sarah would absolutely berate him in front of others every chance she could. She didn't even mind berating him in front of their sons. The poor man could do nothing right!"

I had nothing to say and looked at Liam by the boathouse as I sipped silently from my glass, trying to imagine that he would deserve such treatment or that he would even stand for it.

Elaine sipped her Champagne as she said, "For example, on a night like tonight, she would have criticized the jumper he is wearing, but *she* would have waited until we were all standing there in the kitchen to hear it. She might even go as far to insist that he go change it immediately. Then, we would all know that he should have used the chilled flutes and that he poured the Champagne too fast, obviously causing two of the glasses to overflow. You just silently grabbed the kitchen towel for him, but she would still be cross and complaining about his mistake and wasting the Champagne. Then, we would all know by now that the outdoor heaters and fireplace should have been on at least ten minutes before guests arrived. He would catch hell on that fact for sure, and she would have stood out there with him, giving him an earful in full view of us all!"

She sipped her glass once more and said, "Christ above! She would have stood in the kitchen giving Chef Dan a run for his money on the cook and plating of the burgers or the fry on the chips. Nothing was ever good enough for her and she wanted everyone to know who was truly in charge of *her* house! Again, it was about power. Sarah wielded what power she could, and that was at home. Lee had power elsewhere but not in his own house."

"I realize I am just getting to know him, Elaine, but Liam does not seem to be the type of man to be treated so. I mean, to be as successful as he is, how could he tolerate such behavior? Especially against his oldest and dearest friends, not to mention himself."

She just looked at me and said, "I mean no disrespect to him in any way when I say this, but despite his natural intellect and his clear business success, he is still an awkward, nerdy, lad at heart. My husband is the same! Lee loved a woman who had very little love to give, and he took every little bit she offered because frankly, she was the only woman he had been with. From the beginning he felt like he was lucky to have that. I suspect he could never imagine that there *was* anything more than that."

"I did not know," I said. Of course, I did know Sarah was the first and only one, but did not want to let on fully. I just met Elaine Preston.

"The lads think I hate Sarah, and maybe I do."

She thought more about her words and said, making the sign of the cross, "No, Father God, *hate* is such a harsh word! I do not want to carry that burden. But I resent her for what she did to Lee and how she came between friends. I believe she loves her children—absolutely wonderful lads. I say all of this not to disparage her as a woman or as a mother, but because I want you to know you have a good man in front of you. A good father. A good friend. Tommy and I only want the best for him."

"I can see that. I have so enjoyed talking with you. Should we rejoin the men and have our dinner?"

"Aye, but here is the last bit of this bottle. We should keep this goodness for ourselves, lass!" She poured us each the last tiny sips of the bottle.

"We should!"

Elaine is honest. I am certain she and her husband are wealthy, but there is no pretense with her. She is a real person, and she clearly loves her husband and her friend. In the short time we have been here together, I can say that I like her a lot! I still cannot understand how Liam would have such insecurities or be married to a woman that treated him or his closest friends so. But I hope he knows he has genuine friends who love him and that starting tonight, they will all reconnect.

The men read our minds and joined us on the patio before we could meet them at the dock. When he arrived, Liam and I kissed each other quickly in front of his friends. I would not normally be one for such public displays of affection, but I only wanted to be with him tonight and whatever he was talking about with Tom, he felt the same.

+++

We filled the evening with excellent beer, burgers, and chips from Chef Dan. It was nice to have such a casual evening. Like Liam says, sometimes you just want a beer with a friend and tonight I feel surrounded by friends.

They told stories of each other as young people and their misadventures at university. We laughed a lot together. *A lot!* So much so that my face hurt. It was nice to see Liam be himself. He was not the wounded divorcee, not the successful titan of business, and not the father carrying the weight of the world on his shoulders for his sons. He was just a lad with his best mates, and I loved seeing this side of him.

"Chef, you made milkshakes!" I said as Dan placed the tall glasses with red-striped paper straws before each of us.

"Aye, Miss Corrine, I made you all chocolate milkshakes to go with your burgers. I wanted to include something sweet for you on tonight's menu."

"A chocolate milkshake is most welcome tonight! Thank you, sir!" I said as I immediately began dunking my chips into the shake and not my mayonnaise and ketchup.

Everyone at the table stopped eating and Liam asked, "What on earth are ye doing?"

"Have you never put a salty chip into a milkshake? It is the perfect sweet and salty combination." Everyone looked at me as if I were from another planet and shook their heads. "Try it just once. Take your chip, dunk it, and eat it."

Elaine was the first to try it and said, "That is *good*!"

Tom was next to agree to try this perceived abomination. "It *is* good, Corrine! It is not just a sweet and salty combo. It is also hot and cold."

I put my hand to Liam's cheek and said playfully as he was trying to decide, "You cannot stand to admit it, can you?"

"It is *actually* good," he said, finally resigning to the fact before kissing my cheek.

+++

When the night ended, we walked Tom and Elaine to the front door together. This is not my house, but they were also my guests tonight.

Tom spoke first, saying as he took my hand sweetly, "Thank you both for a grand dinner and even better conversation. It was so nice to be here again! I am so glad to have met you, Corrine! I wish you nothing but the best with your novel—and with *this one*."

"I appreciate you both welcoming me the way you have," I said, holding Liam's hand tight. He squeezed it. "I was so nervous, and you put me at ease straight away!"

Elaine came to me and said, kissing me on the cheek, "We are all friends now and I have my book signed by a famous author!"

"We must do this again," I said with my hand on her shoulder.

Elaine smiled at me and nodded her head, but then hugged me tight. "Thank you, Corrine. You made tonight special, and I thank you for it."

Liam said, "Remember, the gate will open on its own, but do *not* get too close, man!"

"Oh, there must be a story there!" I said, laughing that this was his parting instruction to Tom.

"The last time we were here, this fool practically took off the entire front end of a brand-new Audi Q7 at the gate," Elaine said, hitting Tom in the shoulder. "If he ruins my Defender tonight, I will kill him!"

Once Liam shut the door, he exclaimed, "Tonight was an absolute triumph! A triumph, Corrine!"

"I adored them both and hope we can see them again soon! Should we have one more beer in front of the fire and talk?"

"Of course, I will get them for us."

Once seated for our nightly ritual to connect in front of the fire, Liam and I sipped our newly filled pints.

"I assume Laney gave you an earful."

"She did, but you should know that she did so respectfully." Liam laughed a little at this as I said, "No, I mean it! She loves you and she made that point very clear."

"I love her, too! She has always been a good friend and she and Tommy are such a fine match. I loved being with them. Tonight was fun for me. *Really fun!*"

"I could tell! You smiled all evening and I have never heard you laugh so much!"

"I am so glad you could meet them!"

"Old friends are the best, because they always love you and they never let you stray far from who you are as a person."

"That is so true, and I felt every bit of their love tonight. I think I needed it. No! I *know* I needed it. Love, perhaps I am finding my heart again as well."

I just held his hand tight in mine and smiled at the thought. We were open to each other from our very first meeting and it seems we have both silently been looking for the same thing—to find our hearts again.

Liam never mentioned how they were kept apart and never asked me anymore about what Elaine said about him or his ex-wife. Likely because he already knows. I respect he left our conversation between us and trusts that I would tell him if I wanted to. He also never said what he and Tom talked about down by the boathouse, and I believed the same. It was a private conversation among friends, and he will tell me about it if he wants to.

+++

FIFTEEN
The Path Forward

Crichton House
Loch Leven, Scotland
December 2022

Perfect for a cold, dark, and rainy day, Chef Dan's magnificent dinner was homemade Cacio e Pepe. We had grilled chicken and langoustines, if we wanted to add protein to our dish, but the fresh pasta with Pecorino-Romano cheese and pepper on its own was a warm comfort for me this night.

Enjoying our nightly ritual, Liam and I sat in front of the fire silently for a bit. We spent tonight listening to the music on the house sound system and the pouring rain outside.

"I want you to pack an overnight bag."

"For what?"

Liam leaned in to kiss the top of my head and said softly, "I want to take a drive tomorrow… to Aberlour."

"You *do?*" I said, sitting my glass on the table. I began kissing his cheek over and over while hugging him tight.

"Aye!" he said, laughing at my appreciation, landing repeatedly and enthusiastically on his cheek.

"We can see the marker for the lads," I said, smiling through the tears that started forming. I did not want to cry before him again, but I was so touched that he would think of this on his own. I never once even thought to ask him about the possibility, though it should have been part of my plan from the very beginning. As much as I read and researched with what Andrew provided and a quick visit to the library in Edinburgh, nothing can beat seeing a place in person.

"We know the orphanage doesn't exist anymore, but we will drive to the town, see the marker, and anything else you need to see. We will then drive up and stay the night in Inverness before returning here the next day. I had Jenny book us a suite at Ness Walk."

"I *love* that hotel!"

"You have stayed there before, then?"

"Yes. I stayed there when I was here researching one of my first novels and needed to visit Culloden Battlefield. The hotel has a great location and even better staff. I loved walking along the River Ness!"

"I thought this would be good for your work."

"It is so good for my work and even better for my spirit! Thank you, Liam! Thank you so much!" I said into his ear after kissing his cheek again.

"We will leave at eight o'clock tomorrow morning. It is going to take some time to get there, and we will want to get to Inverness in time for dinner."

"I will be ready!"

+++

Liam drove us beautifully through all manner of Scottish weather and around the twists and turns of what felt like all the villages of Aberdeenshire and Morayshire. It was a joy for me to ride with him so I could enjoy the scenery without the focus required behind the wheel on my own. Normally, I would not enjoy being a passenger—but today, I did. I got to absorb even more of beautiful Scotland on our drive without the stress of navigating the roads myself.

"Who knew that the Walker's Shortbread factory is based here? I would have had you bring me here for that alone!"

"We can pop in if you want. I am sure they have a shop, and perhaps even a tour."

"No, I was just being silly! We have no shortage of shortbread for tea. But is an impressive complex and good on them for putting themselves here in the middle of Speyside distillery country. I might have to look at their website to read more about their history and how this is headquarters."

"Perhaps we get something to eat and visit the town first. We can go to the Aberlour Hotel for lunch and get directions to St. Margaret's."

"That is perfect! I know where the church is. In fact, we may have just passed it on the left. But I welcome the local support and guidance. I would also like to see if we can find flowers to leave there."

"That is lovely," he said, thinking about what I was saying.

"It is a marker for the dead. We should have flowers to pay our respects."

"We absolutely should, and we can ask about a florist at the restaurant."

After turning around at the top of the hill just past town, we found parking directly across the street from the Aberlour Hotel. Liam asked, "What great luck is this?"

"Princess parking, as I call it!"

He leaned across the car console for a kiss as he said, "In this case, love, it is *prince's parking*."

"Well done, my prince," I said, patting his cheek and kissing him.

We walked across the street and shared a lovely lunch together. The manager set us back out from the hotel to St. Margaret's Church and the tiny market on the way that had flowers. We purchased a small spray of flowers and walked hand-in-hand all the way through the iron gates and up the long, narrow drive to the church.

As we reached the top of the hill and the churchyard, I said, "Liam, that's it! Right there! On the front! The very first one!"

There stood the tall stone marker with the Celtic Cross on top and three small poppy wreaths at its base placed after a recent rededication. We read the words on the front silently to ourselves.

To The Glory Of God
And In Honour Of
The Old Boys Of
Aberlour Orphanage
Who Fell In The Great War
1914—1918
Requiescant In Pace

The three other sides of the base had all the names of the young men from the orphanage that died in the Great War. Another stone slab of names attached to the front of the memorial reflected the *'old boys'* who perished in World War Two. I teared up immediately and let go of

Liam's hand to place our flowers next to the ceremonial wreaths. We stood silently for a moment in honor of the lads, both saying our own silent prayers of respect.

"I am so sorry Liam, I feel you have seen me cry more than I would have liked since we set out together from Edinburgh, but I am so moved by this story, I cannot help it," I said wiping my tears from my face.

"I understand and I can tell you are thinking deeply about it," he said, taking my hand again. "I admit I am moved myself seeing the marker with the names. I am proud of the poor lads, respect their service, and honor their sacrifice."

I went around the entire base and read each of the names silently to myself before saying on the last side, "The line after the last name says, *'And all others whose names are not known.'* Like Andrew mentioned, this must have been most of the letter writers or lads that they knew because of their connection back to the orphanage once they left."

"Makes sense. During this time period, there was no easy way to track people who left the orphanage or village if they did not stay in touch themselves."

I was again thinking intensely about the story and how I could make it work in my novel. I have been trying to leverage as much work from what was in the original manuscript, but being here today has unlocked even more ideas. I tried to record what I could in my notebook and took many photos on my phone while we were there.

We walked hand-in-hand back to the car in silence and when Liam opened my door and helped me into my seat, he kissed my cheek and said, "Do you have what you need?"

"I do, and more," I said, kissing him back.

We drove to Inverness in silence. Liam focused on navigating the drive out of the countryside, and I typed furiously on my laptop in the passenger seat. I wanted our time together at the hotel to be special and this would likely be the only chance I would have to capture my thoughts of the day.

Liam put his hand around the back of my neck and rubbed it and my shoulders, saying, "I can feel all of your stress over here."

He immediately wiped away my tension-laced silence with his touch. I smiled at him and said leaning back into his hand, "Bless you! I wanted to capture all of my notes about today before we got to the hotel. I am merging research notes into my manuscript, but I have a new idea about how to rewrite my novel based on our visit today."

"Can you do that this far along?"

"I can, but I will need Kate to bless it. She approved the premise of my last version and would need to accept such a drastic change in the story and plot. Even though I am trying to preserve what I can, this is not an edit of my first draft. It will be a new manuscript—a new story. I am still going to try to meet my deadline. I owe her that much."

"You know I can get you back to Edinburgh again if you need to do more research at the library or the university. And I can always stop at the office. In fact, I know Tommy would actually appreciate me stopping by the office."

"Liam! I am not here to keep you from your own work."

"I know. It is a slow time. We are still working a bit in the hybrid mode between home and office, so we are both representing the choices that many of our employees are making. But I need to focus more than I have. You have been a welcome distraction for the last few weeks."

I smiled, thinking about how he was an unexpected and welcome distraction for me from the beginning. I said, "I have all the information from my last visit to the library when I looked up the book Andrew told me about and some of the letters. Visiting the town and marker today, however, was a revelation."

He just nodded in understanding as he focused on the road ahead. "I also want to finish my notes here so that I can give you my *undivided attention* when we are at the hotel."

"I never want to impede your own work, but confess that I was hoping for that."

I reached out for his hand and smiled. He smiled back and kissed the top of my hand. Of all the ways I have grown to love this man, his genuine support of my work has to be at the top of the list.

+++

We dressed for a fabulous dinner at the Torrish Restaurant at the hotel. Based on their own description, the Torrish fly is commonly used for salmon fishing, which is natural in the salmon pools in the river before us. Naturally, we both chose the salmon course for dinner.

We sat together and talked about our amazing day and genuinely took another opportunity to get to know each other better. We talked about how we were both only children and our parents were no longer with us. We are so fortunate that our parents lived long enough to see us each have some manner of success, which we considered a blessing. In Liam's case, that meant seeing him also have a family of his own and know his sons. It was a touching conversation. One that brought us even closer.

We talked about our favorite music, debating, and eagerly sharing our favorites, all of which reflected the handful of years between us. We both love *The Clash, The Smiths, New Order* and more. I tried to make a case for more bands from the Eighties, but he was not in complete agreement with my selection. Each band name I rattled off was met with polite derision. We laughed throughout the entire conversation. We agreed on loving the symphony but not so much the opera. Though we broke apart at our preferences for theater. I love the classics and Shakespeare, and he likes all theater. I shut the conversation down when I said I hated musicals. He was clearly unhappy with my absolute declaration, but did not argue with me.

We had a delicious dinner and even more fun just talking with each other about ourselves and our lives. Talks that had nothing to do with lost loves, divorces, business, or books.

We moved into the bar area for one more glass before bed and were fortunate that we had the entire bar to ourselves. I had my spritzer, and he had his whisky. We held hands and looked at each other across the small table, both realizing what we felt was deeper than we could ever imagine.

Each conversation and discovery validated what we felt in an instant. *We belong together.* Since we met, everything had been pointing to that fact. Even though we both seem to check ourselves against our own nerves, personal insecurities, and conventions of time, our feelings have been powerful from the start. They have only grown stronger in this short amount of time together.

"*Corrine,*" Liam said, leaning in and putting his hand to my cheek, "I do not know how this all works or if it is too soon, but I *have* to say what I feel... *I love you.*"

I kissed him and said through my smile and my hand stroking his bearded cheek, "You told me once not to be afraid to show my heart and I would say the same back to you, Liam. *I love you too!*"

I cannot believe he would say the words to me and that I would say the same words back to him. I have never said them to any other man other than David. We have only known each other for a few months, but I do love Liam and knowing he feels the same made me happy.

I confessed to him, "I have not said those words in a very long time."

"I was thinking the same thing. It has been a *very* long time."

Still holding hands across the table, I leaned in and said, "I feel no need to define our relationship or put it into a box for now. I just want to be with you. Let the future be what it will be. In the short time we have known each other, you have made me happier than I've been in many years!"

"My darlin' I can say the same. Though I do not know that I have *ever* felt this way. Every minute with you has been a revelation of emotions and a new happiness I cannot put into words. If I did, they would certainly be inadequate—especially to an author. I only want to be with you, love." He looked at me and immediately felt my emotions shift upon his words.

"What…?"

"It is Christmastime. You will navigate the first holiday since the divorce, and you will have your boys with you at Crichton House for part of that time. I should not be there. Not now. It is too soon."

"Corrine," he said, starting to pre-empt my words. He knew what I was about to say.

"No. We can decide not to worry about what might be perceived as too soon or not for us, but we cannot rush children. I am sorry I did not tell you before, but I could not find the right time or even make myself say the words. I knew they would hurt too much. I am going back to London for Christmas. You should be with your family—your sons."

"I want to be with you," he whispered under his breath.

"I know, and I want to be with you. But we should not rush this just yet. I can give you the time you need with the boys, and I can settle what I need to with Kate and the book. You know I owe her the manuscript by the end of the year, and it has opened up in so many ways now. We can talk every day and I can come back to the house once the boys return to their mother."

He said nothing and hung his head in resignation.

I wrapped my hands through his hair and said, kissing the top of his head, "Liam! I am not leaving you for long. You will be able to be with your sons for Christmas. I just told you I love you, and I do."

"I understand, and as much as I want to fight it, I will not. You are thinking of my lads, and I love you even more for it. When do you want to go?"

"Tuesday the twentieth. Four days from now. I booked the open ticket I had pending for a flight out of Edinburgh and was hoping I could convince you to take me to the airport."

"So soon?"

"It was difficult with Christmas and New Year bookings, but the hotel helped me secure a room at a very busy time, so I will need to arrive a bit earlier and maybe stay a bit later. Like I said, it will help me finish the book and I can spend more time with you after the holidays without the distraction of this deadline looming over me. The manuscript will be in Kate's hands then, and I will have to wait for her feedback. *I will be all yours!*"

"If you have the hotel booked, then let me fly you to London. Please cancel your commercial flight." I nodded in agreement to him as he continued, "I will call Nate, my pilot, tomorrow to make it happen and we will ensure you have a driver get you to the hotel from London City. Jenny will see to it all for you! Let us help you here."

"I tried to take care of myself and did not think to ask for help."

"You are independent to a fault, Miss Hunter," he said, lightening his mood and mine.

"That I am, Mr. Crichton! Thank you and Jenny for helping me."

We just looked at each other and thought about being apart. We have grown so close being at the house on Loch Leven, our trip to Aberlour, and now Inverness. This is the right thing for all of us, for now. We have moved quickly, but we both agree that bringing his sons into this new relationship is the one thing that cannot—and should not—be rushed.

+++

We walked out of the lift to our room hand-in-hand but in silence. I was thinking about new declarations of love, but I know Liam is still not completely happy about me going to London for Christmas. I can tell he is still thinking about it. He stood behind me as I faced the suite door, waiting for him to open it. Instead, he brushed my hair aside and began kissing my neck.

After a few moments enjoying his welcome attention, I said, "Babe, please open the door."

"Did you just call me *babe*?"

"*Maybe…*" I said slowly before I started giggling uncontrollably and leaning back into his chest. "I have clearly had too much to drink! I have never called anyone *babe* in my entire life!"

He whispered in my ear, "*I like it.*"

"Then, please open the door, *babe*!"

"I am not sure where the key is."

I turned around to look at him, his hands now affixed to the doorframe. One on each side of me.

"You have the key card. I saw you take it from the table when you signed the bar bill."

He just looked at me with a smile and kissed the tip of my nose. I realized that this was another playful game. I immediately put my hands in the pockets of his sports coat. Nothing.

"Cold."

I looked at him sideways. I already know where this game is going, but I will play along if for no other reason than to get in this room with him. I ran my hand slowly up his chest to the breast pocket of his shirt. Nothing.

"*Colder,*" he said, breathing in my ear and returning to his kisses on my neck. I then moved my hands down and around to the back pockets of his trousers.

"Warmer, but not terrible if you want to linger for a bit," he said with a wink and a smile before kissing my nose again. Nothing.

I pinched his ass as hard as I could as he flinched and said, laughing, "Ouch! That hurt! *But in a good way.*"

"Enjoy it all you want, but you cannot make love to me in the hall of this hotel. I am certain there are laws against indecency in this country."

I could see him process my words and my slight reprimand just as I moved my hands slowly to the front of his trousers. I found my target and pulled it from his front pocket quickly. Just as he leaned in to kiss me, I turned back toward the door and opened it. He seemed stunned for a moment that I would reject him so. I walked in, kicked off my shoes, and began undressing myself before him with the door still open.

Finally, he moved from the hall, shut the door, and said, picking me up and carrying me to the bedroom, *"I love ye, my darlin'!"*

"And I love you, babe."

+++

We spent the remaining days together, loving each other, and continuing to grow as a new couple—making it all the harder for me to leave him. I made considerable progress editing my book and continued to merge the stories together as I planned. We spent nights learning more about each other, only increasing our connection, and bringing each other pleasure. Our relationship has been open and honest in a way I have never experienced in my life. While David and I also connected quickly, this new relationship was its own. And it was welcome.

When the day finally came for me to leave, the unnamed young lads, who I still had not met or even seen much of while here at Crichton House, placed my luggage in the back of Liam's Range Rover. Miss Betty and I just smiled and nodded to each other politely. I am certain she was thankful that I was leaving before Liam's sons arrived, but she said nothing to me, and I had nothing to say to her.

I was slightly ashamed that I could not even muster a courtesy, *'Happy Christmas'* to them before I left, but I could not pretend that any of them were kind or warm to me during my visit. I may have to remedy this if I return to this house in the future, but felt no need to settle it today. I already had enough emotion brewing inside.

Liam and I rode to the small private airport in silence. We held hands and occasionally looked at each other, but neither of us could speak. When we pulled up next to the jet on the tarmac, I immediately hopped out of my seat and waited in the back of the car for my luggage. Before opening the tailgate, Liam pulled me to him and said in my ear, *"I will always regret you leaving me."*

I kissed him and with his cheek to mine, I said back to him with tears in my eyes, "I remember those very words. You said them to me once before. This is the right thing. I will see you after Christmas. Enjoy every minute with your sons! They need you as they adjust to their new world of two households. I love you."

"I love you more," he said, now holding my face in his hands. "Travel safe and Happy Christmas!"

"Happy Christmas!"

I kissed him again and willed the tears to stay put for now. This was my decision, and I needed to own it. He handed my luggage to the pilot, and I walked up the stairs of his jet without him. I did not look back at him. I could not. I cried off and on the entire way to London but was happy to be back at the hotel I love. It was a welcome comfort today.

Somehow, Liam's assistant Jenny upgraded my last-minute reservation to a suite and not only filled the room with white flowers but also a small, lighted Christmas tree by the fireplace with an assortment of beautifully wrapped packages underneath. A note on the hall table next to one bouquet read:

I miss you already.

Love, LC

I called Kate and told her I had arrived. She and Luke agreed to meet me for drinks in the hotel tonight. As much as I missed Liam, I looked forward to seeing my dearest friends, and hoped that they would help me through my first night without him.

+++

"Well, that is perfect timing!" I said as I met Kate at the same moment as she was also walking into the double doors to the bar and hugged her.

Luke was already in the bar and arrived with martinis for them both. "Corrie, my girl! We have missed you," he said, before kissing my cheek. "What can I get you?"

"Nothing. Let's sit. Tommaso will take care of me."

We sat at a table in the corner by the window and my spritzer kit was delivered almost immediately. I raised my glass to my friend across the bar and winked at him. He nodded to me and smiled. I love my friends in this bar and they love me.

"Tell us *everything*," Kate said. Her demeanor was much more supportive than the last time we talked in this room, but I know she could see that I was not sitting before her brokenhearted. I am happier than I have been for a very long time. She would never deny me any happiness, no matter her own reservations about my relationship with Liam or how she thought it started. Perhaps his divorce being final helped, but I suspect Luke also talked her down a bit. She also knows that I have spent almost a month with Liam at his house on Loch Leven and have told her nothing. I know her well enough to know that she is dying to know the truth of it all!

"I do not even have the words," I said, sipping my wine. With tears in my eyes, I continued, "You both know better than anyone how much I loved David—how much I will *always* love David."

They both looked at each other and then back at me and nodded. Kate said, "We do, my darling. We do!"

"Liam told me he loves me, and I said the same back to him. In my life, I have only said those words to one other man." They knew what it meant to me to not only say those words to another, but what it meant for me to tell them about it.

Luke spoke first and said, "That is wonderful!"

"This has all happened so quickly, but I needed to give him the holidays with his boys who have just gone through their parent's divorce. I would have not left him for any other reason. I *could not* have left him for any other reason."

"Corrie," Kate said softly, taking my hand in hers.

"I love him, and he loves me," I said, smiling at her through tears of happiness and longing for the man I left back at the house at Loch Leven. Luke took my other hand but said nothing. David was his dearest friend and like Kate, I suspect he has always grieved how the loss of the man they brought into my life hurt me—how it has hurt all of us.

"Kate, there is more. I finished the book."

"*You finished it?*"

"You sound surprised," I said, laughing at her and smiling at Luke, who winked at me in support and squeezed my hand still in his.

"I admit, I did not expect it. I told Luke on the ride here that I fully expected another request for an extension tonight because of this new relationship. One that I would have given you, by the way. *How?*"

"Liam did exactly as you hoped with your introduction. He connected to me with a historian who gave me a nugget of information that changed *everything*. But Liam himself gave me *even more*."

"What do you mean? I always saw him as a connector, but not that he had anything to add to your novel himself."

"The entire book was missing *heart,* and Liam gave mine back to me. I struggled to find the emotion in the story, and his love and support unlocked it all."

"Well then, I cannot wait to read it over the holiday!"

"Kate, you gave me an extension for my last manuscript, but this is so changed, I want you to consider this a first draft. The book I am handing you is not an edit of what you started with. Yes, I reused what I could, and you will read some things you recognize, but this has changed."

"Give me a little more than that, my darling!"

"I have woven two stories together—my original and the story of the lads of Aberlour Orphanage."

"I'm sorry, what? Who?"

"You will see. Instead of writing just about the female journalist during this time, I also wrote from her beloved's point of view who was sent to war. He was an *'old boy'* from Aberlour Orphanage. Liam took me to the town, and everything just came together. I am completing one last edit pass now, but it still needs a solid pass with my editor having switched the story and perspective up so. The story is there, though I am certain there are some glaring errors and inconsistencies because of the quick rewrite. I will send the file to you by Christmas."

"This is a cause for celebration, friends," Luke said. He left us to get the next round of drinks at the bar.

Kate took my hand again and said, "I am so happy for you! But more than that, I am *proud* of you!"

"You know better than anyone that I never expected this. I never expected Liam in my life, but I am happy for the first time in many years. And I am proud to give you my work for the first time in as many years."

"Take your time, my darling! You have until the end of the month. Send it when you are ready."

Just then, Tommaso joined Luke in bringing all new glasses for the table. We raised them to each other in celebration for our beloved David, the promise of new love, and the hope that this may be one of the best novels I have ever written.

+++

SIXTEEN
The Last Gift

**The Corinthia Hotel
London, England
December 2022**

Each package under the tree had a gift tag with gold numbers embossed on them. Dates. I had five special gifts for each day from my arrival here in London until Christmas Day. As happy as that made me, it only made me miss Liam more. I could see how many days we would be apart before the holiday and knew that we likely had many more days apart after that.

I am certain his assistant Jenny coordinated this holiday bounty, but I could tell Liam was involved. Each card was in his own handwriting. How the two of them pulled this off before my arrival with such short notice is a wonder! I can only assume that Liam's pilot, Nate, made a quick trip to London, delivering these packages before he delivered me.

The card for the very first day of my arrival, **December 20th,** read:

I know that as fine a hotel as this is,
you still need a taste of Scotland for tea.
Love, LC

Inside the box was a beautiful basket filled with an assortment of Walker's Shortbread and Tunnock's Tea Cakes. Both are not only a welcome reminder of the country I just left but also sinfully delicious! They will be a most welcome addition to my in-room tea service. But I am going to have to take many long walks around London to get my steps in and make up for these sweet treats.

+++

The card for **December 21st** read:
Something is to be said for the handwritten word.
I hope this helps you capture ideas and
moments of inspiration.
Love, LC

Inside the package, I found two black Moleskine notebooks and a Tiffany & Co. silver ink pen. I thought about this man continuing to charm me from afar, and I appreciated his thoughtful support for my work.

+++

The card for **December 22nd** read:
You have not learned to fully appreciate whisky,
but you should have your own when you need a dram.
Love, LC

I had a small bottle of Laphroaig and a small whisky glass with my initials–CH–etched on it. I smiled to myself, because I spent some time in the city that day collecting a few of my own gifts for the man that had given me so much already. He will definitely see his favorite whisky returned to him.

+++

The card for **December 23rd** read:
Winter in Scotland requires a fine wool jumper.
Now you have one for your return to Crichton House.
Missing you and loving you, Liam

Inside the box, I found a gorgeous wool Fair Isle cardigan in lovely shades of brown, ivory, and lavender. How this man even knows my size is astonishing on its own. I suspect someone spent a moment with my clothes hanging in the closet. It is truly stunning!

I took note for a moment that his signature changed from *'LC'* to *'Liam,'* and it warmed my heart. Everything he has given me is becoming progressively more personal. I know he is not just blindly signing cards; he had a hand in the planning of these beautiful and thoughtful gifts.

+++

The gift for **December 24th** was a bottle of the 2010 Dom Perignon that we shared the night we met and that he bought for my birthday celebration in this very hotel. The card read:
Happy Christmas, my love!
Know that I will raise a glass of my own to you tonight.
I love you, Liam

Jenny must have alerted the staff to this gift as I returned to my room in the evening after turndown service to find the bottle on ice, along with an incredible assortment of pastries and cheeses.

I ordered a Christmas hamper from Daylesford Farms in England, and had it delivered to Crichton House with a card that read:

Wishing the very best for you and your family this Christmas!
Love, Corrine

I wondered if he would even know what I sent to the house, or if it landed with Miss Betty or one of her unnamed lads. We could not talk as much as I hoped beyond text, but I knew he was with his sons, and they deserved all of his attention. I hoped I would hear from him to tell me he received it, and he finally did on Christmas Day.

+++

Are you there?

I am.

Ready for you to come
home. Calling now.

Before I could reply, the phone rang, and I loved seeing **'My Scot'** on my screen once again.

"Happy Christmas, my love," he said when I accepted the call.

"Happy Christmas, to you! How did Father Christmas find you all?"

"We had a delightful visit for sure, though I think I may have indulged a bit with gifts this year. I am certain Sarah will not be pleased."

"Divorce guilt can be a difficult thing to navigate sometimes, though I doubt Eric and Ewan had many complaints."

"That is a fact! They are off changing out every XBOX in the house and playing the new games they asked for. I suspect I will not see them again until they get hungry. Dan and I decided not to set a time for supper. We will just see who ventures downstairs."

"God bless! A house filled with men!" I said, laughing at the thought of them all in the house I have grown to love. "But, I admit, I am glad you have Dan there with you."

"We joked that at least we have wine and whisky to survive it! I *will* tell you I had a good talk with the lads at dinner last night. I told them about you."

"Oh my! I did not expect you to say that!"

"I wanted to respect them by being honest, and they are old enough to understand. I wanted them to know the truth of it from me and not from the press, their friends, idle gossip in the city—*or their mother*. I do not want to act like you do not exist or that you are a secret."

"That is fair. How did they take such news?"

"Eric is thoughtful and sensitive, and he stayed quiet for the most part. He will always protect and defend his mother, as they are very close, and I do not fault him for it. He just nodded his head as I talked, but said nothing to me. Ewan said that he supported it and already knew that I was different—that I seemed happier. I *am* happier! Still, part of me was shocked the lad noticed. Maybe he is the more sensitive of the two and I have had it wrong this entire time."

"Or perhaps they are *both* sensitive and aware, but express it in different ways."

"Aye, I did not think about it that way."

"I am glad it has been a good visit for you all. As nervous as I am that you told them about me, perhaps they *are* of an age to understand,

and it should come from you first. It is especially important if I am to return to your house."

We sat in silence together for a moment, thinking about the transition all of us were going through together. We have remained shielded in our own world for the last several weeks, and the thought of his family made me nervous. Old friends are one thing, but ex-wives and children are not something I have ever had to deal with before. This is uncharted territory!

Liam changed the subject and said, "The Christmas hamper was over the top, but most welcome. You did not have to do that, but we all thank you! The lads and I fought over the sweets immediately, and Dan worked to incorporate many of the items into our menus."

"Did he really?"

"He did! He wants to reach out to them about their fine cheeses. They were all incredible! He said that as much as you and I like a meat and cheese board to snack on, they would be excellent suppliers for the house."

"We should go there sometime with Dan. It is a most amazing place in the Cotswolds. I think you both would love it. They know who they are, and it shows across all elements of their brand, and in the quality of their products."

"I know we would enjoy that. My darlin', I have to go because I hear two braw lads barreling down the stairs—likely in search of food—but I had to talk with you today. Have you opened your Christmas Day gift?"

"I have not. Wait just a second. I can open it with you before I let you go."

I retrieved the last package from under the lighted tree that has kept my room cozy the last few nights and set about opening it.

"I told you on text how much I have loved all the gifts. They have been so thoughtful. I know you had a hand in this plan, and it was not all Jenny. Am I right?"

"She helped me coordinate, of course, before you arrived! But I listed out what I wanted and wrote all the notes myself."

"You have both done an extraordinary job! I will be certain to thank her as well," I said, pausing for a moment because I felt emotional as I opened the box. "Oh, it is lovely! *Liam*…"

Before me was a silver ornament in the silhouette of a Scottish piper engraved with the year and our initials LC and CH intertwined and then adorned with a red ribbon to hang it.

The card for **December 25th** read:

Our next Christmas will be together, my love!
Liam

"I am going to hang it on my precious tree right now. And yes, sir! Next Christmas, we will be together! Enjoy the rest of your time with your sons and thank you again for making my own Christmas so special this year. I love you."

"Och, I love you more. Goodbye!"

+++

I struggled spending Boxing Day alone, but did so by joining my friends in the hotel bar in the afternoon. Thankfully, both the bar and restaurant were open only to residents of the hotel, so the room was not as crowded as you might expect. Sitting at my favorite barstool in the far corner, I had my computer and spritzer. I was content with my final edit pass and sent the file to Kate straight away.

The bar staff today was fun and festive, and I would not want to be anywhere else! They were working but clearly enjoying being with each other. Some exchanged personal gifts and indulged in special treats made just for them by the pastry chef. I did not hear from Liam today, but reassured myself that he was celebrating the last of the holidays with his sons, and I should not despair.

I was in the middle of writing in a new manuscript when two soft lips kissed the back of my head. I smiled, breathed in, and said calmly over my shoulder to the culprit, "Sir, you should know that my boyfriend has a *very* jealous nature."

His mouth made its way to my ear, and he whispered, *"Boyfriend? First babe and now boyfriend?"*

I turned to look at the man I wanted to see more than anything today. I said, clutching his face in my hands, "I almost said *my lover*. Do you like that better?"

He smiled and kissed me on my mouth before whispering, *"Much."*

"I wanted nothing more than to see you today," I said to him while placing my hands around his back. "But I did not think it would be possible! *How?*"

"I sent the boys to their mother this morning and had to deliver your last Christmas gift, lass."

I kissed him again and then said, grinning from ear to ear, *"You* are my last Christmas gift."

He kissed me quickly before he sat on the stool next to me at the bar. Tommaso placed his martini in front of him almost immediately.

With one hand around the back of my chair, he pushed toward me a small red box with a gold ribbon.

"What is this?" I asked as I untied the ribbon and opened the distinctive Cartier box to reveal the largest princess-cut diamond earrings I have ever seen. "Oh Liam, they are stunning! Do you know I don't own a pair of diamond earrings? Let me put these beauties on now so you can see them!"

I took out my mother's pearl earrings that I wear every day and put the diamond earrings in. I asked, pulling my hair back and showing off my new jewels, "What do you think?"

"I think you are beautiful."

"You better be staying in my room, sir."

"My darlin', I would not be anywhere else."

+++

I perched myself up over Liam's chest and said, "The last week has been so hard without you."

"I feel the same. Did you make the progress you needed?"

"I did. The manuscript is in Kate's hands now and I am all yours until she responds. I have other books in progress that I will continue to work on, but I have no deadlines."

"Och, love," Liam said, bringing my hand to his lips to kiss. "That makes me happy. Have you thought more about living in the city or country?"

I sat up and faced him, clutching the bedsheets across my chest. "I love the house at Loch Leven. Can you remain out of the city for your work?"

"I can. But I asked about *your* preference. I need to do both, I'm afraid. I told you I have been looking at houses in the city for months. Though the country house is not that far of a drive, I will have times during the school year and sport schedules for the boys or for business that it is best to be in the city and I do not want—nor do I always have advance notice—to book a room at The Balmoral every time I have to be there."

"Though they would welcome you in a second."

"They would. But I want my own home."

"Also, while Sarah and I agreed not to disrupt them this school term, we agreed to negotiate times where they will be in both houses next year. They will need to be in the city. Why don't we go look at a few homes together?"

He could see me thinking and finally asked, "What?"

"You just got divorced, and this is so new. Are you sure you want to do this… *together*?"

"I do. Do you have reservations?"

"I am just checking myself. I don't want us to move too quickly." He looked at me as I continued, "Those are my rational thoughts when my heart wants nothing but to move quickly. I told you I love you and I do! I told you I do not want to be apart from you, and I meant every word. But are we ready to merge our lives so soon? Would it be better for me to have my own place in the city? Even if it is near yours? Or should I stay in the country, and you have a place in the city for you and your sons as you need?"

"Let's look together. I can give all the scenarios to my estate agent and let her show us the options available. We can see them all and then decide."

"I can agree to that. You need to think about your sons first, then we will figure out my plan. I have no problem being in a hotel, as you know."

"You do love a fine hotel, that is absolutely true!"

"What I *love* is that you are a one-woman kind of man!"

"I am and I found my woman."

+++

I thought about how things progressed so quickly with David and now Liam. I was so determined that I did not want or deserve this kind of love that I ignored the possibility of it. When it happened to me finally, it happened in an instant. Now, two times over. I could not be more blessed with the incredible men brought into my life.

I kissed the top of Liam's head, as it was my turn to hold him in my arms. Running my fingers through his thick, dark hair, I finally asked, "Did you see that you have gifts under the tree as well?"

"No, I did *not!*"

Like a child that just woke up on Christmas morning, he leapt out of bed, put on his hotel robe, and headed straight for the lighted Christmas tree before the fireplace. He sat on the floor, and I, now in my own hotel robe, sat next to him.

He opened the first package that revealed a glass flask in a leather holder with his name embossed on it next to a bottle of his favorite whisky—a twenty-five-year-old bottle of Laphroaig.

"Och love, that is wonderful! We can take it with us on our walks."

"To the old stone wall, you mean?" I asked, smiling, and then kissing his cheek as I thought about our country walks and the memories we shared there more than once.

"Aye!" he said slyly, before kissing me back. "And you remembered my favorite whisky."

"Of course! And thank you for providing me with my own bottle."

He opened the next gift and then saw the same red box he handed me earlier. He just looked at me before opening it, acknowledging what he was thinking in the moment, "We apparently have the same taste in jewelers."

"Och, Corrine," he said, admiring the gold cufflinks with his initials *LC* engraved on them.

"I chose the LC because so many of your friends call you that, and you often sign your messages with it. I also admit that I did not know your middle name for a full monogram, but then I also thought it works perfectly for Liam and Corrine."

I heard myself saying the words and realized that I sounded so nervous rattling off my rationale. This gift means so much to me, and I wanted him to love it as much as I did.

"My darlin', thank you for these," he said as he kissed me sweetly. "All of my other cufflinks represent Scotland with thistles or flags on them. Those are perfect for business situations, but these are incredible because they are *personal*."

"What is your middle name, by the way?"

He hesitated for a moment before saying, "*David*. Liam *David* Crichton."

He saw me tear up immediately and kissed me again before I could cry. I said in his ear as I hugged him tight, *"All this time, I thought David was protecting me, but he guided me to you, Liam! I know he did!"*

"I cannot explain it, but the minute you told me the story, I felt like there was more at work here than just the fortunate timing of Kate's email introduction. We were so silently and unintentionally open to each other from the start. I do not know what I believe, Corrine, but I suppose I would like to think that your David guided you to me as well. And I thank him for it."

It took me a moment, but once I could recover from the emotion of it all, I asked, "What are the plans for the New Year? Do you want to stay here in London, or would you prefer to go back to Scotland?"

"I would like to go back, but I want to honor your stay here at the hotel."

"I paid upfront to book the dates for the busy holidays, so I am committed whether I stay here or not. The hotel will not complain about having a gorgeous suite handed back to them. I want to go back with you to Scotland as soon as we can."

"Then let me reach out to Nate now and see if we can go back tomorrow or the next day. Is there anything you need to do in London before leaving?" Liam grabbed his phone and started typing.

"I was just going to shop tomorrow. I would like to have a few more clothing options since I am still living out of a suitcase, but I can shop in Edinburgh just as well. There is nothing keeping me here in London."

The pilot came back at once. Liam said, "We can leave at nine o'clock on the 28th. That gives us one more day in the city."

"Let's explore and shop tomorrow. If we have to stay one more day, perhaps I can show you some of my favorite places in London."

"I would love that!"

"We have to be at breakfast before eleven o'clock... *unless...*"

He said, kissing my neck and slowly untying my hotel robe, *"Unless?"*

I said breathlessly in his ear, *"Unless we just want room service."*

+++

I needed new clothes to wear. I am so tired of my current selection and the sales after Christmas were good. Liam indulged me a little during our tour of London, where we had sushi at my favorite restaurant on Charlotte Street and then spent an insane amount of time and money at my favorite High Street shops. We followed each other to each of our favorite shops on Bond Street before we landed at The Kings Arms in Shepherd Market.

Sitting across from each other and looking over our pints, I smiled at him and said, "I loved spending today with you in the city."

He looked at all the bags we had underneath the table and said, "Same, but you are a terrible influence, Corrine. We both spent a small fortune today. But I love this pub. How did you find it?"

"On my very first trip to London many years ago, I stayed at a hotel nearby in Mayfair and randomly walked the area, trying my best to both understand my surroundings and stay awake after my flight. I found this spot and fell in love. I always try to stop in when I am in town. There are so many good pubs in London, but this one is sentimental. And... the flat David had was not far, so we would often come here together."

"Thank you for sharing it with me."

"You are welcome! Kate likes to tell me I am a creature of habit, and I suppose I am. It is the same as the Rose & Crown in Edinburgh. It was the first pub I went to there, and I fell in love in the same way. If I like a pub, and good people work there, I am incredibly loyal. Maybe it is my way of paying tribute and I feel comfort being in my favorite places with friends."

"You are loyal, that is a fact," he said, kissing my hand. "We should walk back to the hotel. I want us to have a fine dinner tonight before we leave, and someone will need to press the shirt I bought so I can wear my new cufflinks."

"I can press your shirt, my love," I said, laughing and intentionally teasing him. "It is not that difficult, and you do not need a Miss Betty everywhere you go."

"No, I guess I don't."

+++

"You look so beautiful," he said as I put my shoes on in front of the mirror of the walk-in closet before checking my hair. I put it up tonight to show off my new diamond earrings. I had on a black silk jumpsuit that had a sleeveless, tuxedo-style top and cigarette pants and heels at a height that I have not worn in quite a while. It was exciting to get dressed up for a dinner date, and my man looked quite dapper in his dark grey suit and new shirt.

"Thank you," I said, smiling at him as he watched me finish my shoes. "I am not sure if it is this new outfit or the incredible diamonds I have on my ears tonight."

I walked to him, and he kissed me on my forehead as he said, "They both help, of course, but I think you are *beautiful* on your own."

"Do you need help with your cufflinks?"

"Aye! I fixed the left but cannot seem to get the right."

Once we were set, we walked hand-in-hand to the lift in silence, just enjoying being with each other, how fine we both looked, and how confident we both felt.

I could feel the change in Liam, and the change in myself. We talked of a renewed confidence in our fifties, but there is more to it than that. We were both walking taller, and our happiness and confidence showed on each of our faces. I hoped that everyone could see what I did.

We not only love each other, we make each other better.

+++

After a wonderful dinner, we found ourselves in the hotel bar before returning to our room. Glass in hand, I swiveled my chair to face him and said, "Liam, I wanted to talk more about where I will live in Scotland."

"Aye, yer rethinkin' yer plan then?"

Before I could answer, I just smiled at him because I love how even the slightest amount of alcohol makes his accent even stronger than it already is. It is the most charming thing!

I stood up for a moment and took his face in my hands as I kissed him. I stroked his beard as I said, "No. I am not rethinking it, but wonder about Edinburgh. I do not want to rush things, that is a fact. I told you I might want to have my own place, but I just want to ensure I have my own *space*."

He just looked at me, clearly confused by what I was saying.

"I love the house at Loch Leven because you gave me my space to live with no assumptions. That space became my workplace, and I love it. I could not have made the progress I did on my novel if I didn't have a place to retreat to and make my own. This whole time I told you I needed to feed off of the energy of a pub or a bar, but this book was different. The view and the room helped calm me. It helped me focus. If you find a place in Edinburgh, I need the same. You know I want to be with you, and it doesn't have to be an entire suite, but I need an area of my own to work and yes, even just retreat to when I need a moment to myself. I am so used to being on my own."

"Absolutely, I would never deny ye that. I just want us to be together and we can find the right home that gives ye what ye need. But ye also know that I can easily get you an office at my company."

"That is kind, but I do not think being in a corporate environment would be good for me or my process."

"Understood."

"Also, Liam. We have not discussed it fully, but have you considered what it means to have me in a home that you will eventually share with your sons when they are with you?"

"They know about you now and yes, I have. I do not know when the right time is to introduce you, but Sarah and I agreed they will stay home with her during this current school term and not have to go back and forth. I will visit them in Edinburgh for sporting games or school events and we will have a regular lunch and afternoons together on Sundays. I thought it would give me some time to figure out how they are coping with all of this change. It was also the reason I was looking for a larger house. I will need rooms for them there so they can also have their own space, as well."

"Then I do not want to look for my own flat. Know that I am happy to stay at the house on Loch Leven on my own when you need to be here in the city."

"Och, love," he said, kissing me. "I would be heartbroken with you only at Crichton House, but I respect your decision. However, if you are telling me that you want to be with me, then I want you to be with me in the city and in the country when you want to be. I will ensure you have your own space."

I smiled and said, "I only want to be with you—wherever you are."

I meant the words I said, but we both knew that the real barrier to being open to living in both homes was knowing his sons. It is something we will have to navigate together. Like he said, we have some time, but that time will catch up with us at some point.

+++

SEVENTEEN
My Home

Edinburgh, Scotland
February 2023

Suddenly, I am afraid to answer my phone. I could see that Kate was calling me as my phone vibrated on the table just under the watchful eyes of Flora MacDonald and I was nervous. She must have finally finished reading my revised manuscript. I am in the middle of the Rose & Crown pub waiting for Liam after his day of work and mine at the library researching my next novel, focused on a lost Scottish distillery in the early 1920s. I took a deep breath and answered.

Before I could even say hello, she said, "Corrie, it is just so beautifully written! I cried so often while reading it. The brave young lads!"

"Well then, that is saying something because you are not one to cry!"

"The merging of the older manuscript with the new story was absolutely brilliant and I believe this will be your best novel yet!"

"Do you really love it?"

"I do! I am going to push this book forward in the schedule this year. I thought with your extensions that we would publish later than I planned, but I want to stay on course with the original schedule to publish in late summer. You and your editor will have to prioritize this and work on an accelerated timeline and I will have to battle our printers, marketing, and distribution in parallel to include it in their schedules. But I will need you to do press for this one."

"You know I *hate* doing press! I prefer being behind the scenes."

"I know you do. We won't make it heavy lift for you, and I will not make you travel the world for it, but will try to get you in front of a few key reviewers and publications pre-publication. We will build a set of marketing and social media campaigns for you that help tell the story and extend media, so you do not have to carry it all yourself. I would ask nothing more than a series of interviews over a few days. We can do them in London or even in Edinburgh or maybe even a few remote. I wouldn't ask if I did not believe in the story, my darling."

"I can agree to that. I just do not want to be far from home for long." Kate caught my words at the same time as I did.

"Scotland is *home* now, is it?"

I looked at the double doors to the Rose & Crown just as Liam walked in. He walked to me, kissed my forehead, and then went to get his own pint.

"I am building my home here, yes," I said, smiling at my handsome man at the bar rail. "Liam is my home now. I know why you are asking this of me, and I will not argue with you. Press helps me sell books, and I should be invested in selling as many books as I can, but I am not good at it."

"That is where you are wrong! You *are* good at it, but you hate it, and it shows to every reporter and reviewer you sit in front of," Kate said. "You have not had to do it for a while, but you are the best spokesperson I have for your own work. I will minimize it as much as I can. Please, Corrie, this novel deserves your discomfort for a moment because it is so good. You *have* to support it!"

"I agree," I said, giving in to her argument, "just make it easy for me. If we can do interviews here in Edinburgh, I will be even more willing to do a good job for you."

"Done," she said, laughing at my lame attempt at negotiation.

Liam, now seated before me, and I just looked at each other as Kate said in my ear, "Marketing will set up meetings with you on the cover and then the promotional plan. We can do those online. I might even ask that Dr. Marshall take an interview or two to cover more of the actual history. Have you shared the latest draft with him?"

"I have. Well, not the whole novel, but I had Andrew read some of the key chapters to check my historical account of Aberlour Orphanage and the letters during editing. He was very supportive, and the version you have reflects his feedback on the parts he read. We can get the full copy to him when you are ready."

Liam sipped his beer and nodded his head in agreement. Andrew was very complimentary and supportive of the revised story. I put my hand out to his across the table and mouthed, *"Kate."*

He whispered, *"She liked it then?"*

I nodded back with a smile, and he squeezed my hand tight as he said, *"Well done, love!"*

She must have heard us both whispering to each other and asked, "Corrie, is Liam there with you?"

I smiled at him and said, "He is. He just arrived at the pub to meet me after work."

"Put me on speaker."

I did as she asked and said, "Alright, Kate. You are on speaker."

Still holding Liam's hand, he just looked at me with a furrowed brow, uncertain of what was happening. I just shook my head at him that I was unsure myself.

"Thank you, Liam!" Kate said, as we smiled at each other. "Thank you! I asked you to help Corrie with this novel and you did so brilliantly!"

Liam kissed my hand and said, "It has been my pleasure, Kate. I am proud of Corrine's work, but I believe I got more out of your introduction than she did."

I shook my head at him in disagreement. We have both benefitted from Kate's introduction months ago in ways neither of us could have imagined, and much of it has nothing to do with my wayward novel.

"Well done again, my darling! I hope to see you both again soon and we will reach out on press schedules and marketing once I can get you confirmed in the publication queue."

"Goodbye, Kate!"

"I am so proud of you!" Liam said, holding my hand tight as I disconnected the call.

"We will see how this goes, but all I could think while she was talking to me is that I am so happy that I did not give up on this manuscript. I am *proud* of this story! I am *proud* of what I have written, and you know I could not say the same about my last two novels."

"I remember, but there was so much pain and turmoil surrounding you that had nothing to do with your writing… or your ability to write."

"I know, but this is a moment where I feel restored… to who I am as an author, to who I was before." I wanted to say, *who I was before I lost David,* but I did not.

+++

"Look at you, handsome!" I said to Liam as he entered the bedroom of the suite we booked at The Balmoral for the night. My Scot was standing before me in a formal black-tie kilt and jacket. He looked very dapper and smiled at the compliment.

"Och, you flatter me, but I know well enough that you are only looking at my knees."

"Those knees—on the verge of peeking out from under your kilt—do make me weak. Come here. I need your help to zip up my dress."

I stood before him in my formal black dress with a lace boatneck top with three-quarter sleeves, and a sleek floor-length silk skirt with a slit just above my own bare knee. He came to me as I turned around to expose the back zipper.

He said softly as he gently ran his finger down the skin of my lower back, "You look stunning, but honestly, I would prefer *not* to zip up this dress."

"The good news is that when we come back, I will need your help to get out of it."

"Then I will gladly save my reward for the end of the night," he said, completing his task.

After he zipped up the dress, I turned to him and said, "Let me kiss you before I put on my lipstick. I am wearing a dark red tonight."

I kissed him and smiled. I am nervous about attending a public benefit with other members of Edinburgh society, but we both look so good that I truly welcome a fancy night together.

"You are wearing your new cufflinks," I said proudly.

"I am! They mean a lot to me," he said as he watched me put on my lipstick. This is definitely not an everyday shade, but it suits my dress. I just smiled back at him in the mirror, and it was then that he pulled a red box out of his jacket and placed it on the vanity in front of me.

"What is this?"

"I wanted to get you something to go with your earrings. Tonight is your first social event with me and when I saw your beautiful dress, I knew it would be a perfect match. It is platinum and has just over eight carats of diamonds."

I opened the box to find a diamond bracelet that matched the earrings he gave me for Christmas. "Oh, Liam! It is gorgeous! Love, I don't want to get red lipstick all over you, but I must kiss you again!"

I kissed him quickly, trying my best to not get lipstick all over him. As I tried to wipe the traces off of his lips with my thumb, he said, "I do not mind a little lipstick because every person at this benefit will know that I was kissed by the most beautiful woman in the room."

"Will you help me put it on?"

He wrapped the diamonds around my wrist, and he was right. The bracelet was simply perfect for this dress. I am starting to appreciate his fine taste in jewelry. I smiled and kissed him once more as I admired the new sparkle on my wrist.

"The car is here, and we should go."

I put my lipstick in my evening bag and grabbed my wrap from the corner of the bed. "I am ready if you are."

+++

We walked through the lobby of the hotel under the watchful eyes of everyone there. We looked good together in our formal dress for the evening. Everyone who works for the hotel and knows us wished us well on our way out, and I am certain I saw one or two hotel guests take pictures of us on their phones.

Our driver met us outside and as soon as he got out of the car to get the door for us, he recognized me and said, "Miss Hunter! It is good to see ye again, lass!"

"Paul! My goodness! It is good to see you again as well! How are you, sir?"

"You know each other?" Liam asked us both, surprised.

"Aye," Paul said instantly.

"We do. Paul has driven me to and from the airport many times and has been not only an excellent ambassador for Scotland, but a tremendous help to me personally. He has often given me instruction on driving across this beautiful country."

"Well, Paul works for me for part of the year now, when he is not needed for some of the TV shows filming during the other half, that is."

"Good for you!" I said, knowing full well that Paul does like driving the actors and producers for the TV shows and movies filming in Scotland. It is good for him to have a gig that he loves and a solid employer during other times of the year. He has been a support on my travels, always making certain I knew where to go and how best to get there safely. With each of my drives to pick up a rental car, he gave me the instruction I needed to get out of the airport and across the Queensferry Crossing Bridge. While I know how to get there, I let him tell me every time because he is kind and has always cared for my safety. Before my nerves about tonight could return, Paul instantly proved to be a welcome, fatherly comfort.

"Mr. Crichton, the gallery is close, but they have closed the portion of Queen Street right before the entrance for drop offs, so we will go around and come back down so that I can let ye both out on the red carpet."

"Red carpet?"

"Aye, I drove the route this afternoon before picking ye up, lass. We will be in a queue with other cars, and they will stagger entrances for the photographers to get their shots. Ye will have to walk the short red carpet and take pictures at the press stand before entering the gallery."

"Oh my!" I said, looking at Liam as my nerves returned with a vengeance. Somehow, I thought this would be a quiet benefit where wealthy people just patted each other on the back for their sizable donations and drink Champagne in the stunning location that is the National Portrait Gallery of Scotland. Now it seems there is more required for our appearance tonight, and I am not certain that I am ready.

Liam took my hand in reassurance and said, "If there is a photo call, then Corrine should be on this side of the car and I will open the door and escort her out, if you don't mind."

"Not at all, sir. I expected that. Since the lane is closed, ye can exit safely on the driver's side before helping the lass out. I will stay behind the wheel to move the queue forward for the next car when ye are done."

"Miss Hunter," Paul said, directing me to the now open door on the left side of the car. Liam joined me in the back seat and took my hand again immediately. With a smile and a squeeze of my hand, he tried to reassure me. He could feel all the nerves and tension growing in the pit of my stomach.

He brought my hand up and kissed the inside of my wrist before saying, "You will be just fine, love."

I listened to the men chat mindlessly in the car about traffic as I repeatedly checked that my hair was still in place in my sleek chignon, powdered my nose, and reapplied my lipstick. Somehow, I did not expect all of this, and the butterflies in my stomach were working overtime. I am so nervous, I feel sick!

As we pulled up to the gallery, we were the third car in queue. I reached out and squeezed Liam's exposed knee, willing myself to smile at him. Liam grabbed my hand and smiled reassuringly. If this is the life he has, then I need to be open to it and represent him, his name, and his reputation. As our car inched closer, I tried to calm myself. I will be just fine. *I will be just fine!*

"I promise, this will be a fleeting moment. Wait for me to come around and open your door. I will help you out of the car. You are with me, and I will not let you go until we are inside the gallery. And even then, I make no promises."

He kissed my cheek quickly. I smiled and nodded in understanding of his instruction. Liam exited his door when the event coordinator gave Paul the signal, and to keep from focusing on myself or my own nerves, I said, "It was good to see you again, Paul. I am just going to leave my wrap here."

"Aye, Miss Hunter! Have fun tonight, and I will take you both back to the hotel when you are ready."

Just then the car door opened and save for the blinding flash of cameras, all I could see was Liam's welcome hand reaching in for mine. I turned to put my feet on the ground, took his hand, and stood up to meet him with a smile.

We walked to stand before the cameras hand-in-hand and then posed with our arms around each other. Thankfully, as I could not see anything, Liam steadied me and kept me standing upright while steadily moving us toward the stairs leading up to the door. We smiled at the cameras and at each other as the photographers shouted many things at us, looking for some sort of reaction.

"What is your name, miss?"

"Liam, put the rumors to rest. Is this your new love so soon after the divorce?"

"How long have you known each other?"

"Did you leave your wife for her, Liam?"

"Will Sarah also be at the benefit this evening?"

I followed Liam's lead and kept my mouth shut with the intrusive questions and just let them take their photos. I thought to myself for a moment that they could look me up. I may not be as famous as Liam Crichton in Scotland, but I am not a complete unknown.

Once inside the gallery and away from the mayhem outside, I said blinking my eyes repeatedly, "I am not kidding, I cannot even see you right now!" Somehow, I thought that the advancement of digital photography would reduce the flash, but the sun was setting, and the light required it. "Did you *hear* what they asked?"

"I know. It is disconcerting with all the flashes and the provocative questions. But you were brilliant. Where is your wrap?"

"I left it with Paul in the car. I decided that since it was a short walk in, I did not want to carry it all night."

"Then love, I owe you a glass for running the gauntlet and here is the man who can help us both right now," he said as a young server held a tray of Champagne flutes before us.

This is exactly the reward I needed. We clinked our glasses together and the first sip calmed me instantly. Being together openly at the Rose & Crown or at Bar Prince, is one thing. There is now photographic evidence of the fact that we are a couple. We are out for all of Edinburgh at this very moment, and it feels like another milestone in our new relationship.

I met government officials and members of Edinburgh society, all of whose names disappeared further from my mind with each glass of Champagne. Liam was in his element, charming the socks off of everyone in a room filled with people that seemed to have been waiting for him to arrive all evening. He kept me close, and I appreciated him for it. At one point, I saw our glasses were empty. He was talking to members of Scottish Parliament, and I stealthily took his empty flute and mine to the bar for replacements. I am not sure anyone noticed my departure from the conversation, including Liam.

At the bar, an older woman joined me. I just smiled at her briefly as I waited for my new glasses from the bartender.

"Good evening to you," she said to me with a broad smile and a thick Scottish accent.

"Good evening to you, as well."

"I told myself that I had to welcome the woman that arrived on the arm of the most eligible divorcee in all of Scotland tonight."

I just looked at her, uncertain what to say in response. She was well into her seventies and seemed not only entrenched in Edinburgh society, but quite wealthy. In fact, she was dripping in diamonds and emeralds, perfectly suited against her black evening gown. She proved me right as she said, reaching out her hand to shake mine, "Mrs. Meredith Cox, I am the chair of this benefit tonight."

"It is a lovely event and in a location I have grown to appreciate more and more on my travels to Edinburgh."

"What is your name, lass?"

"Oh, I am sorry, Mrs. Cox. My name is Corrine Hunter."

"The author?"

"That is correct!" I said, taking my two newly filled flutes from the bartender, hoping to walk away from her cordial interrogation at the edge of the makeshift bar. "Liam has been helping me with my latest novel."

"I did *not* expect that," she said. "I did not see him as a writer."

"He did not help me write the novel. He helped me with connections for my research and did a fine job."

She looked at me through narrow eyes trying to gauge the real relationship between me and Liam though I suspect based on our entrance and her first words to me she believes it has very little to do with my upcoming novel—which she asked nothing about, by the way.

"I would expect nothing less from Mr. Crichton. He is most *helpful* to others."

"Thank you again for a wonderful event. I hope you have met your goals tonight."

"I have *indeed*, Miss Hunter," she said, smiling at me over her glass as I walked away with both of mine. Whether those goals were the benefit fundraising or her newly gained bits of information, I may never know.

I handed Liam his refilled glass without a word and found my way back to the glass lift to the second level. This was my opportunity to revisit some of my favorite Allan Ramsay portraits—all old friends I have dearly missed. I cannot even remember when I was here last.

+++

Standing before Master Ramsay's portrait of David Hume and admiring the artist's work, I heard Liam's voice echoing in the empty gallery, "I thought I would find you up here, my darlin'."

This time, he handed me another glass of Champagne as I said, "You were deep in conversation, and I wanted to sneak a private moment in the gallery. I have not been here in a while, and I missed some of my old friends."

Liam nodded in agreement as he sipped from his own glass and looked at the paintings himself.

"Liam, who is Meredith Cox?"

"Aye! She is the chair of this benefit and one of the wealthiest women in Scotland. She inherited millions from her father's Speyside whisky empire, and she married into even more whisky money—two times over, in fact—with each of her late husbands. Why?"

"She cornered me at the bar and introduced herself by saying she wanted to welcome the woman who accompanied the most eligible divorcee in Scotland herself."

Liam laughed at this designation and asked, "Did you tell her your name?"

"I did, but why do you ask me that? Should I not have? Did I make a mistake?"

"Not at all! Stop worrying! You have your own name and your own career, but I would bet you she went right out to those photographers and told them who you are."

"Liam, I did not know! I just answered her question," I said apologetically. "This is such an unfamiliar world for me."

"You did *nothing* wrong! I just wanted the bastards with all of their cheeky questions to research you themselves, but I suspect we are in the tabloids now. It was going to happen, eventually."

He took my glass and put it on a catering tray in the corner with his. I thought about his words and my own irrational insecurities. We walked together to the glass lift. Once inside, he took my hand and asked, "Are you ready to go home? I can text Paul."

I released all of my worries the minute he asked, because nothing else mattered to me in that moment. What I said to Kate was true. Despite being in the hotel for the night, Liam was *my home,* and I did not want to be anywhere else.

I held his hand tight in mine and said, "Yes, please!"

+++

EIGHTEEN
An Unwelcome Offer

Crichton House
Loch Leven, Scotland
March 2023

Sitting before the fire after dinner one night, Liam asked, "What do you think about having a dinner party with some of our friends?"

"What?"

"I think it would be good to let some more people into our circle. You know Tom and Elaine, and now I would like to know some of your friends."

I nodded at his thinking. I do not have more than a handful of friends, so my list will be small. Liam will not have to work all that hard to know them. And I am certain they will love him as much as I do.

"I thought about a housewarming at the townhouse in Stockbridge, but I do not think they will finish the electrical upgrade for another few weeks and we need to hire a designer. The house needs everything, right down to cutlery and linens. You know we are starting from scratch, and I admit, I want to preserve that space for us for now."

"I respect that. If that will be our home and the second home for your sons eventually, I am not sure I want to share it just yet myself. We have not even enjoyed it together."

"While it takes a little coordination to get here, this house is better suited for parties. Nothing big, but maybe it is time."

"I would want to invite my friends from London. That includes Kate and her husband Luke, of course. Then I would also like to invite Mark and Colin. But can we identify where they can stay in town and maybe secure the room for them?"

"They can stay here, love."

"I thought we could offer the guest room downstairs to Kate and Luke."

"We have a guest house on the property."

I looked at him dumbfounded and asked, "You do? Where?"

"*We* do, aye!" I smiled at him for saying '*we*,' and including me. He said, "I can see how you would not know this, because we have a fondness for only one side of the trail along the old stone wall."

"*Liam!*" I exclaimed, almost embarrassed, thinking that we do in fact have an affinity for a certain spot on this property.

He laughed at me before saying, "Past the boathouse and about a three-minute walk along the trail is a small cottage for guests. I think it will be perfect for them. It is simple, but very modern. One bedroom, one bath with a small open living space with a kitchen and bar. Miss Betty can see that it is stocked for them. She will want your direction on that since you know them best. We can direct anyone else to the tavern in town. If we invite people that stay there, I can hire someone to transport them by boat or car."

"I absolutely adore you!" I said. "Should we reserve anything for Tom and Elaine?"

"You are kind, but no. Tommy likes to sleep in his own bed. He will hire a driver. I am certain of it."

"Then that is that for me! Thank you for offering the guest quarters here for my friends."

"They are most welcome!"

"Besides Tom and Elaine, who would you like to invite?"

"They are my closest friends, but I have one more friend from work. James MacLaughlin is our CFO and Tommy and I have worked with him for over twenty years. He and his wife Diana are lovely people. They live nearby and will probably also have a driver."

"That is manageable! Two couples each. A party of ten it is!"

"Jenny will be here in the morning to deliver a contract for me to sign that has to go out tomorrow. I will ask her to work with you on invitations and planning. She knows all the people we have hired in the past and is a pro at event planning. She helped Sarah with all of our parties and can handle the logistics and billing. I am happy to weigh in on anything you want, but thought you should assume your role here at Crichton House and lead the planning of this event."

"That is kind. I cannot wait to meet Jenny in person, but if we are merging our friends for the first time, plan this with me."

"No, love! I trust you and I want you to feel like you can do this here on your own."

I breathed in and nodded my head in acceptance. He was not absolving himself of work for the party but was trying to make me feel like this was also my house by giving me the responsibility. I finally asked, "Do we have a budget?"

"No," he said, kissing my forehead. "We never have a budget."

I just smiled again and thought of the creative freedom that comes with such a task, unincumbered by restrictions or budgets. Every day offered me new surprises and wonders with this man.

+++

My guests from London arrived and were already in their accommodations getting settled and dressed for dinner. Liam and I agreed we would be ready early so that I could walk him through everything planned and we could have a moment to ourselves before our guests joined us for the evening.

Jenny and I settled on an incredible idea to create a Scottish version of a winter house outside on the patio. With the fireplace on one end, we set a long table for our guests covered by a woodland shelter. The look was inspired first by *Hygge*—the Danish version of cozy comfort–which soon evolved to *Coorie*—the Scottish version which embraces the comfort of the outdoors.

Jenny led all the logistical planning with vendors responsible for the set up and was here to direct them earlier today on everything from the lights and flowers to the place settings. She was an absolute wonder! I do not know how she kept Liam coordinated during the day, but added being a full-time party planner to her responsibilities. She clearly knew what we must do right down to the most basic details, and she had no problem directing me when she needed to. She knows this house, and she knows better than I how to navigate or even bypass Miss Betty on certain decisions. I learned a great deal from Jenny. Miss Betty wants nothing to do with a dinner party, though she helped get all the guest quarters set and I thank her for that!

Attendees were sent a copy of a book about how to bring the *Comfort of Coorie* to their own home with their invitation and instructed to dress *Winter Lodge Chic* to help stay casual and comfortable and, quite frankly, to help stay warm. Even in March, the air is still quite cool at night.

We got a local whisky company to relabel some bottles for Crichton House and the labels matched the invitations, and we created a custom drinks menu with some signature cocktails along with a fully stocked standard bar inside.

Before our guests arrived, I walked Liam through the bar set up and then to our woodland inspired shelter filled with cozy seats, tartan throws, and pillows. We had fairy lights throughout the branches surrounding us overhead and candles on the long table. We had the large fireplace on one end and small heaters warming the shelter.

"Here is the menu Chef Dan and I worked on together." I smiled up at him while he read the card at each place setting. I then looked at our friend and his team working furiously in the kitchen and settling everything for the bar. "He was an incredible partner for me, Liam! I love him and his food!"

"Aye, he is a good man," Liam said, looking at the menu card.

Assorted Starters For The Table
> *Whisky Smoked Scottish Salmon Trio*
> *Caviar Blinis with Crème Fraiche and Dill*
> *Scottish Venison Skewers with Onion and Peppers*

Tomato and Basil Tartlets

Choice Of Main Entrée
King Scallop Risotto
Smoky grilled Scottish scallops, served over Parmigiano-Reggiano and asparagus risotto
Beef Wellington
Traditional Scottish beef, new potato mash with chives, steamed haricots verts, served with a bordelaise sauce and horseradish cream
Mushroom Ravioli
Fresh ravioli with local wild foraged mushrooms and spinach, served in a light butter and Parmigiano-Reggiano sauce

Assorted Desserts For The Table
Rustic Apple Tart Tatin
Served with cinnamon ice cream and a salted caramel sauce
Selection of Scottish cheeses
Served with honeycomb, fig spread, fresh fruit, and oat cakes

"Everything here sounds absolutely delicious," he said. "How will I choose a main?"

"I *might* have already told Dan that I want a little risotto on the side for later, but I am going straight for the beef myself. I saw it earlier, and it is gorgeous!"

"Aye! He will leave us everything that is left, and we will feast like kings and queens again tomorrow!"

"Please tell me you are happy with what we have done! Jenny and Dan did such an amazing job."

Liam held me tight around my waist and kissed the top of my head as he said, "You *all* did! Some of our parties here have been over the top and this is just perfect for this small group. It is not pretentious, and it celebrates Scotland. Well done, love! *Well done!*"

"Thank you! I really want you to be happy. I am so nervous about tonight. I mean, doing this together for the first time with our closest friends…"

I leaned into his shoulder, and he held me tight as he said, "You have made it beautiful and welcoming. We might retain the shelter. We can sit out here under the fairy lights for our talks together in front of the fire. It is so *Coorie*!"

I laughed, knowing he was embracing the theme and heard in his voice for the first time how close the term was to my own nickname.

"It is cozy, isn't it? Oh! I forgot! There is a reusable tweed tote at each seat. It includes a small bottle of our custom house whisky, a whisky glass etched with each attendee's name at each place setting to note seating arrangements, a locally made lambswool tartan scarf, and a small seedling of a Scots pine tree in burlap, with instructions on how to plant."

"That is perfect for the theme of this evening!"

I laughed nervously and said, "I am so glad you are happy. Can we get a glass of wine now? I am afraid my nerves have gotten the best of me."

"We absolutely can, but *stop* your worrying," he said, taking my hand, kissing it, and leading me back to the bar in the kitchen. "Tonight will be a triumph! I know it!"

+++

Our Crichton House resident guests were the first to arrive, and my friends from London immediately put me at ease. I directed them to the young bartender Chef Dan had for us at the far corner of the kitchen. I loved knowing that we could see all the activity in the kitchen as Dan expertly led a small team from his newly-opened restaurant to deliver on tonight's fabulous menu.

Liam took over his role as co-host and chatted eagerly with my friends. He reconnected with Kate, and met Luke, Mark, and Colin. Within minutes, they were all laughing loudly in the corner when the front doorbell rang.

Liam took my hand as we walked together to meet Tom and Elaine at the front door. True to form, Elaine had a bottle of Champagne in her hand. This time, only one for the hosts.

"Corrine and Lee," she said, taking Liam's hand and placing her other on my shoulder, "we are so happy to be here with you both tonight!"

Elaine *was* happy. I could see it on Tom's face as well. They walked in grinning from ear to ear and I could tell that they were absolutely over the moon to be included in such an intimate affair at this house and to see us again. If I can help bring old friends back together again, then this party would indeed be a triumph.

"We are so glad you are here. Let me take your coats, and then I want to introduce you to my dearest friends from London over by the bar."

The bell rang again. Liam said to me, "Go, love! I will bring in James and Diana."

The MacLaughlin's were the last to arrive and were a lovely couple that found their way into the group in an instant. Everyone mixed beautifully at the bar inside and once everyone had drinks in hand, I led them all to the outdoor space where even more conversations were had around the table before the fire and under the fairy lights.

No one was ready to sit just yet, and Chef Dan noticed immediately. He directed his staff to bring some of our first starters around on trays. I stood at the opening of the enclosure, surveying our guests, and smiled.

Suddenly, I felt Liam's hand around my waist as he said in my ear, "See, I told ye! It is a lovely venue with lovely people who are having a lovely time."

"You were right."

"Say that again."

"Stop it! You heard me!"

"You were so nervous, and it is perfect, love! Look at all of our guests. They are relaxed and having fun out here in the beautiful space you created."

"That is what *Coorie* is all about! Relaxed comfort in the outdoors."

"Let's join our guests and enjoy it ourselves," he said as he playfully patted me quickly on my bottom, before we walked hand-in-hand to join our friends.

+++

It was amazing to watch two distinct groups of friends connect with each other so easily. The entire night was fun and reinforced that Liam and I both have good people surrounding us, loving us, and cheering for us as a new couple.

After dinner, my dear friend Luke and I walked back inside together to refill our drinks at the bar, only to be confronted with another conversation happening between Kate and Liam in front of the stone fireplace. I felt the air of discord hanging in the room the minute we walked in.

"Did you know about *this*, Corrie?!" Kate yelled to me across the room.

"Know about what?" I asked as I took my refilled wineglass from the bartender.

"That Liam wants to buy my company," Kate said. I could tell she was not only angry, but she was also hurt.

I looked at Liam and then Luke, before answering her, "No."

What I said was true. I did not know that this was his plan. I invited Kate and Luke here as my friends and they are staying here in this house. To have an issue with Liam tonight is not good for any of us.

"I did not discuss this with Corrine. I do not make a habit of broadcasting my business intentions."

Now I can tell Liam is angry, and it is not something I have seen—or heard—before. I asked him innocently, trying to diffuse the situation, "Why would you want to buy her company if it is not for sale? And if it is not for sale, why is this a conversation… *tonight*?"

Now Liam can see and hear that I am not happy with this negativity at our first dinner party together and I am willing him to end it. This is a small group of friends and I do not need this conflict. Why he felt this was the night to do this, I will never know!

He said plainly, "I do not have publishing or media in my portfolio and Kate has built a solid company. I am not trying to take anything from her. I just wanted to invest further in her successful business. Kate, you would continue to run it as you have."

Kate was not having any part of what sounded to me like a reasonable rationale on the surface. She yelled to me, "He is a primary shareholder in one of my original financiers. My business doesn't have to be for sale. He could make a case for a hostile takeover if he wants it bad enough! He will own me, but what he really wants is to own *you*, Corrie!"

"That is a harsh accusation!" Liam said, almost laughing and looking at me and Luke for sympathy. "I have no intentions of a takeover. Kate, I just wanted you to know that I am interested in buying your company. And this has *nothing* to do with Corrine."

"Does it not? You just told me you want to publish all of her books going forward!"

"What *I said* was that I would like to help her as much as I can going forward. I have learned so much about writing novels from her and I find it all fascinating. I wanted to invest in a successful business. I meant it as a compliment, so I am unclear how that become contentious!"

"Perhaps you also know that her next book will be her best and you just see another money-maker before you. That is all you look for. Am I correct?" Kate asked, as angry as I have ever seen her. Luke touched my back gently to tell me silently that he knew something had gone seriously wrong here and he would handle it on his side. I nodded to him because I clearly needed to handle it on mine.

I cannot be in the middle of this, and I am so confused about what is happening now and why. We were all having such fun tonight. Why Liam did not tell me his idea and why he felt like this was the perfect time to spring this on Kate baffles me. He had to expect that she would not react well.

"Liam, Kate is my publisher, and her company is not for sale. That should be the end of the discussion."

"*Corrine,*" he said softly, willing me to see his side of this argument.

"No, that should be the end. Kate and Luke are our guests here and we have other friends still outside. Let's rejoin them and leave business discussions to another time, love."

Liam just nodded in agreement. He crossed the room and took my hand to lead me back outside. I could tell he was sorry to upset the mood of our party or our guests, but I could also see that Kate was still fuming as I left her in the capable and calming presence of her husband.

+++

After talking to as many people as I could around the table, Kate came to me later in front of the fireplace and said, "I believe you knew nothing about his ridiculous offer, but Liam is *wrong*!"

"Wrong about what?"

"His intentions. He owns everything else. Why wouldn't he own you?"

"He does not own me, nor is he trying to. You are judging Liam because of his wealth. He sprung something on you tonight that you did not expect and clearly do not want, but you are insulting *me* now with your words! You know I would not be with a man that wants to *own* me."

"I do not mean to insult you, but he blindsided me!"

"I understand, I do! Let's talk about it all rationally and without drinks tomorrow." I put my arms around her shoulders and said, "You and Luke are my dearest friends and our guests. It makes me so happy that you are here with us. *Please, Kate!* Please, let this go—at least for tonight."

I wanted to tell her to talk to her husband again, who would surely calm her better than I could. But I did not. The dinner party continued, and we all made it through. Kate and Luke seemed to have fun with the other guests but retreated early to their room with cordial goodnights to us all.

+++

Tom and Elaine were the last to leave and did so, having had a wonderful time and plenty of drink. We sent them off under the safe care of their driver, who hopefully did not get too close to the gate on his way out.

I immediately went to take a shower. I wanted a moment to myself and to relax under the hot water and steam jets. I had built up so much tension worrying about my first dinner party here with Liam and needed a moment. I hoped he would just go to bed quietly, and I would not have to talk to him because I do not yet have the words I need to address the situation with Kate, and I am still confused by his actions.

Instead, he joined me and wrapped his arms around my waist, and I wrapped my hands around his. He could feel my emotion instantly. I was disappointed, and he knew it. He put his head on my shoulder and said softly, "I am sorry, love."

"What you did tonight was wrong. Do you know that?"

"Aye, but…," he said.

"But nothing. Why did you not tell me this was your thinking? I could have saved us a lot of anger and heartbreak with our friend." He kissed my shoulder and kept his head to the back of mine under the hot water, but said nothing. "Liam, I *love* you and I so need your loving support. But for this relationship to work, I want our business lives to remain separate."

"I understand."

"I am not certain that you do."

He held me tight and did not argue with me on this point. I continued, "Kate's feelings and angry reaction aside, *I do not* want you to own my publisher. You already know that my last two novels failed miserably. If we are together, it could be seen that I only publish from here on out, because *you* own the company. I want to recover from my last failures and this book will help me do that. I am certain of it! Please give me this! My career is important to me. I want to stand on my own as an author. So I am asking you to abandon thoughts of owning Kate's company and make it up to her tomorrow."

"I did not think about how it would land, and I was wrong. It is as simple as that."

"If you believe publishing and media is an industry you want to add to your investment portfolio, you can look for another company to invest in. Be the best competitor you can and maybe one day, she will want you to buy her out."

"I am sorry I caused such a row. I miscalculated that Kate might have welcomed an offer. I saw it as investing in her as I would have wanted her to keep running her business. But you have helped me see how that looks for you. I did not think about it from your perspective."

"Make it right tomorrow," I said, before turning to kiss him.

"I will. I owe you that. I should have talked to you first. I am just so used to operating on my own and having a partner at home that does not care what I do."

"I understand that."

We got ready for bed and turned out our lights in silence. I understand his thinking and his own sense of independence where business is concerned. He was not trying to sow discord. He was truly sorry, and I know he respected my independence by asking to keep this part of our lives separate.

Liam wrapped himself around me and said in a whisper over my shoulder, *"I will make it right to you both. I promise. Sleep well, lass."*

"*Sleep well, my love.*"

+++

I sent Colin and Mark off early this morning with my hugs and kisses as they left to drive to Skye for a well-deserved holiday together. I am so glad they joined us here for a night on their way. Chef Dan made them a hearty care package of egg sandwiches, coffee, and smoothies for their travels.

Luke and Kate sat across from me and Liam at the dining room table. We all over-indulged the night before and need a moment to recover ourselves before speaking. Every person at this table had only one goal, and that was to devour our breakfast feast and to stop the incessant pounding in our heads.

Over a most welcome and fully fried Scottish breakfast from Chef Dan after a party, we all sat in silence over our plates. I was thinking this morning that in all the planning he and I did together on menus, breakfast was by far the best.

Liam spoke first.

"I owe you an apology, Kate. You have built an incredible publishing company. I made an offer to buy, but I did not ask if you were willing to sell. I am truly sorry. As friends, I owed you that respect and consideration."

I took Liam's hand under the table and looked at Kate, as her demeanor was quite changed from the previous night. Whether that was because of her husband or her healing morning breakfast, I will never know.

"I also apologize, Liam. My reaction was over the top because I was so caught off-guard. I was embarrassingly defensive and did not intend to make a scene in your own home. Corrie, I apologize to you as well, my darling. I should not have said to you what I did."

"There is no need for that."

"No, there is. I made it sound like Liam was trying to own *you* and I did not mean my words the way they came out. I was truly just thinking as a publisher and owning your books and your name as an author. You know I love you and respect this new relationship you both have. Luke and I are here to celebrate that with you. I am sorry to you both for saying the words that I did, and in the manner I did. I was out of line."

"We are fine, Kate," I said, reaching to her across the table. She put her hand in mine and smiled. "Do not think another thing about it!" Luke is an incredible husband for Kate, as I am certain this display of contrition is genuine and one that perhaps only he could have brought about.

She took my hand in hers across the table and then said, "I am not looking to sell, but I know you were not trying to insult me with the offer."

Liam nodded his head. I spoke up to change the subject and end this episode by saying, "We would like to take you both on the boat to town for lunch before you have to travel back to London."

Luke said immediately, putting his hand on Kate's back, "We would love that, Corrie, my girl!"

I smiled at him. I love Luke and his kind heart. Kate held my hand tight, and Liam squeezed my other hand in his. I knew that all was righted with the apologies and that friendships were restored.

"Meet us at the boathouse at noon," Liam said.

I winked to Liam before saying to Luke and Kate, "Bundle up! The air on the water in the middle of the loch is *cold*!"

+++

After much searching, Liam and I settled on a recently remodeled townhouse in Stockbridge. It was originally two neighboring homes in the historic area of New Town that were turned into one house just a few years ago. We upgraded the electrical system before we moved in to accommodate the same room control panels, Wi-Fi, and security Liam has at the house on Loch Leven. This work prevented us from having our dinner party with friends there and it was for the best.

The house is quite large and has a back room overlooking the garden for me to have an office and lounge space of my own and plenty of bedrooms for guests and his sons.

I made a case for Colin to be our interior designer and Liam did so without question, having met him at our dinner party. Colin started with our bedroom and the living spaces and turned them quickly. Only our bathroom and the kitchen needed full upgrading and the rest was truly décor, essentials, and furniture. We each had our own artwork, books, and clothes, but that was about it. We were starting from scratch with the basics in this house, and Colin and his team worked quickly to get us everything we needed.

Using a custom questionnaire, the boys worked with Liam and Colin on what they wanted and are excited to see their new rooms when the school term ends. On his last trip to Edinburgh to complete my workspace and their bedrooms, Colin and I had tea together at the sprawling granite kitchen island.

"Tell me you are happy, Corrie."

"Oh, Colin! I am *so* happy! You have done such a magnificent job. The house feels like a home now—*our* home—and I am loving my new office! Or should I call it my own *parlor*? It is a comfortable place to work or just go to when I need my own space as an independent woman. When I think about being here, when this house will be filled with men, I might really need that cozy retreat! I also can't wait to spend time on the patio enjoying the new garden. You and your team have done incredible work inside and out!"

"When Liam hired me, I was over the moon, of course! To have a house this historic and gorgeous that also needed absolutely everything was a dream. You and Liam have the same fine taste, which made that dream job all the easier. Not to mention he has no budgetary restrictions!"

I smiled and nodded at these words, as Liam will notice absolutely everything and do the math in his head in an instant, but places no budgetary restrictions on creative endeavors.

"I am pleased that you, as my client, are happy with my work. But I meant are *you* happy, love? Are you happy here in this house, in this city, and with this man?"

Before I could answer him, he explained, "When I got this assignment, I was instructed by Mark straight away to ensure that you were truly happy and settled here."

"Really?"

"Mark has always grieved David. We all have. But his pain has mostly been for you." I just looked at him as the tears welled up in my eyes. "Mark and Luke, especially, have worried for you for so many years. You know that they both love and adore you! It was difficult with the pandemic and you being in Vancouver for most of that time, but they want to protect you, as David would have. They made a commitment to each other on that matter, in fact. Caring for you and protecting you is how they honor the memory of their dearest friend."

"Oh, my! I did not know," I said, with tears falling onto my cheeks. I reached out for his hand. "I have never doubted their love—your love—for a second! But I will be just fine and yes, I am happy here with Liam. He has been an incredible blessing in my life."

"I know that now, being here and talking with you both. We saw it first at your dinner party. I can tell he is a good man, and I can tell that you both love and respect each other."

While I am so blessed to have Liam in my life, I am also blessed to have my dearest friends loving and caring for me. I always looked at the ring still on my right hand and thought of David protecting me, but it has truly been everyone around me, not just him. Even if I was unaware of their pact, their love, friendship, and support have been a comfort to me.

"I told Kate once that I thought that maybe I only deserved this kind of love and happiness once in my life and I would have been content with that. Liam *is* a good man, a supportive partner, and he makes me *very* happy. I love him with everything I have!"

"You deserve this kind of love and more, as Luke says, *Corrie my girl!*" Looking at his phone, he said, "My car to the airport will be here in two minutes. All we have left are the additional linens for the bedrooms and the custom pillows and throws for the media room. All will be delivered directly to you here."

"Thank you, Colin, truly! I will let you know about the reactions from the boys when they see finally get to see their rooms."

"Please do! I hope they will be happy and see how their own visions came to life. We can adjust anything that they need," he said as he put on his jacket and walked to the door.

"The rooms look absolutely amazing! But I am not a fourteen-year-old boy! Liam told me they have loved the photos taken throughout your progress. He is saving the final view for when they walk into their rooms for the first time."

"Thank you and Liam for letting me have my photographer capture some images for my portfolio and website during my work. It is a stunning home!"

"Of course! You have helped make it even more so," I said, opening the door for him. His driver was already outside waiting for him. "Safe travels, my friend! Please give Mark a big kiss for me. I love you. And I love how you both have cared for me."

He paused for a moment and said before kissing my cheek, "Trust me, it has been an effortless task. I love you, Corrie! We *all* do."

+++

NINETEEN
We All Win, In The End

Edinburgh, Scotland
May 2023

I stood in Boots, trying to replenish my stock of toiletries and makeup. Now that I am no longer living out of a suitcase every day, I needed some full-size items for the new house. While Liam is used to his new Edinburgh house manager doing this for him, I am not. I want to buy my own supplies. I also kind of enjoy having chores to do—especially shopping chores.

I saw a woman out of the corner of my eye come and stand next to me. I paid her no mind but after a moment, I realized she was incredibly close to me. Uncomfortably close. So much so that I moved from the shower gel aisle to the neighboring toothpaste aisle. I looked at my list on my phone, trying to check everything off that was already in my basket and what I had left to find.

Suddenly, the woman was standing next to me again. She was shorter than me and stood before me in yoga pants, a hoodie, and with her hair up in a messy bun. She looked as if she had come straight from a workout class. She had no make-up on but did not need any. Her skin had good coloring, though it was clear that she was older than me or spent too much time in the sun when she was younger. The lines around her eyes told me that much.

She said in a thick Scottish accent, "I know who ye are, *Corrine*."

"I apologize. Have we met?" I asked as politely as I could, thinking that if she was a fan of my books, I wanted to be respectful. I usually never remember a name, but rarely forget a face, and her face was not familiar to me.

"No, we *have not*," she said as coldly as she could. I felt every ounce of her judgment and I knew who she was in an instant. In a stunning reversal, I did not know her face, but I *absolutely* knew her name.

"*Sarah?*" I asked in a whisper and as politely as I could.

"Aye! Sarah Crichton. Perhaps you have heard of me!"

"I do not mean to cause any trouble here in the middle of the shop with you, Sarah," I said, stepping away from a woman who seems not only hurt but angry. She followed me back to the shower gel aisle, seething that I walked away from her once again.

"Do you not? Fucking my husband and making a name for yourself in this city? *My city!*"

I could barely speak and just looked around the store, almost apologetic to the others near us. I finally said, "I am just shopping today like you are. There is no need for a scene. I do not want that for you, Liam, or your family."

"You are an absolute whore and a horrible author! And do *not ever* speak of *my* family!"

I looked around again as she became louder, to the point that other shoppers left the aisles on either side of us. I could feel my cheeks burn bright red with humiliation, but I tried to remain calm. She did not want my direction and seemed quite comfortable causing a scene in public, as it has clearly been her intention from the moment she saw me.

"Liam is not your husband anymore," I said softly, reminding her of the current situation and not even bothering to remind her I have a built a name of my own well before arriving in Edinburgh—horrible author or not. "Like I said, this is not the time nor the place for this. I wish you only the best—*truly*."

"I bet *you* do! *Truly*," she said, mocking me and my words. "You are quite right! This is not the time or place."

Before I could feel any sense of relief that she was walking away from me, she turned back around and yelled to the entire store with her arms held wide before pointing directly at me, "Dear shoppers, the *fucking whore* standing before us all in the bath and shower gel aisle is Corrine Hunter. She is not only a mediocre author, but she *stole* my husband!"

I stood completely mortified until she walked out of the double doors back onto the busy pedestrian pavements of Princes Street. I kept my head high and still bought the items in my basket, only to walk all the way to the Rose & Crown with hot tears laced with anger and embarrassment streaming down my cheeks. I tried to hide what I could behind my sunglasses but texted Liam the minute I secured my pint and sat down at my table.

+++

>> Meet me at the Rose & Crown! Now!

What is wrong?

>> Please, Liam!

Give me a moment to settle
work and walk across town.
I am on my way.

Within the hour, Liam joined me. He just held me until I could compose myself and actually tell him what happened in the shop with his ex-wife. Once again, I had to finish my crying spell before I could speak fully.

Finally, I said, wiping my own tears from my cheeks, "I am sorry for crying, but I can't help it. I have not felt so shamed since I met Mrs. Giles at the wine shop in Kinross!"

"You are just fine! Cry all you need! I told you to never hide your heart."

"*Liam*... Sarah confronted me and called me a *whore* in the middle of Boots! No! She said it more than once and then screamed that I was a *fucking whore* and a *mediocre author* at the top of her lungs across the shop! I can never show my face there again! But I am not just embarrassed, I am angry at myself that I *keep* crying! Why can't I *stop crying*!?"

He kissed my forehead as he said, "You know her words are not true. And no one in the shop will remember this scene. Based on the location, I would bet they have seen and heard worse. If it had been in the middle of Harvey Nichols, I might have different advice for you."

I laughed with him through my tears and appreciated that he was trying so hard to comfort me and lighten my mood with humor.

"There you go, love. Laugh it off. We know the truth."

"It *is* funny that she advanced me from a *horrible* author to a *mediocre* one by the end." He just smiled at me and wiped the last remaining tear from my face.

"I have to ask, why would she do this to me if she did not want to be married to you? I know you do not have to answer for your ex-wife's behavior, but her words to me were not that of a woman who did not want to be married anymore. She accused me of stealing her husband. She sounded not just angry… but wounded."

"I told you the truth about it. She filed for divorce nearly six months before I ever met you. Despite the words she said, I can tell you that this has nothing to do with me at all! Sarah does not love me. She loves her lifestyle and position in Edinburgh society. She has likely seen in the press that you are with me, and she is mourning a change in her own social standing."

"It is in the press?"

"Aye, when we attended the benefit together, a photo of us was printed in the paper and it was noted as a debut of us as a couple."

"I did not know. I mean, I obviously knew that we walked the red carpet on our way into the gallery, but I have been so consumed with the last edits and decisions on my novel that I have spent almost no time looking at the news of the day and certainly not the society gossip of the day."

Liam handed me his phone and sure enough, there was a photo of us holding hands and smiling at each other with the caption, '*At the annual Cox Arts Benefit at the Scottish National Portrait Gallery in Edinburgh, newly divorced Liam Crichton wasted no time debuting his new love, Canadian author Corrine Hunter.*'

I smiled briefly and said, handing him back his phone, "We look good."

"We not only look good, we also look happy! They did not invite Sarah to the benefit, and that had to hurt her. In fact, I am certain it did hurt her. Many of her friends were there and she was not. As much as I would like to second guess Mrs. Cox and her motives, she only sent me the invitation this year. I am not saying she picked a side, but she is smart enough to know where the check is actually coming from and perhaps did not want the tension between us at her event. Sarah also probably knows I bought the townhouse in Stockbridge. The purchase amount and the fact that you are living there is public knowledge as well."

"How is that?"

"The sale and price were recorded and one of her friends directly asked me the night of the benefit if you would live there. I told her it was not really any of her business but could tell by the manner of her question, she already knew the answer."

I don't know what I think about him not telling me this story. I can only assume he did not want to upset me on a night I was already so nervous. I said, "This is not the life I want for us. This is not the life I want for your sons. I am not naïve to the ugliness and resentments that can come with divorce, but I only want to operate from a place of respect—even if it all has to be superficial. Sarah is not of the same mind. Not yet anyway!"

"I love you so for saying that. You are always thinking of others. I will talk to Sarah."

"*No, please! Don't!* I don't want her to think I ran straight to you after her confrontation—even though that is *exactly* what I did. I also don't need you two to have any additional animosity between you for this one episode. She said what she felt, and I hope it gave her the satisfaction she needed in the moment. If it didn't, then I am sure she will give you an earful on her own when she talks to you next. But Liam, have we made a mistake being here together so soon? Should I have stayed at the house at Loch Leven? We are so sheltered and protected there. I knew Sarah was here in Edinburgh, but somehow, it never occurred to me that our paths would cross. I do not want to be constantly looking over my shoulder. You know we did that once before."

"I am learning to navigate this just as you are, my darlin'. But no, we have absolutely not made a mistake—Sarah did! You and I know the truth of how and when we met, and how we have connected. Sarah and the entire country of Scotland can judge us all they want for how quick it has been, but we will *never* look over our shoulders again. *Never!*"

+++

Liam joined me at The Balmoral Hotel after a marathon day of press interviews. Kate and the publicist she assigned to me scheduled hair and makeup before the interviews, as we expected most publications to ask for photos in the gorgeous suite, with the incredible view of Edinburgh Castle, booked for the day. I figured it would be a waste of a Glam Squad triumph not to have a few celebratory drinks in the bar with my loving man at the end of a long day.

"Look at you, beautiful," he said as he kissed me before sitting down in the seat across from me. I do not know what makes him smell so sweet, but it makes me happy. Living together now, I have smelled all of his soap, cologne, and beard oil and can only believe it is his own scent. Pure sweetness and sugar… *at least to me!*

"Thank you," I said, putting my hand up under my coiffed hair and batting my false eyelashes at him.

"How did everything go today?" he asked as the waiter instantly brought him his dirty martini.

"I did twelve interviews and filmed a few items for the social marketing campaign. I am tired, but for the first time, I had fun doing press because I love telling this story. I want to share it because it honors the old boys of Aberlour, and they are deserving of such honor."

"I am so proud of you! When will the articles come out?"

"Likely during the weeks leading up to launch planned for later this Summer. Some reviewers will get advance copies of the book in the next few weeks to help them add to their articles. I am sure Kate, or the publicist, will come back to me when confirmed and, of course, they will send me electronic copies of each so we can read them. Let's just hope they are better than the last! I would hate to think I spent all day in press for another round of *'What Happened To Corrine Hunter?'* headlines!"

"Don't make me laugh! You said that last part just as I was taking a sip and I nearly lost my drink!"

I looked at him with all the seriousness I could and said, "If you laugh, then you *lose!*"

"Och no! You are not seriously going to play my own game against me!"

"If you laugh, Liam Crichton, you have to buy the bottle of Champagne I am about to order."

Before he could say anything back to me, I stopped the server and said, "Sir, I would like a bottle of Cristal for the table."

"Aye Miss Hunter! Right away!"

"So much for restraint," he said, mocking me for my expensive choice. At £500 a bottle, this man will be a fierce competitor. Perhaps he also knows that with my audacious selection, I have absolutely no intention of losing the game this time. I will *also* be a fierce competitor tonight! The server immediately presented us with the bottle and poured two glasses before placing it in the silver ice bucket next to the table.

"To our future!" Liam said, raising his glass to mine as we sipped our beautiful bubbles, staring at each other intently. Just as I had before, I reached my hand up and stroked his cheek, and he lovingly took my hand to kiss the inside of my wrist.

"When is the game over?"

"When *I* say it is," I said, mimicking his original instructions.

He just smiled at me and nodded his head in understanding that I managed the rules of the game tonight. Despite not having a nosy neighbor to watch us, it is still fun, and Liam is playing along perfectly. We sipped in silence and stared at each other until I took a large white envelope out of my bag and placed it on the table in front of him.

"What is this?"

"Open it."

The server stopped by the end of the table to top-off our glasses. Liam waited for the lad to leave before he carefully opened the envelope and pulled the proof copy of my latest novel, *The Old Boys*. It reflected the cover art Kate and I approved weeks before. The publicist delivered the copy to me this morning. I was so emotional seeing it that the makeup artist had to redo my eye makeup and lashes. It is always an emotional event to see your work, your words, in book form. Even though this was my twenty-first novel, it felt exactly like the first, and I was beaming with pride! I also know what it took for me to get here. Liam was a part of that process.

"Look at this wonder! It is absolutely incredible! *Incredible!*"

He read the back cover and flipped it back around so that he could admire the artwork representing the memorial marker in Aberlour with a haunting image of a young man in a uniform of the time with his head bowed in reverence on one side and that of his beloved clearly mourning him on the other.

I composed myself and said calmly, "Look inside at the dedication."

I could not keep the smile off of my face for much longer and kept trying not to give myself away by nervously sipping my glass and biting my bottom lip as hard as I could. He flipped each page forward slowly, finally arriving at the dedication.

For My Scot
who helped me find my heart again
and with it, the heart of this story

Liam was overcome and said with tears forming in his eyes, "*Och, Corrine!*"

He took a moment to collect himself before saying, "I am so touched by this. *Truly touched!* But more than that, I am so proud of you! The book is finished! Look at this magnificent thing!"

He reached his hand out for mine across the table. I squeezed his hand and looked him in the eyes. When I could collect myself, I said, "You changed me, Liam. You did not just introduce me to Andrew, who gave me the inspirational gift of this incredibly moving story, but you encouraged me every day to finish this novel and you provided me with a workspace that helped me keep my focus. But my darling man, you opened my heart. You opened me up to the new hope of a love that I never thought I would see again in my life, and it is reflected on every page. *Every. Single. Page.* I thank you so much for it and I love you so much for it."

He took a moment to steady his own emotions and said, "I love you more!"

Then, looking back at the dedication page, he said, shaking his head and laughing, "Remarkable! I have never had a book dedicated to me before and I never expected such a thing!"

Despite his genuine show of emotion at the dedication, I leaned across the table and said through my own tears and a mighty triumphant grin, "You laughed, so you *lose*. You just bought yourself a bottle of Champagne, sir!"

Liam stood up and came to sit next to me and kissed me passionately. I could not help but smile at him through the whole thing.

With his warm cheek next to mine, and his arms wrapped around my shoulders, he said softly in my ear, *"No, my darlin'. I bought a bottle to be sure, but I **won**. We both did."*

I kissed Liam again through my own tears and smiled, thinking that he was absolutely correct.

We *both* won in the end.

+++

GRATITUDE

So many of the staff at the restaurants, pubs, and hotels mentioned in this book have been an inspiration to me. I admire their resilience during COVID restrictions, lockdowns, and ongoing staffing shortages. On my multiple journeys across England and Scotland, I have found a home with the people who cared for me and encouraged me along the way. Much like Corrine Hunter, I also like working in a bar and also prefer a white wine spritzer.

I would like to thank my dear friends at **The Rose & Crown** in Edinburgh. On a trip to Scotland for my historical fiction novels in September 2021, I stayed in a nearby hotel in New Town. I found the pub the night I arrived. I was trying my best to stay awake with a brisk walk—literally around the block—and I fell in love. Being a creature of habit, I found my favorite table on the very first night and on every subsequent visit to Edinburgh, regardless of my hotel location, I worked as often as I could there. **Rebecca, Rachel, Marco**, and many others, always take good care of me. The regulars have been a quiet comfort.

The pub is featured in this novel as a tribute to their hospitality and my own love for its role in completing this novel.

Yes, I do know that with the recent remodel of the pub that the portrait of Flora MacDonald is no longer over my favorite table. She has joined Bonnie Prince Charlie above another table on the opposite side of the room, but I left her where she is described for sentimental reasons.

At **Gleneagles Resort**, the entire staff are five-star all the way! You get the first hint of this incredible team in prep for your trip. It starts with all the basics of dining reservations and activities, including golf and spa, but it is also about paying attention to the clues of *why* someone is traveling. From the very beginning, I felt like everyone was celebrating with me and cheering me on. I would like to acknowledge the team at the **Century Bar—Declan, Cameron, Will, Teresa, and Michele**. They made me feel welcome and took care of me while I spent my evenings editing. They also ensured I had a back of house tour for the bar, wine cellar, and incredible restaurants that was most eye-opening and special.

Emanuele and Francesco at The Corinthia Hotel in London have always gone above and beyond for me. First, they both remembered me from my Christmas stay there in 2019. Emanuele not only remembered my name (*Cinzia* in Italian), but my drink preference. I was most impressed!

Both made my own 50th birthday celebration the night before with my dearest friends special. On my actual birthday, they gave me a small cake with a candle. Emanuele taught me that in parts of Italy you make a wish, blow out the candle, but then you have to break the candle in half.

Who knew!? Could this be why all my wishes have not come true… until now?

I would like to thank the **National Library of Scotland** and the **Aberlour Child Care Trust**. Upon hearing the story of the *'old boys'* of Aberlour, I was determined that my next historical fiction novel would be about this incredible story. But as my first novel, HOLD FAST, grew from one book to a trilogy, and now to perhaps five novels in a series, I sat in the Special Collections Reading Room in the National Library of Scotland and had a bit of a panic attack. I know I looked a fright, silently crying in the corner. I decided in that moment to abandon a project that would require years of extensive historical research to make it right. I regretted that I could not do it.

The plot for this book revealed an opportunity to honor this story—even in a small way—with another author. I visited the marker at St. Margaret's Church in Aberlour on my trip to Scotland in May 2022 and was as moved in that moment as I was the first time I heard the story. I hope that I honored the memory, service, and sacrifice of the old boys of Aberlour Orphanage who fought and died in the Great War. Their story was an inspiration to me and one that perhaps, I hope to revisit again fully in the future.

+++

ABOUT THE AUTHOR

Cynthia Harris is the author of the recently released *HOLD FAST Series* of historical fiction novels set in Eighteenth Century Scotland. She celebrates Scotland once again with her first contemporary romance novel, *Fun & Games*. All of her novels are available in paperback and Kindle versions on Amazon.

Cynthia has built a career in storytelling. From leading advertising and marketing strategy for some of the world's most recognized consumer brands, international news organizations, and major league sports teams—to leading internal and external communication strategy and speech writing for technology, human resources, gaming, and entertainment executives—words have not only been her passion, but her livelihood. With her novels, Cynthia now focuses her time on finding and sharing her own voice.

As a proud graduate of The University of Georgia, Cynthia made a home in the Pacific Northwest sixteen years ago. She keeps her gas tank full and her passport current, so she can escape to the incredible places near and far that allow her to revisit history, fuel her creativity, and find peace. But Scotland is calling, and she is currently looking for a new home in the country that she loves.

FROM THE AUTHOR

Thank you for reading!

If you liked *Fun & Games* (or even if you didn't), I'd appreciate an Amazon review. Your feedback helps me improve, helps me know what you want to read from me in the future, and also helps other readers discover my work.

If you want sneak peeks of future novels or learn about my journey as an author, visit me at cynthiaharrisauthor.com or follow me on Instagram cynthia_harris_author.

Cynthia Harris Novels

Fun & Games

HOLD FAST
Book 1 Of The HOLD FAST Series

A STRENGTH SUMMONED
Book 2 Of The HOLD FAST Series

RAISE YOUR SHIELD
Book 3 Of The HOLD FAST Series

Coming Summer 2023
The Regulars
Observations From The Bar

Made in the USA
Monee, IL
01 May 2023